A WHISPER
OF SUSPICION

A WHISPER OF SUSPICION

Jane Edwards

Five Star • Waterville, Maine

Five Star First Edition Romance Series.

Published in 2002 in conjunction with Jane Edwards.

Set in 11 pt. Plantin by Elena Picard.

Printed in the United States on permanent paper.

Library of Congress Cataloging-in-Publication Data

Edwards, Jane (Jane Campbell), 1932–
    A whisper of suspicion / Jane Edwards.
        p. cm.
    ISBN 0-7862-3747-3 (hc : alk. paper)
    1. San Francisco (Calif.)—Fiction. 2. Trading companies—Fiction. 3. Australia—Fiction. 4. Smuggling—Fiction. 5. Orphans—Fiction. I. Title.
    PS3555.D933 W48 2002
    813'.54—dc21   2001054330

To Star Helmer . . .

The way the story was meant to be told

ACKNOWLEDGEMENTS

Many, many thanks to Hazel Rumney, whose friendship and confidence in my work has boosted my morale enormously over the years. Her brilliant editing of this manuscript made all the difference in its quality.

My humble appreciation to Sensei Nivette Jackaway. Learning the story of how she earned her own black belt in karate provided a wonderful role model for my heroine, Penny.

Love and thanks to my daughter, Sheila Ann Edwards, for responding so quickly and helpfully to my questions—as always!

Finally, my most sincere thanks to Tedd Caldwell, First Officer for Alaska Airlines, for his expertise and patience in leading me step-by-step through possible events which might lead to an air emergency and its aftermath.

I am so very grateful to you all.

PROLOGUE

Damp and grey the fog drifted in, creeping up the front steps of the old house, curling around the ankles of the children huddled on the porch. Penny Lasko shivered, wishing she had something warmer to wear than the ugly brown hand-me-down sweater.

The boy beside her scooted a bit closer. It looked as though he was trying to shield the small girl from the chill with his own rangy little body.

"Maybe we should go back inside," he said reluctantly. "They'll ring the doorbell when they get here, you know. There's no good reason why you have to wait outside."

Matt Devlin's eyes looked very blue and earnest in his ten-year-old face. The skin around one of them was puffy and discolored, as if someone had punched him. They had, Penny knew. She also knew that Matt had started the fight. As usual, he'd been trying to protect her when he clobbered Victor for yanking on her pigtails.

She hated the pigtails. When her mother was alive she had brushed Penny's hair into long, fat curls every day. But here at the Home, seven-year-olds were expected to take care of themselves. Without braids, her hair always wound up a tangled mess. Every time she wove the slippery, carrot-colored strands of hair together she vowed that when she got older she would cut her hair short and keep it that way.

For now, she settled for flinging the despised pigtails back over her shoulder and giving her head a firm shake.

"I'd rather stay out here with you," she insisted. "Oh, Matt, I wish you could come to Texas with me. I asked Mr. Farnsworth if he wouldn't please adopt both of us. He said his wife would have con-nip-shuns." Penny gulped, not sure what the strange word meant, but figuring it couldn't be anything good. "He didn't exactly say she wouldn't want me, either, but that was what it sounded like."

"She's going to like you a lot, I'll bet." Matt tried to sound reassuring. "You'll have your own room, and nice new stuff to wear, and ice cream and everything. Why, getting hit by the car that man was riding in was the luckiest thing that ever happened to you, Penny."

Penny stuck out a cold little hand and wrapped it around his. Matt's knuckles were skinned, and black dirt rimmed his fingernails. But it was a good, strong hand and she held tight to it.

"No, Matt," she told him. "Meeting you here at the Home was the luckiest thing that ever happened to me."

For the first time since he was four years old, Matt Devlin came close to bursting into tears.

"Me, too, Penny. Me, too."

Peering through the fog, he saw a car painted bright yellow pull up to the curb and stop. He grabbed a deep breath.

"You go have a good life in Texas, now. Just—just never forget me."

Matt was her best friend. Her only friend. The skinny, freckle-faced little girl wanted to cling to him and howl that even if they offered her all the ice cream in the whole city of San Antonio, she would still rather stay here in San Francisco with him.

10

But the other kids would hoot and holler and make his life even more miserable than it already was if they heard her causing a fuss. Deliberately, Penny pressed her bandaged wrist against the chipped porch rail and kept from crying by concentrating on the pain.

"I won't," she promised. "As long as I live, I'll never forget you, Matt Devlin."

CHAPTER ONE

Seventeen years later . . .

The morning appointment left her in a state of shock; the rest of the day shot past in a hectic blur. It wasn't until she stepped inside the restaurant and inhaled the savory aromas of chili peppers, cumin and cilantro that Penny Lasko Farnsworth realized she hadn't had a bite to eat since breakfast.

Suddenly starving, she hurried toward the table Leeann Jarvis was holding down in the no-smoking section. Dropping into her seat, she eyed the empty tortilla chip basket with hungry dismay.

"Well, I'm glad to see you, too!"

The laughing young woman in the opposite chair wore the uniform of an Air Force captain. Following their graduation from the university, the former classmates had gone their separate ways. Lee wasn't about to see one of their rare reunions marred by the fact that she had munched down all the appetizers while waiting for Penny to arrive.

"Relax. They'll be along with refills in just a minute," she promised.

"It's my fault for being late," Penny took the blame. Her pretty lips curved into a smile as she gazed across the table. "You're positively glowing, Lee. Piloting military jets all

12

over the world obviously agrees with you."

"I've never been happier in my life. You, on the other hand, look as though you could use a good vacation." The tendency toward blunt honesty was a handicap Lee had never been able to overcome. "Are you still putting in a lot of overtime to pay off your student loans?"

Penny shook her bright head. Even at nearly twenty-five, freckles still dappled her upturned nose. Her once-carroty hair, however, had darkened over the years to an eye-catching shade of auburn. The short, fluffy curls made an attractive frame for her triangular face with its wide-set hazel eyes and firm, pointy chin.

"No, I managed to climb out of debt last year." Penny didn't mention that the heavy liabilities she had struggled for so long to pay off also included the costs of Ethan's final medical and funeral expenses. "Today was unusually chaotic, that's all. First thing this morning I received some news that knocked me for a loop, then right before lunch we had a bomb scare. That turned out to be a false alarm, thank God. Even so, I could have made it on time except that just as I was getting ready to leave, an eight-year-old needed help transferring to a connecting flight."

During college Penny had worked part-time as a security officer at San Antonio International Airport. Upon graduation she accepted a position with the U.S. Geological Survey. But following the terrorist attacks on the United States she had responded to pleas from her old boss to return to work at the airport. There she became part of a team charged with the responsibility of installing heightened security measures to safeguard the huge southwestern gateway and the crews and planes that served it.

The first few months of this duty had been extremely stressful. By now, though, with the new procedures operating smoothly and specially trained dogs working with humans to inspect the passengers and their luggage, Penny was occasionally able to take time off to shepherd youngsters traveling alone from one section of the vast air terminal to another. Today wasn't the first time she had stayed on past the end of her regular shift to see a child safely aboard a plane. Nor was it the first time that she had continued to worry about her young charge after handing him into the care of an already-harassed flight attendant.

The arrival of more munchies provided a welcome diversion. Both women dug in enthusiastically, dunking the warm, crisp tortilla chips into a bowl of spicy salsa with the gusto of true lovers of Tex-Mex fare.

"So," Lee murmured, when the basket of chips was again depleted and the waitress had taken their orders for steak fajitas with all the trimmings. "What happened this morning to kick off your havoc-strewn day?"

"Something incredible. I'm still pinching myself to make sure I'm not dreaming." Penny took a calming sip of Sangria. "You knew I was adopted, right?"

"Sure." Back in their dormitory days, Penny had confided the story of how an elderly Texas oilman visiting San Francisco on business had taken a small orphaned girl under his wing after the taxi in which he was riding struck and slightly injured her. "Your adoptive father died several years ago, didn't he?"

Blinking back a quick rush of tears, Penny nodded.

"Ethan had been badly hurt financially when all those savings and loan institutions failed," she said. "I'm sure that's what brought on his first heart attack. Not long afterwards, Arletta sued for divorce and wheedled the judge into awarding her the house and most of the other assets remaining to him. At his age, he wasn't strong enough to weather a series of blows like that."

Ethan's much-younger wife hadn't wanted to put up with a husband whose health was failing and whose fortune was gone. Penny saw no point in mentioning that she herself had never been wanted by Arletta, even in the beginning.

Thrusting aside these bitter recollections, she brought her thoughts back to that morning's startling interview in the lawyer's office.

"Anyway, where this is leading is that Ethan had a twin sister."

Penny explained that Ethel Farnsworth was an anthropologist who had spent most of her seventy-nine years living among the people of primitive societies and studying their cultures.

"She and I never had a chance to meet until Ethan died. When she flew back to Texas from an island off Borneo to attend his funeral, she told me that her brother's letters had always been full of my doings. Adopting me had made him a happy man, she said, in spite of his dismal marriage."

"That must have helped cheer you up." Lee raised her eyebrows quizzically. "The news you were talking about earlier—it had something to do with Ethel?"

"Uh-huh. She died recently and left me a legacy of about forty thousand dollars," Penny blurted. "According to her will, I'm to use the money for something that will make me happy."

Lee's jaw dropped. "Good heavens, where did she pick up a fortune like that? I've visited a few of those remote islands. Some of them still use seashells for currency."

Laughing at the whimsical notion that she might have inherited pirate chests full of money cowries, Penny explained.

"These are the kind of assets that come from crude oil, not seashells. When Ethan first became a geologist, his sister Ethel lent him the money to drill a wildcat well in a remote region. They hit a gusher and sold the rights to one of the giant petroleum firms. Ethan went on to develop other oil wells with his share of the profits. But Ethel tucked her half into the bank for a rainy day."

Penny rummaged for a tissue. "Oh, Lee, there was the most touching letter addressed to me among her effects. She said that all her days had been sunny because she'd spent them doing the work she loved. There was never any need to tap her emergency fund. Instead, she was leaving the money to me because I'd been the sunshine in Ethan's life. When I read that, I broke down and bawled right there in the lawyer's office."

A loud sizzling noise announced the arrival of their dinner. Platters containing crackling hot strips of marinated beef sautéed with onions and peppers were set before each of them. Several tasty side dishes accompanied the fajitas: guacamole, sour cream, pico de gallo, and thick, chewy flour tortillas kept warm between the folds of a towel.

Tucking into the delicious food gave Penny's emotions a chance to simmer down. Her composure had been restored by the time Lee asked about her plans for the windfall.

"I've been thinking about that all day," she admitted. "Now that the enhanced security precautions at the airport are up and running, I can resign without feeling I'm letting my country down. But I'm really not anxious to resume my career in geology. In retrospect, it's easy to see that I chose that particular science as my major because I knew how pleased Ethan would be to have me follow in his footsteps, not because of any passion for rocks."

Truthfully, she admitted, she found people far more interesting than minerals. "For months, I've been mulling over starting a business of my own. I want to be involved in my work heart and soul, like you are, Lee. This little legacy has given me the push I needed."

Her friend bit into a tortilla. "Tell me more."

"A lot of kids are flying alone these days," Penny said. "The rules keep changing, but most airlines accept unaccompanied children as young as five on nonstop flights provided they're ticketed at adult fare. By the time they're eight, like the little boy today, kids are considered old enough to change planes without assistance—sometimes more than once, if they're headed for some remote location that's served only by feeder flights."

Lee protested, thinking of her little niece. "Eight is awfully young to handle that kind of responsibility."

"Even so, they're traveling." Penny spoke from vast experience. "Families split up and the parents head in opposite directions. If mom and dad share custody, the kids are shuffled back and forth. Or someone wants their little darlings to visit Grandma, but is too tied up with business to accompany them.

"Usually, it turns out fine," she added. "Most children arrive at their destinations without any major problems, even though they might be scared to death the whole trip. But some have special health problems that rule out their being able to travel alone, and others simply aren't mature enough to manage by themselves. Having an adult companion can make a critical difference for kids like that."

"So you want to start a travel/escort service for youngsters?" Lee considered the idea, then nodded approval. "I think you'd be perfect for that sort of job, Penny. Are you going to open an office down by the River Walk?"

Penny laughed off the locale as being far too rich for her blood.

"Get real! Besides, I'm not sure I'll even be staying in Texas. With Ethan gone, this doesn't seem like where I belong anymore. But in any case, there's something important I need to do before making permanent plans."

She picked up the bill, insisting that dinner was to be her treat. "Let's go home. I'll make coffee and tell you all about it."

Both the other women with whom Penny shared a duplex in a pleasant neighborhood had been assigned late shifts that week, so the former classmates had the house to themselves. Penny set the coffee machine to brew, then kindled a log in the living room hearth. Spring came early to South Texas, but late February evenings still tended to be on the chilly side.

"Funny," she said, staring into the dancing flames, "I can never look back at my childhood without remembering the fog in San Francisco. Most every day during the summer we could peer out the window and watch it billow in from the Bay. It was doing that the day I said goodbye to Matt Devlin."

Unbuttoning her jacket, Lee sank into a cushy armchair near the fireplace. "Who was he?" she asked.

"A boy I knew at the Home for kids without families where I was sent after my mother died." Penny swallowed the lump in her throat. "It was an okay place, I suppose. They kept us clean and gave us enough to eat. But nobody really cared about you there, you know? No hugs. Matt was my only friend. He was about ten. I was seven. If one of the bigger boys picked on me, he'd punch them out, then wind up being grounded for starting a fight."

Her warm hazel eyes looked troubled as she turned her

wrist over and gazed down at the thin white scar traced across it. The blemish was almost invisible after all these years. Nevertheless, the memory of how she had come by the scar was as vivid as if the accident had taken place only yesterday.

"It should have been Matt who was hit by that taxi. If so, he'd have been adopted by Ethan Farnsworth instead of me," she told her friend. "He and I used to save part of our dinners every night for this half-starved dog across the street. We'd take turns dashing over to feed him. That night it was Matt's turn to go. But since he was confined to his room for smacking the boy who'd yanked my pigtails, I took his place. I remember calling to the dog at the very instant the taxi barreled around the corner and knocked me down." She gulped. "Really, Matt ought to have been the lucky one instead of me. It just wasn't fair!"

"Heavens, Penny, that's the way fate operates," Lee remonstrated. "Have you ever considered that your friend Matt might have been killed if he'd been the one to dart in front of that cab instead of you?"

Penny refused to be comforted by this worst-case scenario. "Seventeen years ago I got lucky at his expense. Now it's happened again with this legacy from Ethel Farnsworth. I'll never be able to spend a dime of it unless I go back to San Francisco first and make sure that Matt Devlin is all right. Not—not in need, or anything."

She poured out the strong, freshly brewed coffee and handed the other woman one of the mugs. Lee stirred in sweetener, then sipped appreciatively.

"Why don't you just write him a letter?" she suggested.

"That was one of the first things I did after arriving in San Antonio." Penny could still remember how painstakingly she had printed the chatty little message, and the disdainful reaction of Ethan's wife when she had asked for a stamp to send it on its way. "Arletta tossed it straight into the fireplace. She insisted that keeping in touch with the 'riffraff' from my old environment was sure to have a bad influence on me."

"She sounds like a shrew. Didn't Ethan stick up for you?"

"He was usually a strong supporter of anything I wanted to do. But there at the beginning I suspect he'd expended all the energy he could spare in simply getting her to agree to the adoption." Penny gave her head a sympathetic shake. "Poor guy. He must have made a lot of concessions trying to keep peace on the home front."

"So you never had any contact with this boy again?" Lee asked, as they carried their coffee to comfortable seats near the fireside.

"Not then. Not ever, really."

Sheepishly, Penny admitted that as time went by, her once sharply focused picture of Matt Devlin had grown fuzzy around the edges. "To be honest, I think I purposely tried to put him out of my mind. I felt like someone harboring a guilty secret whenever I remembered that my lucky break should have been his. Maybe I would have kept the memory of him buried forever if my eighth-grade English teacher hadn't assigned our class the project of corresponding with a pen pal. Just like that, his name popped into my head."

But by then, she added in a forlorn tone, the attempt to get in touch with Matt had been in vain. "My letter came back stamped 'Moved. No forwarding address.' "

"Oh, what a shame!"

"I felt terrible. Simply terrible." Tears shimmered in Penny's bright eyes. "Matt had been a good friend to me when I was little. Yet after promising never to forget him, I postponed trying to reach out to him until it was too late. Now, it's likely to be a real challenge to learn where he went."

"Sounds to me like a lost cause. Besides, people change, you know," Lee cautioned. "Even if you did succeed in locating Matt Devlin and find that he still remembers you, he might have turned into someone you'd no longer want to associate with. Or he could have moved to New York or Los Angeles—anywhere."

"If he's moved, I guess I'll be out of luck," Penny conceded, ignoring the more drastic warning. "But I won't know anything for sure until I start hunting for him. I'll try all the obvious alternatives first—phone books, the city directory, stuff like that. If I run into a dead end there, I'll track down the people who ran the Home where we lived as children. And if that doesn't work, I'll think of something else!"

Her friend's stubborn determination worried Lee. "What if it takes a posse to round him up?" she asked bluntly. "Or is that what's frightening you? The notion that he might be wanted by the police or even actually in jail?"

The sudden rush of color to Penny's cheeks proved that the guess was accurate. "Good Lord, Lee, I don't know how you do it without a crystal ball. I must admit that such a possibility did occur to me. Back when he was ten, Matt did constant battle on my account. Once I even heard our housemother, Mrs. Cicerone, threaten him with Juvenile Hall. So yes, it's remotely possible that he might have wound up behind bars."

She straightened her shoulders. "But Matt Devlin stuck up for me when I didn't have another soul in the world on my side. I don't care what he might have done since the last time I saw him. If he needs a helping hand now, I intend to hold it out to him!"

Someone had been nosing around the warehouse.

Eight years in the Navy had reinforced the tall young man's natural tendency to keep his possessions shipshape. Ignoring the sonorous blare of foghorns out in the Bay, he stared around the tidily arranged corner he used as an office, and felt the crisp black hairs stir slightly on the back of his neck. In his absence some uninvited visitor had stood here, riffling through the neatly stacked orders and invoices and bills of lading. Afterwards, the snoop had replaced everything almost exactly the way he'd found it.

Almost. Not quite.

A scowl dragged his level dark brows together. Beneath them, eyes of a startlingly vivid shade of blue narrowed in uneasy speculation. At the moment, the warehouse held nothing of any particular value. But as soon as the next shipment arrived, it would be a different story.

There'd be plenty worth stealing then.

Ken Noriega, Chief of Airport Security, objected strenuously to Penny's announcement that she intended to resign. Again! He'd understood her reasons for leaving his security staff after graduation to accept a more prestigious job. But following the attacks on the east coast when he'd waved the flag, declaring that the need for experienced officers to protect the airport was vital, she had agreed to return as his second in command. The anti-terrorist safeguards she and her team had devised proved extremely effective. He was reluctant to lose such a valued associate a second time.

Gently but firmly, Penny countered his arguments. Now that Operation Gatekeeper was functioning smoothly, she was determined to move on to less stressful, more person-ally rewarding work.

During the next month she trained an efficient replace-ment to take over her duties. She also found a suitable young woman to share the duplex with her housemates.

In spare moments she pored over every phone book from the cities comprising the San Francisco Bay Area she could locate. None contained a listing for the childhood friend she was attempting to trace.

Penny had been prepared for the possibility that Matt might have moved away. What she hadn't bargained on was the return of the letter she wrote to the Home children's Home where he and she had once lived. Only days after being sent off, it was returned to her by the post office.

The words "No Such Address" were stamped across the face of the envelope in indelible red ink.

After double-checking the street and house number with the data recorded on her adoption papers, Penny concluded that the letter's return must be due to some postal clerk's oversight. It seemed as if even the government was trying to discourage her from following through on her resolution to trace Matt Devlin.

She sighed, wondering whether it would be best to try to deal with the Home by long distance, or simply show up on its doorstep. Or maybe it was a futile task she'd taken on, and she should just follow Lee's advice to give up the search.

Suddenly, as if listening to distant thunder, she seemed to hear the rumble of her adoptive father's voice. "Hell's bells, girl!" Ethan would roar, whenever she started to back away from a task that seemed too difficult for her. "Nobody ever hit a gusher by letting some puny hitch in their plans keep 'em down for long!"

Penny looked down once more at the defaced envelope in her hand. Then she turned toward the closet where her suitcases were stored.

"You were absolutely right, Ethan," she murmured, with a stubborn tilt to her chin. "No puny hitch like a little sass from the United States Postal Service is going to stand in my way!"

(HAPTER TWO

Even in fading twilight, California didn't look at all like Texas to Penny. San Antonio was wide and flat, with a river swirling languidly through its center. San Francisco seemed poised on its toes, a slim ballerina pirouetting between purple chains of foothills and a vast ocean surging in from the other side of the world.

The contrast went deeper than geography. Enthralled, she stared around as the taxi sped north on Bayshore Highway, conveying her from SFO to a downtown hotel. No languid southern pace here, she noticed. Even inanimate structures seemed possessed of a crackling energy. Streets roller coastered up hills, then cartwheeled deep into valleys. Bridges trapezed across the Bay, their spans outlined against the darkening sky by strings of amber lights.

It took her hours to fall asleep that night. Next morning she piled out of bed before the sun had barely crested the horizon. Hastily, she dressed and hurried outside, much too excited to eat. To her surprise it was not the grand, dramatic views that first gripped her attention. Instead, it was small details that captivated her senses, the unique vignettes that made San Francisco special.

Inhaling, she could almost taste the just-baked sourdough French bread whose tantalizing aroma wafted through the red, white, and blue doors of a delivery truck.

Music seemed to quiver just beyond the breeze when a pair of street mimes piped a duet on invisible piccolos. There was nothing imaginary about the flowers, though.

Daffodils were everywhere!

Tables in the sidewalk cafés along Maiden Lane were topped with baskets of the vivid yellow blossoms. More lavish bouquets hung from lampposts and decorated the display windows of shops and travel agencies rimming Union Square.

Unable to resist, Penny bought a long-stemmed bloom for herself at one of the street-corner flower stands. Swinging across Geary with it in her hand, she caught sight of her reflection in a polished marble façade. She looked ready to burst with joy.

How glorious to have come home just in time to welcome the arrival of spring!

Her bright auburn head swiveled around as the Powell Street cable car clattered past. The rapid clickety-clack of its sunken wheels provided a rhythmic background for the gripman's exuberant tattoo on its bell. A block further down, Market Street's wide, diagonal swath marked the end of the line.

Hopping off there, passengers scattered in all directions. Those who had been waiting for a ride in the opposite direction flocked into the center of the street to help the crew spin the gaily-painted tram around on its turntable.

Penny had caught up by the time the cable car was facing the right way for its return trip to Fisherman's Wharf. Slipping onto one of the outer benches facing the street, she clung tightly to a pole as the car rattled back up the hill at a stop-and-go rate of nine miles per hour.

Absorbing the passing scene, she couldn't resist a delighted exclamation upon spotting pagoda-style rooflines

and signs splashed with flamboyant Oriental characters.
"Chinatown!"

Penny's Texas accent caught the ear of the well-dressed
matron seated to her left. "A tourist, are you, dear? Too
bad you weren't here for the celebration a few weeks ago,"
the woman declared. "There's always a spectacular dancing
dragon parade along this street, complete with firecrackers
and red confetti, to cap off Chinese New Year's."

"Lucky me," Penny replied without a moment's hesitation. "I'll be here to see it next year."

Gripping the edge of her seat as the cable car swung
around the corner onto Jackson Street, she marveled at the
confidence with which she had spoken. It sounded as if she
had already made a decision to relocate to San Francisco.
Looking back, she realized that from the moment her flight
touched down, perhaps even from the day she first heard of
Ethel Farnsworth's bequest, the matter had never been in
doubt.

This was where she belonged. The city she intended to
call home from now on. But there was an even more urgent
matter to attend to before she began hunting for office
space and a place to live. There could be no postponing her
search for Matt Devlin.

At Lombard Street, Penny kept her seat while would-be
sightseers alighted to walk a block uphill for a view of "the
crookedest street in the world." Then, before the tram
reached Fisherman's Wharf, she transferred to a Muni bus
whose route passed close to the neighborhood where she
had once lived.

Matt Devlin had monopolized her thoughts during the
past few weeks. Now, stepping off the bus, she found herself peering around, straining for a glimpse of a boy running
to meet her as Matt had often done so long ago.

But at this time of morning children were all in school. The sidewalks were empty. Penny chided herself for wishful thinking as she started down the block. Time would have no more stood still for Matt Devlin than it had for her. It wasn't realistic to keep on thinking of him as the rangy ten-year-old he'd been when she saw him last. By now, he'd be a grown man.

What sort of man? Trying to shield her from disillusionment, Lee had cautioned that in the intervening years, Matt might have become a thoroughly disreputable character.

"What if he ran off to live on the streets?" she'd posed a possibility. "Teens often do, you know. If so, that would explain why he was no longer at the Home when you wrote that last letter."

Picturing her childhood friend homeless and destitute weighed on Penny's spirits. Battling dejection, she'd pointed out happier alternatives.

"He could also have left because he was adopted, just like I was."

Too late, she realized that she had given Lee the wrong impression of Matt. By mentioning the battles he'd waged on her behalf, she had unwittingly portrayed him as an unruly young devil. That wasn't the case at all, she thought. To her, Matt had been a pint-sized Lancelot, her small Knight in Shining Armor. No doubt he had become a model of good behavior after Ethan took her off to live in Texas.

Unless, of course, he'd met some other little girl who needed a defender against pigtail-pulling bullies.

Penny discovered that she didn't care for that idea at all.

She paused to unbutton the jacket she had layered over her full-skirted dress of pale green wool. Here there was none of the energy-sapping humidity one often encountered in the Lone Star State. Still, the temperature had climbed well into the sixties, and the clear, warm air was fragrant with the scent of hyacinth. Primrose brightened the walkways, and in the middle of the next block a flowering plum tree in full bloom strewed fragile pink petals across her path.

Penny was still thinking of Matt as she strode toward it. Suggesting to Lee that Matt might have been adopted had been wishful thinking, pure and simple. Lucky breaks like that seldom happened to orphaned boys who'd reached the age of ten. Still, stranger things had happened. And it would have been perfect if he'd found a good home with a nice couple.

Except—

Her pace faltered as the obvious drawback to this rosy scenario occurred to her. What if Matt had been adopted? And what if his new parents had decided to change his name to theirs?

This was exactly what had happened to her. For the first seven years of her life she had been plain Penny Lasko. Afterwards, Ethan's name, Farnsworth, had been legally added to hers. She had used it ever since.

Penny groaned. It would complicate her search enormously if the boy she was trying to find had undergone a similar experience. How could she ever hope to locate a Matt Devlin-Something-Else?

Common sense intervened before her morale could descend into gloom. If Matt had been adopted, a record of the proceedings would be on file, Penny reminded herself. His name along with those of his new parents would be right there in black and white on the official documents.

Straightening her shoulders, she walked on through the drift of falling blossoms. It was self-defeating to conjure up dilemmas before they arose. Undaunted at failing to find a directory listing for Matt, she had turned hopefully to Plan B. Even after her letter to the children's Home was returned unopened, she hadn't given up. Instead, she had decided that her first priority upon arrival in San Francisco would be to visit the Home in person and speak to whoever was in charge. Whether or not they had solid information regarding Matt's current whereabouts, they would know where to send her for answers.

By the end of the next block the neighborhood had begun to look familiar. A strong sense of déjà vu nearly overwhelmed her when she caught sight of the house on the far corner. Its low, encircling fence wore a different color paint these days. Still, she knew beyond question that this was where the dog had lived, the wretched, neglected dog that she and Matt had befriended.

Her footsteps sounded as energetic as those of any fast-lane Californian's as she hurried toward the corner. From there she'd be able to see the big, rambling house on the opposite side of the street that had once been her home. She and Matt used to take turns racing down the front steps every evening after dinner, tearing across the pavement—

In her eagerness Penny darted into the crosswalk. Momentum carried her halfway across the intersection before shock halted her.

"What on earth?"

Feeling as if she had just been doused with a bucket of cold water, Penny gaped around in confusion. Had she taken a wrong turn? Walked too far? No, the sign at the corner confirmed that these were the cross-streets she had pinpointed on the map. Something was out of kilter, though. While this side of the street was much the same as she had remembered it, across the way nothing looked familiar.

There wasn't a single house to be seen. Nothing at all, in fact, except trees and grass and low green bushes covered with tiny white blossoms.

A horn blared, rudely jolting her out of her trance. Scuttling for the safety of the curb, Penny vividly remembered the occasion seventeen years earlier when a taxi had careened around this same corner and struck down a small girl.

Yes, this corner. Automatically, she ran her thumb across the faded scar on her wrist. She had come to the right place. Inexplicably, however, part of the neighborhood had changed beyond recognition.

Trying to get her bearings, Penny took out the letter she had mailed to the children's Home almost two weeks earlier. When it had come back defaced with a blurred red stamp declaring that there was no such address, she'd assumed that an error had been made, and resolved to follow up in person.

But now to her dismay she realized that the post office hadn't goofed. The address she was seeking had simply ceased to exist.

Intent on acquiring some answers, Penny marched across the street. It was easy to see that the small park that had mysteriously replaced the Home was fairly new. Though carefully tended, the bushes and saplings were far from mature.

The babble of shrill young voices caught her attention. Turning, she followed a tanbark path bordered by a low-growing shrub. It led to a small clearing designed to serve as a toddlers' playground.

In the center of the lawn, three preschoolers were engaged in a game of catch. As Penny came into view, one of the little girls crowed in delight as her chubby arms closed around the fat red ball.

A pleasant-looking woman in her late forties occupied a nearby bench. A crochet hook skimmed in and out of a skein of silken yarn as she kept an eye on the children's play.

Penny sat down a short distance away and struck up a conversation. "What a glorious day!"

"Isn't it, though?" The older woman raised her face gratefully to the sun. "We've had such a lot of rain this winter. It's a mercy to have the drought ended and everything green again, but I can't say I'm sorry to see the fair weather arrive. Are you vacationing here in the city?"

It was the opening Penny needed. She blessed the noticeable Texas accent, which seemed to inspire people to go out of their way to be helpful.

"No, I was born here, but I've just returned home after a long absence," she replied truthfully. "I'm still having trouble convincing myself that this is the same street I lived on years ago."

"You hadn't been here since the earthquake?" Seeing Penny's bewilderment, the woman lowered her needlework and explained.

"Here in San Francisco we're used to tremblers, of course. The fault lines shift, and the city rocks. But the quake that hit while the World Series was being played out at Candlestick Park some years back was the most devastating natural disaster since 1906. Freeways were ripped apart, a section of the Bay Bridge collapsed, and countless homes and businesses were destroyed."

Shocked, Penny wondered how such a cataclysm could have taken place without her being aware of it. Further inquiries helped her pinpoint the date, which she then linked with the events of her own life. Realization dawned.

"My Dad suffered his first major heart attack around that time," she confided. "It happened in a remote back-country region of Wyoming. He and his team were on an oil-hunting expedition when he toppled over. The other geologists brought him to a small mountain hospital. I flew north to stay with him until he was well enough to travel, and remember how dismayed I was to find no television in the place. I must have missed the media coverage of the earthquake entirely."

"Well, it was enough to break your heart. Many of the buildings in this part of town were reduced to rubble in a matter of seconds. Then fire swept through the neighborhood in the earthquake's wake, just the way it had in 1906. It was a terrifying inferno, whole blocks of the city burning out of control."

"What a nightmare!"

"That's exactly what it was," the woman somberly agreed. "Quite a lot of people were killed. Many others lost their most cherished possessions. The one redeeming aspect about the tragedy was the way it brought out the community spirit in folks. Everyone pitched in to help. Either the main quake or one of the aftershocks had ruptured the water mains. Volunteers formed bucket brigades blocks long, keeping the blaze under control until the firemen could rig up their equipment to stretch down to the waterfront and pump salt water out of the Bay."

Picturing the scene, Penny found herself wiping away tears. "What happened to the people whose homes were destroyed?"

"The Red Cross set up shelters during the emergency. Aid poured in from all over the world. Afterwards, the victims salvaged what they could, and started over again some-place else. Many of them would still be trying to find a way to rebuild if the city hadn't bought a whole section of lots along this street and turned the acreage into a park."

A yowl erupted from the grass. One of the toddlers had decided to bounce up and down on the ball instead of sharing it with her playmates.

The woman arose, prepared to make peace. Penny stood up, too. "Thanks so much for taking the time to talk with me," she said.

In a downcast mood she made her way back to the side-walk. One mystery had now been cleared up. But she had a horrid feeling that her search for Matt Devlin had just grown even more complicated.

As a former resident, she would have rated at least a mild welcome at the children's Home. Had she been lucky enough to find the same supervisors still in charge, her visit might have turned into a jolly little reunion. Inquiries about "whatever happened to so-and-so" would have seemed quite natural, and possibly elicited the information she so earnestly desired.

But the Home was gone. Undoubtedly, someone at City Hall could direct her to the agency in charge of orphaned children. But individual case histories would be considered privileged information, and social workers didn't open their files to strangers without a very good reason.

Sentiment, she figured, would hardly qualify as a good reason. The bureaucrats downtown would surely have a dozen questions of their own if she showed up looking for a boy she hadn't seen since she was seven years old.

Before tackling the problem from that angle, she decided to canvass the householders on the opposite side of the street. There was always a chance that some long-time resident of a house that was still intact might remember Matt. Maybe even be in touch with him.

Unfortunately, ten o'clock on a Tuesday morning proved to be a poor time for catching people at home. Nobody answered at the first four houses she tried. At the fifth, a young mother was just trundling a baby stroller out onto the porch as Penny ran up the front steps. She shook her head when asked about the children's Home.

"Sorry," she said. "We just moved here from Chicago last fall."

After that, chiming doorbells went unanswered for several more houses in turn. Then in mid-block Penny spied a stocky, grey-haired man digging energetically in a planting area bordering the front walk.

Something about the finicky way he troweled a seedling into a shallow hole, then tamped down the topsoil around it rang a distant bell in her memory. Trying to contain her excitement, she hurried toward him.

The gardener raised his head impatiently as her footsteps approached. "Young lady, if you're selling something, I don't want any. If you're collecting for charity, I gave at the office. And if you have a petition that needs signing, I doubt I'd approve of the cause."

Lucky her, Penny thought glumly. The neighborhood grouch. But she refused to let his truculence rattle her.

"Nope," she denied with forced cheeriness. "None of the above. All I'm gathering is information in hopes of locating an old friend. We both lived across the street years ago."

His mouth twisted into sour disapproval. "Part of that pack of brats the city billeted in that big old Victorian, I suppose. Those young devils were always whacking a baseball into my junipers, or taking a shortcut across the corner of my lawn. Earthquake flattened the place. Good riddance!"

Now Penny remembered why this irascible man seemed vaguely familiar. He had hollered at a small, pigtailed girl years and years ago for chalking hopscotch squares on the sidewalk. Clearly, his disposition had never improved. He was too crabby to be willing to help her even if he could.

She trudged on, spirits dragging. Not even the pretty yellow daffodil she had carried all the way from downtown seemed to help cheer her after hearing the man's scathing tirade.

At the next house Penny hesitated, casting a discouraged glance over her shoulder. The surly gardener was still watching her, a sour look on his face. He would probably cackle with glee if she abandoned her quest and slunk away.

The thought acted like a tonic. No curmudgeonly scowl was going to stampede her into giving up when she'd barely started. She had known from the beginning that her search from Matt Devlin might not succeed. But she had a long way to go before she was willing to accept defeat.

Doggedly she continued, trying each house in turn. By the end of the long double block, however, she had seriously begun to consider returning that evening, when more of the neighborhood residents would likely be at home.

But what could she do in the meantime? It wasn't as if there was any use getting out the phone book and calling Devlins at random. Like herself, Matt hadn't any relatives.

It was a lonesome thought. Luckily, it impelled her to keep on going, because six houses into the next block she got a break.

The tiny lady who hobbled to the door with the aid of a cane must have been nearly eighty. Still, she treated Penny's inquiry with bright-eyed interest.

"Indeed I do remember the children's Home," Flora Roselli declared, after trading introductions with her caller. "Some people are crazy for traveling, but I was always more interested in my own community. After fifty-two years in the same house, there's not much I can't tell you about this neighborhood. Besides, Mary Cicerone and I were good friends."

Hearing the familiar name left Penny light-headed with relief. Gratefully, she accepted the offer of a seat on the creaky porch swing.

"I'm so glad I kept ringing doorbells until I found you," she exclaimed. "Mrs. Cicerone was housemother when I lived at the Home. Could you tell me how to get in touch with her? I'm hoping she can help me locate one of the other children who was there at the same time as I."

An expression of sorrow crossed the lined face. "I'm so sorry, my dear. Mary passed away six months ago."

Six months! Penny felt a crushing sense of defeat. Only six months! If she had started her search for Matt just half a year earlier. . . .

Mrs. Roselli appeared to realize that the bad news had jolted her caller. "Perhaps it would help if you told me a few more details," she invited. "Over the years my husband and I got to know quite a number of Mary's young charges. Aldo always hired a boy from the Home to help him with the yard in the summers. He said they could use the extra pocket money."

"Your Aldo sounds very kindhearted." Penny leaned earnestly forward, resisting the urge to cross her fingers. "I'd be so grateful if you could remember anything about my friend. He was called Matt. Matt Devlin."

After a pause for thought, the old lady gave her head a regretful shake. "I wish I could say the name sounded familiar, but it doesn't. Can you remember what this boy looked like?"

"I've never forgotten him," Penny said simply. Reaching back through time, she saw him with her heart. "As a ten-year-old he was slim and wiry. He had black hair that curled down over his ears, and blue eyes. Such a vivid blue they drew you right in. Back when I knew him, one of them was usually swollen shut. Matt was a battler, I suppose, but he was always loyal to his friends."

Unexpectedly, Mrs. Roselli nodded. "There was someone like that. He was older by the time I came to notice him, though. Fifteen, maybe sixteen. The eyes . . . yes. They were the brightest blue, like a stained glass window in church with the sun shining through from the back side. But it's what you said about being loyal to friends that makes me sure we're talking about the same young fellow. There was something. . . . Let me think."

Penny sat absolutely still, scarcely daring to budge for fear the creaky swing would distract her companion's thought processes.

A maroon van rolled down the street and turned the corner. Next door the automatic sprinklers popped on, sending a hiss of water arcing across the lawn. A mailman plodded into view, canvas bag swinging from his shoulder as he sorted methodically through the letters it held.

"Now I remember!" Mrs. Roselli cried triumphantly at the sight of him. "The boy I told you about delivered the Wednesday afternoon shopping paper. He used to carry the rolled newspapers in one of those wide canvas aprons that slips over a person's head."

This ruled out the notion that Matt might have been adopted after she left the Home, Penny mused. He must have gone on living there for several years afterward. But in that case why had her letter come back, the one she had written to fulfill an eighth-grade English assignment?

"Go on," she urged eagerly.

"There isn't much more to tell. I do recall that he palled around with two other boys. Ben Zimmerman, whose family ran the bakery down on Chestnut Street, was about the same age as your friend. The third boy was a year or so younger. Jerry, I think his name was. Or maybe Jimmy."

A sudden frown creased the old lady's wrinkled brow. "Aldo felt sorry for the younger boy," she added, a bit abruptly. "Took him on as his summer helper that year. They had plans to build a rock garden in the back yard."

Something about the woman's phrasing struck Penny wrong. She had the odd, sharp conviction that she didn't want to listen to any more of Mrs. Roselli's recollections. But it was too late to stop. Too late to pretend that it didn't matter.

It did matter. Terribly.

"The rock garden," she repeated, her mouth dry. "It didn't get built?"

"Not that year." The old lady shook her head. "They ran away, you see. All three of those boys. They ran away and we never saw them again."

Twenty minutes later Penny rounded a corner and found herself in a bustling little business district. Mrs. Roselli had told her that the family of one of Matt's close friends had owned a bakery on this street. Chances were it would have changed hands a dozen times since then. She had to find out for sure, though. This was the only lead she had left.

Nevertheless, she caught herself dawdling. Postponing the evil moment when her search would come to a dead end.

Suddenly, she found herself beckoned by the heady fragrance of apple and cinnamon. In her eagerness to get started that morning she had dashed out of the hotel without bothering about breakfast. The oversight had been growing more and more noticeable. Now, led by the nose, Penny moved down the block a few doors to ogle a mouthwatering display in the bakery's front window.

When a puff of breeze sent the overhead sign swinging, it drew her gaze upward.

ZIMMERMAN'S
Fine Viennese Pastries Since 1968

Her luck had held, Penny thought jubilantly. The same family had owned the bakery all these years!

Snatching a deep breath for courage, she stepped inside. The sparkling glass showcases were more than half empty this late in the morning. Even so, she thought, eyeing their contents hungrily, it would be difficult to choose between the rolls and muffins and plump berry turnovers that remained.

"Hello! Need some help?"

An attractive young woman with thick blonde braids twined around her head like a crown stepped through from the rear premises. The name "Trudi" was embroidered in curlicued stitching on the pocket of her rose and white uniform. It suited her perfectly, Penny decided. Then, catching sight of the tray Trudi carried, she temporarily stopped thinking about anything except food.

Still warm from the oven, sprinkled with a snowy drift of powdered sugar, the apricot strudel looked too scrumptious to resist.

"I'll have a square of that. And coffee, please." Penny

glanced at the little cluster of tables and chairs arranged against the side wall. "Is it okay if I eat it here?"

"Oh, sure. A lot of people can't resist these goodies long enough to get them home."

Trudi scooped a generous square of strudel onto a paper plate, set a fork and napkin on the counter, then filled a tall cup from a carafe on the warming plate behind her. After paying for her purchases, Penny devoted the next few minutes to taking the edge off her appetite. Then she sipped the rest of the steaming brew while trying to think of the best way to broach the subject she wanted to discuss.

"That was just delicious," she said. "I lived just a few blocks from here when I was younger, but I don't remember this bakery. Is it new?"

"Heavens, no." Trudi glanced up from the tray of glazed doughnuts she'd been rearranging. "My in-laws were just newlyweds when they opened the business. Ben and his sisters grew up back there in the kitchen."

"Ben!"

Penny's only thought had been that at least one of the runaways had returned. But when she saw the jealous flare in Trudi's green eyes, she wished she had used more discretion.

"Do you know my husband?" the blonde demanded.

"No, I never even heard of him until half an hour ago," Penny assured her. "Mrs. Roselli who lives across from the new little park told me that someone I'm trying to locate used to hang out with a boy named Ben Zimmerman when they were both teenagers. You probably know him yourself. Matt Devlin?"

"No, sorry." Trudi shook her braided crown. "Reno is my hometown. I met Ben at a ski lodge over the Christmas holidays, and we were married last month. I haven't had time to get acquainted with many of his friends yet."

"Well, I wish you much happiness," Penny said politely. "Uh, do you think your husband would answer a few questions for me? It's very important. I'll be glad to come back whenever it's convenient for him."

"He's in and out a lot."

Trudi moved down the counter to assist another customer. She started back toward Penny after ringing up the sale, all the while keeping an eye on a trio of giggling schoolgirls who couldn't seem to decide what they wanted. "Listen, how about letting Ben give you a call if he knows anything about this guy Devlin and has time to talk. Where can he reach you, Ms. . . . ?"

"Farnsworth. Penny Lasko Farnsworth." She brought out the city map the desk clerk had given her that morning and passed it across the counter. "I just got into town. The hotel's name and phone number are stamped here at the bottom. I'm in room Four-oh-seven."

"Four-oh-seven. Right."

Each of the schoolgirls had produced a rumpled dollar bill, and all now began digging change out of their pockets. Penny turned toward the door as Trudi swung back to them. Hopefully, the jealous bride would decide to relay the request to her husband. With any luck, he'd have good news to pass along when they spoke.

"What did you say her name was?"

"Farnsworth," Ben repeated into his cell phone. "It must be true what they say about sailors having a girl in every port. Imagine forgetting a cute little redhead."

Matt Devlin had known plenty of redheads. Blondes and brunettes, too. None of them, however, had been named Farnsworth.

There was a wary glint in his deep blue eyes as he rested a lean hip against his desk and scanned the cavernous warehouse. At the time he'd signed the lease, the rent had seemed more than fair. Now he wasn't so sure he'd gotten a bargain. Two break-ins in two weeks was a fringe benefit he found highly unwelcome. Worse yet, he still hadn't found a single clue, either to the intruder's identity or to what he had been after.

Or could it be a case of what she had been after?

Considering the possibility, he tilted his dark head to one side. Maybe, he thought. Why else would an unknown female claiming to be an old friend have gone to so much trouble to track him down?

He decided that making it easy for her to find him might work to his advantage.

"You're still on your honeymoon, ole' buddy," he told Ben easily. "I'm sure your bride would rather I talked to this mysterious redhead myself. How do I get in touch with her?"

Brows lifted as he jotted down the name and number of the classy downtown hotel. "My, my," Matt muttered to himself as he hung up. "I wonder what Ms. Farnsworth's game is."

He intended to find out.

CHAPTER THREE

Hurrying across the elegantly appointed lobby, Penny heard snatches of a dozen languages. None of them made the slightest impression on her. Her attention was riveted on the white square of paper visible in the pigeonhole for room 407.

She had come straight back to the hotel after leaving the bakery, pausing only long enough to buy copies of San Francisco's two daily papers before heading for her room. All afternoon, while waiting for Ben Zimmerman to call, she forced herself to concentrate on the want ads jamming the back pages of the *Chronicle* and the *Examiner*. Finding a place to live was an urgent priority. She had already resolved not to spend any of the inheritance from Ethel Farnsworth until she found Matt Devlin and learned his circumstances. But her savings wouldn't last long if she spent many days in her current pricey surroundings.

At 7:30 she finally acknowledged that Trudi's husband might not contact her for days, if ever. She could starve to death, waiting for him to get in touch. But now it appeared that her timing had been abysmal. During the half hour she'd been out swallowing a quick bite of supper, a message had been left in her box.

The room clerk slid a small, flat envelope over the counter along with her key. The words "Ms. Farnsworth, room 407," had been scrawled across its face. The blunt black handwriting had an angry slant to it, as though the writer had harbored a grudge and was taking it out on the paper.

Annoyed at herself for having missed the call she'd awaited the entire afternoon, Penny strode toward the elevators. Her fingers fumbled to unseal the envelope's flap, then reached inside and came up empty. Surprised, she turned it over and searched more thoroughly.

It contained no message of any kind.

Frustration came to a boil. All set to swing around and march back to the desk, Penny glanced up and stopped in her tracks. Just ahead, a tall, slim man leaned against the wall with his arms folded. His stance was nonchalant. His expression was not.

He was glowering at her.

Dark as his crisp black hair, the bold stare seemed designed to pierce and pry, to ferret out her most carefully guarded secrets. The look was so keen, so penetrating, that Penny almost jerked back at the force of it. Before she could manage to wrench free from the scathing contact, the man straightened up.

He took a challenging step toward her. "Ms. Farnsworth? I understand we're old friends."

That was a lie, his tone declared. Feeling rather as if she'd been challenged to a duel, Penny stood her ground and stared back at him.

His eyes opened wider. Their color was striking, the deep, clear hue of sapphires. Penny had never seen anyone with eyes that impossible shade of blue. Except once. Long ago.

"Matt?" she asked, on a glad catch of breath. "Matt Devlin? I wouldn't expect you to remember me, it's been so long. But I've never forgotten you."

He had been braced for any claim the woman might have made except that one. That, and the joyful welcome in her voice. His flint-edged glare softened as he took a closer look. Framed by short, curly auburn hair, her triangular face was more appealing than pretty, but her wide-set eyes with their splashes of gold and green and amber were beautiful. Milky skin, freckles zigzagging across her nose. . . .

From out of the past, memory stirred.

"Penny Lasko," he murmured, his voice elated and incredulous at the same time. "We were kids together, you and I!"

Almost instinctively, Penny reached out to take his hand. But her fingers were already filled with the empty envelope. "Did you leave this in my box, Matt?"

He shrugged an acknowledgment. "I told the clerk that I had a message for Ms. Farnsworth in room four-oh-seven. Then I hung around to see who came to pick it up. Penny, why the devil didn't you tell Ben's wife who you really were?"

"I did!"

A well-dressed couple emerged from an elevator and squeezed past. Other hotel guests were drifting in their direction, their glances curious.

"We can't talk here," Penny murmured in an embarrassed tone.

Grasping her arm, Matt steered her toward an unoccupied couch on the opposite side of the lobby.

The gesture brought a flood of recollections. Visions of a skinny little girl with Band-Aids on her knees and carroty hair slithering out of its pigtails danced before his eyes.

Everything else might have changed over the years, but not that. While Penny Lasko had grown taller and slightly more assured, she still reminded him of the little urchin he'd taken under his wing when he was ten.

Strength and dependability were oh-so-evident in the guiding touch of Matt's fingers. How well Penny recalled the scrawny mite of a girl who had relied so trustingly on a boy not much older than herself. Then, Matt had been her protection against the world. But times had changed. These days she was capable of taking care of herself.

Rather breathlessly, she dropped down on the edge of the couch and began to explain.

"Really, I did tell Trudi that my name was Penny Lasko Farnsworth. But the bakery was busy this morning, and I guess the last part of it was all that stuck in her mind. Farnsworth was the name of the man who adopted me," she clarified the issue. "I've used it along with my birth name ever since Ethan brought me to San Antonio to live with him and his wife."

Apologetically, she glanced up at the solemn young man who seated himself beside her. "I'm sorry, Matt. It was really dumb of me not to remember that I was simply Penny Lasko back when you and I knew each other. Especially since it had already occurred to me that it would be much harder to locate you if you'd been adopted and given a new last name, too."

"You could have spared yourself any worries on that score." Matt's wry tone told more about his unloved youth than he would ever have consciously revealed. "Nobody ever had any yen to adopt me. But here we are, all grown up. Tell me why you came looking for me after all these years, Penny. Are you okay? Is there something I can do for you?"

The questions were as deflating as an oven door slamming on a soufflé. Matt had jumped to the conclusion that she had looked him up to ask for help, Penny realized, rather than to offer it to him in case he needed it.

Embarrassed, she shook her head. From the instant she'd laid eyes on him standing in front of the elevators, it had been clear that her original worries about his suffering deprivation—at least in any material way—were groundless. Though clad in windbreaker, jeans and boots instead of the elegant designer clothing favored by most of the well-to-do tourists occupying the hotel lobby, the outfit was obviously a matter of preference rather than need.

It suited him. So did his short, neat haircut. He looked exactly right: the cool, self-confident master of himself.

"Thank you, Matt, no. I don't need anything. As a matter of fact, I came to see if you—" Her quixotic idea now seemed whimsical in the extreme. She gave a sheepish shrug. "It's a long story. Let's just forget it."

A faint smile tugged at his mouth. "We have the whole evening ahead of us."

From Matt's point of view, that was quite true. Wanting plenty of time to deal with the mysterious redhead who'd turned up in his old neighborhood looking for him, Matt had cancelled an appointment with a prospective client in order to come downtown. He had expected to find a stranger when he left that message as a lure to bring the occupant of room 407 out into the open.

Instead, he'd received a welcome surprise.

"Start at the beginning," he suggested. "Tell me about your life after you left the Home. Did your new parents turn you into a pampered little southern belle?"

"Anything but!" She laughed at the idea, then grew serious. "Ethan was great, Matt. No girl could have asked for a more wonderful father. Even though he was really old enough to be my grandfather, he had a youthful spirit. But his wife, Arletta, disliked me from the start. She even burned the letter I wrote you soon after I arrived in Texas."

"Letter?" A disturbing sensation roared in Matt's ears. It reminded him of the time he'd just come back from shore leave, and a massive wave had hit the carrier before he'd regained his sea legs. "You wrote to me?"

"Of course I did. You were my best friend, weren't you? Don't you remember making me promise never to forget you?"

Penny's jaw clenched as she recalled Arletta's description of him and everyone else she'd once known as "riff-raff." Then she shoved Ethan's snobbish wife out of her thoughts once and for all. Instead, she focused on Matt Devlin, her sweet childhood friend who had matured into this attractive and very capable-looking man.

"Years later I wrote you again." She looked up at him, reliving the embarrassed letdown she had felt as an eighth-grader whose chosen pen pal had apparently vanished into thin air. "They returned my letter. Someone there at the Home marked it 'Moved. No forwarding address,' and sent it back."

Matt closed his eyes to mask the remembered pain of that summer. The three of them had taken off together. Afterwards, only he and Ben had been left to regret the impulse that had turned out so very, very badly.

Feeling shut out, Penny waited for him to tell her why he had run away. After a very long two or three minutes, she realized that Matt had no intention of explaining.

That was his business, of course. Who did she think she was, anyway?

In an effort to smooth over the awkward silence, she picked up her own life story again, covering the remaining high points in a few brisk sentences.

"Which brings us to Ethan's twin sister," she capped off the tale. "Ethel died recently. She had no children of her own, and because I'd been her brother's adopted daughter, she left me some money. The bequest got me started thinking of you."

"Why me?"

"Because for the past seventeen years I've been convinced that Ethan adopted the wrong kid. He should have taken you instead of me."

"That's the silliest thing I ever heard."

"No, think about it." Penny cooled his protest with a hand on his arm. "Remember that dog we fed, who lived across the street from the Home? The night I got hit by Ethan's taxi, it had been your turn to take the food over to him. That lucky accident changed my life completely, Matt. But by all rights the luck—and the inheritance from Ethel—should have been yours instead of mine."

Uncomfortable with the way he was glowering at her, Penny stumbled on. "I thought . . . well, I wondered . . . I figured. . . ." She looked into those stunning, bright blue eyes, grabbed a deep breath, and blurted out what she'd been trying to say. "I didn't know what kind of life you'd had. I thought it was at least possible that things mightn't have gone too well for you. When I was little, you held out a helping hand to me. It seemed only fair to try and repay the favor."

Shock left Matt feeling numb. Not once in all his twenty-seven years had anyone gone out of his or her way to do him a kindness. Because he didn't know how to handle such a novelty, his reply came out sounding gruffer than he'd intended.

"Forget that nonsense. I've gotten along just fine on my own. The legacy's all yours, Penny, just the way the lady who made the will intended it to be. Gonna buy a ranch with it when you get back to Texas? Or is San Francisco just your first stop on a world tour?"

Furious patches of color popped out on Penny's cheeks. Matt was acting as if she had insulted him rather than trying to do him a favor!

"Wrong on both counts," she snapped. "Now that you've assured me you're much too macho ever to accept a friend's help regardless of the circumstances, I can follow through on my own ambitions with a clear conscience. I intend to start a small business of my own based here in the city." In one fluid movement she was on her feet and moving briskly away. "Nice to have seen you again, Matt."

"Hey, wait a minute!"

She had taken him by surprise. Penny got in four quick strides toward the elevator before he caught up with her.

Heads turned. Matt paid no attention. What he couldn't ignore was the hurt expression he had glimpsed on her face. Little Penny Lasko used to have the same look at times.

It stunned Matt to realize that he would be willing to get down on his belly and grovel if it would make up for the distress he'd caused her with his careless tongue.

"I'm sorry," he said in a raw voice. "Forgive me."

Neither anger nor insult could have stopped Penny's headlong rush. Humility managed the trick. Matt's abject tone convinced her that his squelching comeback had been meant as a shield, not a put-down.

Meeting his gaze squarely, she saw regret in those beautiful blue eyes. "I'm sorry," he said again, before she had a chance to sort out her feelings.

He wrapped his strong, warm fingers around her hands in a way she found both petitioning and sheltering. "Thank you for thinking of me, Penny. For offering to share. The idea that you would even consider such a thing knocked me off-stride. Nobody ever . . . I've always just fought my own battles."

"Yes, and quite a few of mine, as well."

Inside the nest of hands, the sharp room key was gouging into her flesh. Penny used the pain as an excuse to

51

free herself, to stand solidly again on her own two feet. There was no reason to feel so upset, she chided herself. The bond they had shared in childhood placed neither one of them under obligation as adults. To be honest, if it hadn't been for Ethel's legacy she probably never would have come in search of her childhood champion.

"Of course I forgive you," she assured him in a cool, firm voice. "And please believe that I meant what I said a minute ago. It really has been good to see you again."

Matt Devlin jammed his hands into the pockets of his windbreaker. He had thought of this long-lost friend often in the first few years after her adoption. Was it that mention of Ethan's wife's 'con-nip-shuns' that had kept him from trying to find her, once he was grown? The notion that he wouldn't have been welcomed in Penny's new home? That was a big part of it, he admitted. Having endured plenty of put-downs in his youth, he wasn't about to go out of his way to seek another.

But the past was gone. This was a whole new start. He had no intention of letting Penny vanish from his life again now that fate had caused her to wander back into it.

"I remember you as being someone who always played fair," he threw out a dare. "I've already listened to your life story. It's only right that you give me a chance to bore you with mine."

Penny recognized the hook in that audacious challenge, but found it irresistible nonetheless. It would be very interesting to have Matt fill in a few pieces of background, she decided. Tonight, before they'd recognized each other, he had looked so . . . so tough and wary. As though he'd suspected that the woman who'd been asking questions about him might represent some sort of a threat. She wondered what hard experience was responsible for that lack of trust, and what catalyst had caused him to run away from the Home in his teens.

Perhaps whatever it had been was what made him so insistent now on ramrodding his own destiny.

"I reckon I might hold still for a spell while you bend my ear," she quoted one of Ethan's folksy sayings. "Tell me, Matt, does your autobiography include a chapter on a wife and kiddies?"

"Not so far. But I do have a few interesting live-in friends." Matt's teasing grin cautioned her not to get the wrong idea. "I have a hunch you'll enjoy meeting the Woolies and Billabong Babies. How about I pick you up first thing in the morning and introduce you?"

Regretfully, Penny shook her head. Upstairs, newspapers were scattered across her bed, a dozen want ads circled in red.

"Thanks, Matt, but my first priority is finding a place to live. From what I've seen advertised so far, I suspect I'll have to settle for a tiny studio apartment. That is, unless I'm lucky enough to stumble across a house or duplex to share with several other women, like the place I had in San Antonio. Compared to what I've been used to paying, the rents here seem incredibly steep."

It occurred to Matt that Penny's inheritance might not be as large as the lavish bequest he had envisioned. If so, that made her willingness to share it with him seem all the more generous.

"The price of housing in this town is astronomical," he agreed. "That's one reason I live on my boat."

"Aha! That explains why you aren't in the phone book."

"I am, but it's a commercial listing at the warehouse under my company name."

Asking questions in the old neighborhood, locating the

bakery owned by Ben's folks, checking through the phone book—she really had gone to a lot of trouble to locate him, Matt realized. But the jolt of pleasure this thought gave him was tempered by uneasiness at the notion of her sharing quarters with strangers.

"It pays to be careful when choosing your roommates," he worried aloud, visions of her being menaced by serial killers and drug dealers clouding his mind. "And want ads can be misleading. You'd do better to contact a reliable rental agent who can steer you to a secure building in a safe neighborhood."

Seeing her again must have activated Matt's old protective instincts, Penny thought, touched yet a bit annoyed.

"That's something to consider," she answered neutrally.

"Meanwhile, I know where there's a terrific bargain to be had in office space," he barreled on, oblivious to the cool reception his last well-meant suggestion had earned. "Interested?"

"Fascinated."

"Great." He had an inkling that she might be teasing him. That was okay. At least she wasn't angry with him any longer. "I'll pick you up first thing in the morning. We'll have breakfast, then get started right away."

Matt was sounding more like a big brother every moment, Penny reflected in chagrin. Apparently, that was the role he saw himself filling in her life.

Though she couldn't have said why, the notion wasn't at all to her liking. She tilted her pointy chin. "On one condition, Matt Devlin. I will take you to breakfast. Interested?"

"Fascinated." Matt grinned, delighted to have the feisty old Penny back. "You can feed me anything but grits."

Over breakfast next morning Matt gave Penny a choice

of traveling around town by bus or taxi. "Right after my discharge from the Navy, I bought a car and put up with it for about six months," he explained. "But parking in this city is such a hassle, and garage space so hard to come by, that I finally decided owning my own wheels was an aggravation I could do without."

Penny reflected that in just those few sentences, Matt had revealed more about himself than she had managed to learn in more than an hour's conversation the previous evening. The Navy? She told herself she should have guessed immediately that his erect posture and neatly cropped hair were the results of military training.

"The bus suits me," she assured him.

Taking her elbow, he guided her around a corner. "We can catch an express two blocks down that will take us where we want to go in no time."

San Antonio was such a spread-out city that Penny would have found it very difficult to manage without wheels of her own, particularly during the years she had attended college while working part-time at the airport. But being the tip of a peninsula surrounded on three sides by water, San Francisco was much more compact. A ride of a few blocks brought them to within sight of the Embarcadero's wharves.

Gazing around with interest as they stepped onto the sidewalk, Penny caught sight of tall orange cranes unloading ponderous containers from the decks of ocean freighters. Nearby docks housed stacks of the huge, colorful rectangles that held imported goods from all around the Pacific Rim.

Matt turned through the gate of a sprawling business park. He set a slow pace, making it easy for Penny to get a good look at the various structures making up the complex.

"This site is perfect for me. Depending on what sort of

office space you have in mind, it might work well for you, too," he said.

"It might," she agreed cautiously. To her relief he made no further efforts to convert her to his viewpoint.

Conveniently adjacent to the front parking lot, two-story office buildings offered sizable commercial quarters for lease. Buildings housing smaller units, each with a private entrance accessible from a covered walkway, were located at the rear of the property. Opposite them stood half a dozen warehouses with energy-saving solar panels affixed to their roofs.

Leading Penny in this direction, Matt pointed out several famous landmarks visible in the distance. Topping the rise of Telegraph Hill to the north, the lovely fluted column of Coit Tower soared heavenward. The classic monument made a benign contrast to Alcatraz jutting granite-hard from the cobalt waters of the Bay half a mile out. Compared to the ultramodern Transamerica building topping a nearby rise, it looked timeless and serene.

"Just south of here is the Waterfront Historic District. Altogether, the entire location has a lot going for it," Matt said earnestly.

"I can see that. On the other hand," Penny mentioned an important consideration, "with the docks so close, the area looks pretty industrial. The clientele I expect my business to attract will be people who are fairly well to do. It's possible they might look down their noses at conducting business in such workaday surroundings."

Not much of the business park's space was allotted to landscaping, she noticed, and the construction, while solid, had a basic, no-frills appearance. Eyeing the buildings closely as they walked, she formed the impression that a considerable number of the office units seemed to be unoccupied.

When she raised the point, Matt explained that beginning in the early 1970's the microchip industry had expanded dramatically in Northern California.

"Rental space was at such a premium that developers bought up every available parcel of land. Both here in the city and down in Silicon Valley they threw up one business park after another.

"Then this latest recession hit," he went on. "Dot-com companies with millions in venture capital invested in them suddenly became known as the 'dot-gones.' Other high-tech firms downsized their staffs and economized on space in order to survive, or relocated to states where commercial property and housing for their employees cost considerably less."

The economic downturn had affected Texas as well, Penny knew. Several airlines had cut back on less popular flights, and San Antonio International had felt the decrease in business travel. But it hadn't occurred to her that the availability of commercial space would also increase.

"So right now there's too much supply for the demand?"

"Neatly stated." Pausing at the entrance to the last warehouse, Matt pulled a bunch of keys from his pocket. "Developers of some of the newer complexes like this one are currently offering space at bargain rates. By next year the pendulum will probably have swung back the other way. I tied up a lot of square footage while the price was still in line with my budget."

Penny watched him deal with two separate padlocks, then key in a formidable deadbolt. Reaching inside, Matt snapped on a bank of fluorescent lights. Then he stepped back, holding the door wide in welcome.

"Come on in and meet the gang."

CHAPTER FOUR

So far, Penny had managed to keep from bombarding Matt with questions. It hadn't been easy. Now, at his invitation she stepped eagerly inside, looking around to see what his place of business could tell her about her childhood friend.

To her disappointment, the cavernous warehouse seemed designed more for keeping secrets than for revealing them. Arranged supermarket-style, it had long aisles of shelving bisected by occasional walkways. Unlike a supermarket, though, the place was so empty it echoed. The only signs of occupancy were a neat office nook in the front corner off to her left, and a dozen or so cardboard cartons clustered on a shelf partway down the nearest aisle.

Leeann's pessimistic warnings squirmed their way into Penny's head.

She shoved them firmly out again, refusing to let her trust in Matt be shaken. Still, it was hard to keep from wondering why two hefty padlocks as well as a deadbolt were needed to protect all this bare space.

She turned to him with a quizzical smile. "Do you suppose the 'gang' went out for coffee?"

Matt realized that most people would think he was suffering from delusions of grandeur if he tried to convince them that someday soon he would have need of every bit of the warehouse's tremendous storage capacity. But Penny had never doubted him when they were children. Her un-blinking faith had carried him through quite a few bouts of self-doubt. He didn't believe she would mock his adult ambitions, no matter how far-fetched they might seem to others.

"No, they have a habit of hibernating when nobody's around," he joked in reply. "Come on down here. I'll show you."

Despite his confident manner, Penny detected a twinge of anxiety in Matt's tone. Her approval seemed to mean something to him. It was the least she could do to offer encouragement . . . for old times' sake.

Once she got a glimpse of the boxes' contents, however, all need for pretense vanished.

"Matt, he's adorable!" she exclaimed, when he brought out a cuddly toy sheep and tucked it into her arms. "His coat feels like real fleece."

"It is. Didn't I tell you they were called Woolies?"

Convinced that Penny's enthusiasm was genuine, Matt brought out three more toy sheep: an ewe, a curly-horned ram, and an engaging black-faced baa-lamb.

"You have a whole family there!"

He nodded. "No two Woolies are exactly alike. They're handmade by members of a church sewing circle in a tiny New Zealand community. Sheep outnumber people several thousand to one in that part of the world. Every year at shearing season, wool scraps accumulate by the binful. It was the rector's wife who got the idea of recycling some of that raw material into toys."

Matt's voice rang with assurance as he described the origin of the unique playthings. Finding his enthusiasm contagious, Penny thought how attractive the contrast of blue eyes twinkling in a deeply tanned face was.

She snuggled the Woolie against her cheek. "Whoever made this one did a wonderful job. I love him! But Matt, New Zealand is a tremendous distance away. How did you get involved with toy makers clear down there at the bottom of the world?"

Seeing the nuzzling the toy sheep was receiving, Matt felt an inexplicable pang. Long ago, he and Penny had been pals. Buddies, that was all. It came as an unsettling surprise to find himself wondering how it would feel to have her hold him that close.

"It's a long story," he warned.

"That sounds familiar," she retorted with a laugh. "As I recall, you didn't let me get away with using any lame excuses."

Penny would have liked to urge him to start from the beginning, as she had done when recounting her own life story. But much as she longed to know how Matt had fared during the years he'd stayed on at the Home, she had a hunch that prying into whatever had caused him to run away might spoil the comradely rapport they had begun to rebuild.

Matt packed the Woolies back into their box as he talked. "While I was in the Navy, the carrier I served aboard was assigned a tour of duty Down Under. We spent several months taking part in maneuvers along with ships crewed by Australians and New Zealanders, or Kiwis, as they call themselves."

Penny was glad that although Matt had left the service, he had retained his trim military haircut. "Did you like the Navy?" she asked.

"You bet. I picked up training in all sorts of skills, and the travel experience was tremendous." He paused to look up with an earnest expression. "But halfway through my second four-year hitch I began feeling a yen to try charting my own destiny."

"You, too? I know the feeling."

Matt reached for another box. "It wasn't until my best buddy became the proud uncle of triplets that I hit on the idea for the sort of career I wanted to pursue. On our next shore leave he asked me to come along and help him shop for gifts to send his sister's babies."

Penny smiled, picturing two dashing sailors inspecting toy stores. "You must have had a ball."

"It was a whole new world to me. Darned few toys had come my way when I was a kid," Matt said quietly. "Jake wasn't impressed, though. At least not at first. We kept running into the same mass-produced stuff in the shops Down Under that are carried by every discount store in the States."

Penny surrendered the Woolie she had been holding so it could be packed away. "But you did find the perfect gift for the triplets eventually, right?"

"In Brisbane, we stumbled across a craft market. One of the displays was decorated to represent the Great Barrier Reef that lies offshore in that part of the world. The woman running the booth had created a collection of toys she called Reefies." Matt grinned at the recollection. "Great-looking fish and crabs, octopuses and lobsters, each one equipped with its own little bed of coral."

"How did you manage to choose among them?"

"We didn't choose, we bought one of each kind. Then, when we got back aboard ship, we had trouble holding onto them. A lot of our shipmates had youngsters at home. They tried to buy the Reefies from us to send to their own kids. We could have doubled our money if we'd been willing to sell."

It was this experience that gave him the idea of importing unique toys as a business, Matt added. "I figured that if I could locate other playthings as well made and imaginative as the Reefies, American parents and their children would snap them up."

"Matt, how enterprising of you!"

"It turned out to be a good idea—eventually." Matt tried not to let her praise go to his head. "But at the time I didn't know what I was letting myself in for. Red tape comes by the yard when you're applying for licenses to import foreign-made merchandise into the USA."

Unpacking the rest of the cartons, he displayed the Reefies to her next. "Meg Limmons, the woman who dreamed up these wonderful creatures, was a great help," he said, handing her a winsome octopus. "She introduced me to several other artisans who were struggling to succeed in the toy market."

In Penny's opinion, each item he demonstrated was a potential trendsetter. She loved the fact that none of the toys had any connection with violence. Another plus was that many, like the Woolies, were made from scrap or recycled materials.

While she liked them all, her particular favorites were the Billabong Babies. Matt told her that the charming little koala bear and the comical kangaroo were marsupials, like many of the animals native to Australia.

"That means they carry their young around in their pouch, right?" She eyed the shallow, free-form dish Matt had uncrated with each of the Billabong Babies. "What are those?"

"Showing's better than telling," he answered with a teasing grin. "If you'll fill a paper cup with water from that cooler next to my desk, I'll give you a demonstration."

After doing as he asked, Penny watched in rapt delight while Matt trickled a few drops of water into each of the dishes. Then he positioned them on the shelf near the toy animals.

"Watch, now." Matt pushed a button in the back of the koala, then another on the kangaroo.

As though drawn by a magnet, each of the mother animals swung toward her own water dish, then bent down. Out hopped a baby from each pouch. The fuzzy little koala scampered over, took a noisy slurp from the dish, then swiveled around again to jump back into his mother's safe, warm pocket. Hopping along on his oversized feet, the young kangaroo followed suit.

Penny clapped her hands at the amazing performance. "That is the cleverest thing I've ever seen! Why are they called such an odd name?"

Matt explained that except for its coastal fringes, Australia was primarily a vast desert. "In The Wet, as the monsoon season is called, they have torrential rains and flash floods. But once summer arrives, the countryside dries up—even the rivers, except in a few of the deepest spots. Those water holes that remain in The Dry are called 'billabongs.' " Matt laughed. "Any smart animal would carry one along with him if he could. And these are very smart animals."

"They sure are."

Actually, Penny thought, it was Matt who was the smart one. He'd had the perception to spot the potential of these marvelous toys, and the tenacity to arrange for their importation to America.

"What amazes me," she continued, "is that there isn't a line a block long outside of shop owners applying to carry the toys for sale."

"Shhh, quiet. Don't give anyone ideas," Matt half joked. "My biggest problem isn't finding outlets for the toys. As you've seen, they practically sell themselves. But as you can also see, I have an empty warehouse. The people I'm dealing with overseas aren't geared for mass production. They're artists who tinker around with toys for the sheer joy of it."

Penny reminded herself that a large part of the toys' charm was that they were unique and limited in availability. "But you will be getting more in stock soon, right?"

A shipment of Reefies had just been dispatched to him the previous week, Matt said. He added that he had backed the Reefies' creator financially with a sizable chunk of his Navy severance pay, and held an exclusive import contract with Meg and most of the other artisans. "Several gross of the Woolies are also en route. But I wish I could say the same for the Billabong Babies."

Matt picked up the little kangaroo. "Neville Baker, who dreamed up these toys, is a real creative genius. He's also something of a recluse who lives in the Outback, a long way from any population center. His work force consists mainly of native people who live in the area. Unfortunately, his Aborigine helpers have a habit of going walkabout."

Penny was familiar with that term from the Crocodile Dundee movies. "Doesn't 'going walkabout' mean just pulling up stakes and wandering off for a look at the countryside whenever the spirit moves you?"

"Too right," the importer grumbled, sounding like an Aussie himself. "As of the moment, Neville's been left high and dry—and so have I."

Discouraging as this state of affairs might be, Matt felt that the Billabong Babies were so unique they were definitely worth waiting for. Meanwhile, he had recently received samples of a new board game he felt sure would interest retailers. Its creators had named it Dreamtime.

"That's sort of a mystical Aborigine concept. I expect it to go over big, given the interest in fantasy themes these days," Matt said optimistically. "I'll know for sure this afternoon when it has its first unveiling."

"You're going to take the game around to toy shop owners to get their reaction?"

"And orders, hopefully. Starting with my best customer."

Matt explained that Russell Kehoe owned an upscale Sutter Street shop called Diversions. "I'm hoping that having the guarantee of a new game for the Christmas season will take the edge off Kehoe's annoyance at having the delivery of the Billabong Babies delayed again," he added, with a wry grimace.

Penny found it odd to be thinking of holiday shoppers in the middle of March. She reflected that in Matt's business, long-range planning must be essential.

"I hope you pointed out that part of the charm of the toys you import is that they're not a glut on the market," she said crisply.

"Kehoe's a shrewd merchandiser who specializes in unusual products. As a matter of fact, he's been pushing for an exclusive on my imports," Matt admitted. "But I don't think it's a good idea to put all my eggs in one basket."

"You sound like a pretty shrewd merchandiser yourself."

Matt had always had faith in himself. But now, for almost the first time since he was ten years old, he experienced the deep satisfaction of having another person share that belief in his worth and intelligence.

He would have liked to let Penny know how much her esteem meant to him. He had never mastered the skill of expressing his emotions verbally, however.

"Thanks for the pat on the back," he said, a trifle awkwardly. "I wish I was convinced that Kehoe is as crazy about these toys as I am, but with him I suspect it's strictly business. Cutthroat business. He has a strong motive for wanting to corner the market on every unusual plaything that comes along. To him, Monopoly isn't just a game."

"Ethan's wife was like that."

Penny sighed, remembering how Arletta had begrudged every minute her husband had spent with the small daughter he'd adopted. Maybe it would have been different if she had been a dainty, feminine little girl with pretty manners. But at the age of seven, Penny was none of those things.

When Ethan learned about the pigtail-pulling bullies who'd made life miserable for her at the Home, he marched her into a barbershop and ordered her carroty hair clipped off to ear length. Then he'd bought her some sturdy denim clothes. Soon after their arrival in San Antonio he took her to a dojo—a studio run by a deceptively gentle-looking Korean—for her first lessons in self-defense.

Finding a local dojo was something else she needed to do without delay, Penny thought. Without regular practice sessions, her martial arts skills would soon deteriorate. Feeling vaguely guilty about the passing time, she stood up.

"I got so carried away admiring your wonderful toys I almost forgot that today I'm supposed to be searching for an office of my own."

"There's plenty of space for lease in this complex," Matt reminded her.

Gazing around the warehouse, Penny found it easy to imagine the shelves filled to overflowing with the sort of wonderful toys she'd just been looking at.

"I can see why this location is ideal for you," she said. "It's roomy and convenient to the docks, and a two-minute walk from the bus stop. But an office so close to the waterfront is likely to be a turnoff for the type of clientele I hope to attract."

"Society leaders and the dot-com millionaires who yanked their money out of the NASDAQ in time?"

"Well, not to begin with." Penny's smile faded. "On the other hand, the service I'm offering would be unlikely to appeal to anyone who wasn't fairly well fixed. Let's face it; people who are struggling to make ends meet don't have the resources to send their children across country by air, with or without an escort. If I hope to make a living through my travel escort bureau, I'll need the patronage of affluent customers. Probably the same type of people who do their shopping at your friend Kehoe's upscale toy shop."

Matt saw her point. But he expressed some reservations of his own when she mentioned her hopes of locating in the Union Square district.

"The Square is ringed with exclusive stores and top-notch travel agencies," he said. "Those outfits can afford the high, heart-of-the-city rents because of the huge volume of walk-in business the location attracts. But you plan on offering a specialized service, Penny. It won't be colorful posters or designer originals in the front window that attracts your customers."

"Of course not. It'll be the assurance that I can deliver their child safely to wherever he or she is bound."

"Then it seems to me your first priority should be to convince prospective clients of how honest and reliable you are," Matt said matter-of-factly. "If they're the kind of parents who want the best for their youngsters, they'll be more

impressed by solid character references than by plush surroundings."

Penny's earnest nod assured him she agreed with this
outlook. "Once I've made a good start, word of mouth will
be my best advertising. But I'll need local references until
I've established a solid client base. Everyone who can vouch
for my integrity is clear back in San Antonio."

"How about offering to pay the long-distance tolls for interested clients to talk with your previous employer?" he
suggested. "The calls would be tax-deductible, and you
wouldn't need to hold the offer open for long. Once you've
accumulated a core group of satisfied customers, they'll
serve as references for later prospects."

"That's a great idea. It really is."

Recalling the hotheaded youngster she had known years
ago, Penny marveled at what a solid citizen Matt Devlin
had become. He'd matured into a self-made man who had
conceived the idea for his own business and followed
through successfully on it. It made good sense for her to
treat his suggestions with respect.

"Since I'm already here, how about if I look into what
sort of office space they're offering in this business park,"
she proposed. "At least I can get a quote on the monthly
rent."

"That way you'll have a basis for comparison with what
you find in other areas," Matt pointed out. "Griff Hazelton,
the developer of this property, has an office here in the
park. I'll walk up with you and make introductions."

Penny noticed that Matt carefully snapped both padlocks, then turned the key in the formidable deadbolt that
guarded the front entry. Why, she wondered again, was it
necessary to take such extreme precautions to safeguard an
almost empty warehouse?

Had he risked his last cent on the prototypes of those toys?

An old-time memory, warm and comfortable as a bowl of oatmeal on a foggy morning, thrummed through her as his lean, strong fingers curled about hers. How often in the past, Penny wondered, had Matt held out a helping hand to her?

Wistfully, she thought how much pleasure it would have given her to return the favor. That was what true friendship was all about. Give and take. Helping each other.

But Matt had made it quite clear that he neither needed nor wanted her help. The notion of paying him back for all the black eyes he'd endured on her behalf was one of those pipe dreams that would never become reality.

Matt interrupted this bittersweet reverie. "Would you like to meet me at Diversions this afternoon around four? My business with Kehoe will be finished by then, and you'll have had a chance to look around the city for rental space. We can compare notes."

"Sounds good."

Penny found herself almost reluctant to let go of his hand when he shifted to take out a business card and jot the toy store's address onto the back of it. She forced a self-assured smile. "If I find a place I like, would you be willing to come have a look at it?"

"I'd have been hurt if you hadn't asked."

Matt felt flattered that Penny valued his advice enough to extend the invitation. But she had made it clear that she intended to make her own choices. He understood. Each decision he'd made when establishing his own business had seemed like a landmark achievement. He didn't want to rob her of feeling the same satisfaction.

The suite of rooms they entered a short time later didn't

actually reek of Gatorade and liniment, Penny assured herself. Nor was the man who rounded the massive desk like a quarterback targeting his receiver really wearing shoulder pads. Nevertheless, she had a hunch that Matt's ebullient landlord would have felt more at home in cleats than in the expensive Tony Lama boots he wore.

Glass-fronted trophy cases filled one wall of the office, showing football players in various action poses. But when Griff Hazelton reached out to grip her hand, Penny realized at once that he was personally displaying the most important trophy for her admiration. The flash of diamonds in the Super Bowl ring he wore would have been impossible to miss.

"Hel-lo, little lady!" he exclaimed, hardly waiting for Matt to finish the introductions. "You-all from Texas, honey-chile?"

Penny bit her tongue to squelch a sharp retort. Did this big, friendly oaf come on to all females in that obnoxious way or had her soft, Southern drawl activated the tendency?

"From San Francisco, originally," she replied in a cool tone and firmly extricated her hand from his grip. Starting today, she meant to begin eradicating that accent. She'd be darned if she would allow herself to be patronized because of it.

"Ms. Farnsworth is interested in discussing office space with you," Matt interjected stiffly.

He felt a sudden flash of anger and realized in surprise that he had come within half a breath of taking a swing at his landlord. In the past, his dealings with Hazelton had always been amiable. But watching the ex-ballplayer ogle Penny had roused some deeply protective instincts.

She was just a kid!

Matt couldn't recall the last time such a juvenile impulse

had assailed him. He supposed it would have been back in the days when he and Penny were close companions. Let anyone tease that skinny little waif and here came Devlin, fists flailing in her defense, setting himself up for a black eye.

He forced himself to relax. It would have been embarrassing to have Griff Hazelton break him in half right in front of Penny. The other man outweighed him by eighty pounds and had the reach of a gorilla. Besides, the wolf in cowboy boots had already backed off. He called a "See you later" to Penny over his shoulder, and prudently walked out.

From the surprised look on Griff Hazelton's face when she dropped his hand, Penny gathered that his advances weren't rebuffed very often. But to her relief, he didn't exactly seem crushed when she backed away. It wouldn't have been tactful to put a strain on the good landlord-tenant relationship that existed between him and Matt.

Having made it clear that she wasn't here to play games, she gave the developer an amiable smile. Despite her petite size, large, muscular people no longer intimidated her.

Those first lessons in self-defense Ethan arranged had been followed by formal martial arts training that continued throughout Penny's school years. Learning to toss a heavyweight over her shoulder might not have been strictly ladylike. The skill had proved the undoing of many a burly hooligan, though, during her years at San Antonio International. In her personal life, it guaranteed that dates never took an unwanted turn.

In response to her question about office space, the developer spread a color-coded schematic of the business park across his desk.

Penny studied it for a moment. "The smallest units lie at the back of the site?"

"Both the smallest and the largest." He gestured, Super Bowl ring flashing. "Six warehouses form our rear perimeter. Now, if you should be interested in acquiring several thousand square feet. . . ."

Penny hastily disabused him of this notion. "Basically, I just need enough space for a desk and a couple of chairs. Tell me about your rates, please."

She jotted figures in the notebook she carried in her purse. After asking if a three-month trial period was available, she set off beside him on a tour of the various-size units. Each was clean and snug, complete with overhead light and smoke alarm. All the basics. Nothing extra. Nothing, unfortunately, to impress wealthy potential clients with her solidity as a businessperson.

Matt's viewpoint made a lot of sense, she admitted. But instinct told her that success would come her way more quickly in a classier location.

Six hours later, Penny found herself hoping that conclusion was incorrect. Matt hadn't exaggerated about the steep rents she could expect to encounter downtown. The dingiest broom closet in the city center seemed far out of reach of any would-be tenant not funded by the Rockefeller Foundation.

Like it or not, she was going to have to settle for one of those no-frills units at Griff Hazelton's business park.

Diversions' animated sign was visible the moment she turned the corner onto Sutter Street. Watching the neon clown attempt to lasso a rocking horse with a lariat made of balloons, Penny decided it was a far more effective bit of advertising than any SALE! banner would have been. It strongly implied that all toys acquired at this establishment were guaranteed to provide fun galore for their new owners.

But a few yards short of the shop's entrance, Penny formed the conclusion that at least two people inside Diversions were not having a good time. A heated argument was audible even through the heavy plate-glass windows.

Suddenly, the door burst open. A small dynamo whizzed out, all ringlets and ruffles and patent leather shoes that hit the sidewalk like shiny little jackhammers.

The child was too upset to heed where she was going. She pelted forward while twisting her head around to shout a mutinous ultimatum back over her shoulder.

"I won't!" she howled, a split second before barging full tilt into Penny. "I won't go without you!"

CHAPTER FIVE

"Whoops! Careful."

Penny thrust out both hands, but the instinctive gesture came a split-second too late to fend off a collision. The child who had just blitzkrieged out of the toy shop cannoned into her with an impact that knocked the breath out of both of them.

For an instant it seemed as if they were both destined to land in a tangled heap on the sidewalk. Struggling for balance, Penny caught sight of the anguish in the little girl's big, brown eyes. Impulsively, she stooped down to the youngster's level. Her hands reached out to the small shoulders, steadying and comforting at the same time.

"You okay?"

A gurgly sob wound up as a hiccup. "Uh-huh, I guess. I 'prologize for bumping into you."

"Maybe it was lucky you did. Otherwise, you might have tumbled right off the curb. Cars can't stop as fast as people can, you know."

As if to prove Penny's point, a delivery van careened past, spewing a hot, evil-smelling exhaust in its wake.

The child inched back looking suddenly wary. "I'm not s'posed to talk to strangers."

"Good. I'm careful about which strangers I talk to, myself."

Straightening up, Penny saw a way to shepherd the little girl back inside without causing her to lose face.

"I was on my way to meet a friend at that toy shop over there," she said. "He had business with the owner this afternoon. If you knew someone there, too, we could ask them to introduce us. That way we wouldn't be strangers any longer."

The youngster bobbed her flaxen ringlets, okaying the idea. She was about six, Penny decided. Petite and pretty, and very self-possessed for her years.

Together, they turned toward the building. It was then that Penny caught sight of the man poised watchfully in the doorway. His tailoring was impeccable, his fair hair expensively styled. Glimpsing expressive dark eyes identical to those of the child who walked beside her, Penny had no doubt that the pair was father and daughter.

But it wasn't he to whom she spoke. As had happened so often in her childhood, Matt Devlin showed up exactly when she needed him.

"Hi, Penny," he called. "I'll be ready to go in a minute."

Hearing the underlying tinge of exasperation in his voice, Penny wondered if the owner of Diversions had been pressuring him for an exclusive to carry the new board game. It wasn't hard to guess the outcome of that confrontation. As many a bully had learned in the past, Matt wasn't one to let either himself or his friends be pushed around.

Since the premises were momentarily empty of customers, Penny assumed that the other man must be Mr. Kehoe. Waiting until Matt had finished measuring a display rack, she asked if he would please introduce her to the shop owner.

Matt didn't hesitate. Any time Penny needed a favor, it was his pleasure to supply it. Turning, he presented her formally to the brown-eyed man who had witnessed her side-walk encounter with the little girl.

"Penny, this is Russell Kehoe, the owner of Diversions. Kehoe, I'd like you to meet my oldest friend, Penny Lasko Farnsworth."

"How do you do?" After shaking hands, Penny gravely requested that her new acquaintance introduce her to his daughter. "Our meeting was on the casual side, I'm afraid. We both agreed that talking to strangers was not a good idea."

The shop owner raised thick, sandy eyebrows in approval. "By all means. Ms. Farnsworth, may I present my daughter, Miss Bethany Kehoe. Beth, this is Penny."

Halfway through their formal handshake, Beth began to giggle. "Now we can talk all we want. You're not a stranger anymore."

"Neither are you," Penny teased.

Watching this byplay, Matt wondered what was happening. Half an hour earlier a dour woman clad in black had escorted the child into the shop, then taken herself off with the mention of a dentist appointment. One look had been enough to tell Matt that Beth and her nanny weren't fond of one another. A few minutes after that, while working in the back room, he'd overheard a sharp argument break out between Kehoe and his daughter.

Now Penny had walked in and restored peace. With an admiring glance in her direction, he remarked that he'd left some papers in the rear of the shop. "Let me collect them and we'll be on our way."

While Matt's tone was unruffled, the rigid set of his shoulders told Penny that he and Russell Kehoe were not on the best of terms just then. Nor were Beth and her father the picture of harmony. In fact, Penny thought uncomfortably, there was so much tension in Diversions that it could have used shelf space of its own.

The shop owner focused on her out-of-state accent as a topic for small talk to smooth over the prickly atmosphere.

"I moved here from Philadelphia last year," he said. "You sound as if you might be a newcomer to San Francisco, as well."

"I was born here, though most of my life has been spent in Texas," Penny answered the implied question. "Now that I've come home to stay, I hope to launch a small business of my own. I've just spent the day looking at office space to rent."

"Are you a toy seller too?" Bethany asked with interest.

Penny felt devoutly glad that such was not the case. Under his suave exterior, the child's father had the steely demeanor of a ruthless competitor.

"No, nothing like that. I intend to offer my services as a traveling companion for children who would otherwise have to fly long distances by themselves."

Kehoe's handsome features stiffened in anger. "Who put you up to this scam?" he demanded.

Shocked by his hostile tone, Penny took an instinctive step backwards. This man was an important business associate of Matt's, she reminded herself while taking a deep breath to keep angry words from spilling out. It would hardly be tactful to tell him exactly what she thought about his rudeness. But neither would she allow herself to be insulted.

"Perhaps you misunderstood," she said icily. "The business enterprise I have in mind offers a legitimate and much-needed service. Until quite recently I was part of a team in charge of anti-terrorist security at San Antonio International Airport. Whenever time permitted, I also assisted unescorted children to change planes. Many of those youngsters weren't mature enough to cross the street by themselves, let alone find their way around a crowded air terminal. But since they had been sent off alone on what was often a cross-country journey, they had no option except to see it through with no one familiar to turn to if things went wrong."

"In that case, I apologize for jumping to conclusions." Though Kehoe's words were conciliatory enough, his rigid expression failed to soften. "Perhaps you'll understand my concerns when I tell you that my daughter is scheduled to travel to Philadelphia soon to spend the Easter holidays with her mother. Only minutes before the two of you met so explosively, she had thrown a tantrum about making the trip in the company of her nanny."

So that was what the argument had concerned. Still feeling aggrieved, Penny couldn't resist a comment.

"If you don't mind my saying so, Mr. Kehoe, it sounded as if *you* are the person Beth hopes will be her traveling companion."

Lugging the boxed game and his briefcase up the aisle from the back room, Matt caught sight of the awkward tableau at the front of the store. For the second time in only a few minutes, he had the feeling he'd missed something.

"Ready to go?" he asked.

The fury of Penny's thoughts had drowned out the sound of his approach. She swung around in relief. Matt had shown up at exactly the right moment.

"All set." Carefully, she concealed the animosity she felt toward Russell Kehoe so as not to taint the business relationship between the two men. "Here, let me catch the door for you."

Matt paused, frowned, then gave in without protest.

78

Standing back, he let Penny handle the chore because she seemed so anxious to leave the shop.

During their childhood at the Home, he remembered, she had always beat a quick retreat whenever trouble threatened. Not being very big or very strong, it had been her only means of self-defense.

She still wasn't very big, he reflected, looking down benevolently at the top of her bright head. Short auburn curls lay in shining clusters, replacing the hated pigtails that had once blighted her life.

Matt felt an inexplicable urge to reach out and run his fingers through her hair. The impulse seemed shockingly dishonorable. He was still trying to figure out what had caused it to pop into his head when the toy seller followed him out onto the sidewalk with a last-minute query.

"I suppose there's not the slightest hope of getting the Billabong Babies in before Easter?"

With an effort, Matt held onto his temper. Irritating as the man's persistence was, Russell Kehoe was also his best customer.

"None at all, I'm afraid. As I've already explained, the inventor has trouble keeping workers because of his isolated location. But hopefully, shipments will start trickling through from him by summer."

Kehoe made an exasperated gesture. "Baker's a genius! He could be a millionaire by now if he'd use his head and move to the city where there's a decent labor pool available. Can't you persuade him to see reason?"

Matt clenched his jaw. He wanted to talk to Penny, not stand here rehashing a sore point he and his client had already threshed out earlier.

"Neville Baker likes living in the Outback," he retorted. "It's his home. The place where his creativity flourishes.

How would you like it if someone tried to dictate where you had to live?"

Kehoe's expression closed like a trap, as if Matt's rhetorical question had been a personal taunt. Noticing his grim stillness, Penny wondered whether the shop owner's cross-country move had been entirely voluntary. Not that she cared. All she wanted at the moment was to move on to an atmosphere that didn't crackle with tension.

The toy shop door creaked as she started to turn away. Glancing back, Penny saw Bethany's unhappy little face peeking out through the opening.

"Goodbye, non-stranger," she called. "It was nice to have met you."

Matt didn't take her arm because his hands were already full. But Penny noticed the way he quickly switched over to walk on the curb side. Ethan had always done that too, she remembered. When as a small child she'd asked him why, he'd explained that in the old days gentlemen had walked on that side to protect the ladies they were escorting from being splattered by mud from the wheels of passing carriages.

She smiled at Matt, wishing he and Ethan could have known each other. In spite of belonging to different generations, they had a surprising number of habits in common.

The straight-shouldered young man beside her didn't smile back. "What was going on back there?" he asked, coming straight to the point.

Penny sighed. She supposed it was inevitable for Matt to have picked up on the animosity that had suddenly sprung up between Russell Kehoe and herself.

"Just an awkward misunderstanding," she explained, hoping to gloss over the matter. "I made the mistake of mentioning my new business. Mr. Kehoe jumped to the conclusion that I was trying to finagle him into hiring me."

"I ought to go back and punch him in the nose!"

It was weird, Matt thought, a little confused at what had happened to his ordinarily peaceable nature. Twice today he'd felt the urge to massacre another male on Penny's account.

"Thanks for the impulse, but I'm glad you didn't," Penny said, smiling up at him. "It would be a shame to let such a picayune misunderstanding come between you and your client. Mr. Kehoe and his daughter had been sniping, and I accidentally blundered into the midst of the conflict. I gather that Bethany is due to fly back east soon to spend Easter with her mother. She's been pestering her dad to go with her, instead of sending the nanny along as escort."

"Poor kid," Matt said sympathetically. "Her parents haven't been divorced long. I suppose she figures that if she can bring them face to face they might decide to reconcile."

"Any chance she could be right?"

He looked dubious. "According to the scuttlebutt I've heard, it was a bitter breakup. As business partners during their marriage, Pamela and Russell Kehoe ran one of the most successful toy outlets on the East Coast. Now, each of them seems determined to make their own shop the country's number one independent."

"Perhaps he's been pressuring you for an exclusive on the toys from Australia to eliminate the chance of his ex-wife getting them for her store."

Matt nodded agreement. From what he knew of the personalities involved, her guess was likely to be right. But he was sorry now that he'd passed on the gossip. As a teenager he had learned to keep his nose out of other people's business. The lesson had stuck.

"Stay out of their affairs, Penny," he advised gruffly.

"Being involved in a family dispute is a no-win situation. Trust me. I know."

What a strange thing for Matt to say, she thought. To the best of her knowledge, he had no family of his own. Not so much as a second cousin.

"I do trust you," she assured him. "I always have. And believe me, I have no intention of meddling in the Kehoe family's affairs."

"Good."

It had been a mistake to invite her to meet him at Diversions, Matt realized now. While not the womanizer he knew Griff Hazelton to be, Russell Kehoe was rich and smooth and as persuasive as the snake in the Garden of Eden. He wouldn't trust either of those men around someone as attractive as Penny.

The notion took him by surprise. Attractive? Penny?

Matt had once overheard the housemother at the Home refer to the two of them as the Ugly Ducklings. He had figured that was one reason no one had ever wanted to adopt him.

Slanting another look sideways, he reflected that if Penny had ever deserved the unflattering nickname, that was certainly no longer the case.

The light changed just as they reached the end of the block. Penny started to plow blithely ahead against the red. Juggling his burden to free a hand, Matt reached out and grabbed her by the arm. His strong grip kept her safely on the curb until the signal turned green again.

"I haven't had a chance to ask you how the search went," he remarked, as they turned south onto Stockton Street. "Did you find a business address that suited you?"

"Ha!" Penny scoffed. "Oh, Matt, you were so right

about the steep rates. Downtown offices don't rent by the square foot. They rent by the square inch!"

"What about your legacy? Could it take up the slack until you got your new business off the ground?"

"I doubt that even the whole forty thousand would be enough to keep me for long at the astronomical prices I ran into today." Penny made a disgusted face. "Besides, Ethel Farnsworth said in her will that I was to use the money for something to make me happy. It didn't mention a word about fulfilling the wildest dreams of some greedy land-lord!"

Knowing that oil wells ran in the Farnsworth family, the modest size of her inheritance surprised Matt. More than ever he was touched that she had come all the way to California intending to share the money with him. What had she called it? Lending a helping hand. A disagreeable thought struck him.

"I hope this doesn't mean you'll be returning to San Antonio?"

"Not a chance. I think I knew this was where I belonged even before the plane landed at SFO. Besides," Penny added cheerfully, "conspicuous consumption is out of style just now. With companies downsizing and all the emphasis on conservation these days, I'm hoping future clients won't balk at talking business in a less-than-elegant office."

"Elegance is one thing; safety's another."

Matt was still as protective as ever, Penny realized fondly. First he'd stopped her from crossing against the light, even though the closest car was a block away. Now he was worried that she might wind up in a crime-riddled neighborhood.

While she appreciated his concern, she was tempted to point out that she was an adult, quite capable of taking care of herself nowadays. Yet he looked so earnest it would have been mean to tell him that Knights in Shining Armor had gone out of style along with the opulent furs every fashion-conscious female once flaunted.

"I doubt you'd have recommended your own business park if you didn't consider it safe," she said lightly. "The one-room offices there rent for quite a reasonable sum, all things considered. Besides, after a bit of haggling your landlord agreed to let me lease one for a three-month trial period. I've decided to go back and sign an agreement with him in the morning."

"That's terrific!" Matt kept his packages clutched tightly to his chest to keep from congratulating her with a hug. "As your oldest friend, I claim the right to take you out for a celebration dinner."

"Thank you. As your oldest friend, I accept with pleasure. Have you someplace in mind?"

"Shanghai Sal's is fun." He spoke absently, his mind on how great it would be to have her working nearby. "I need to finish up some paperwork. Let me take care of that. Then I'll phone for reservations and pick you up at seven-thirty."

He escorted her as far as the hotel's entrance before striding off. Penny lingered, gazing after him before continuing on into the lobby. There was a hard edge to Matt that she found excitingly attractive. Even as a child, his jaw had thrust flintily out to intercept trouble. In maturity, his uncompromising features proclaimed him to be an individual to be reckoned with.

Her childhood friend had grown up, Penny marveled, absorbing that fact fully for the first time. Matt Devlin was no longer the boy she had once leaned on.

He had become the man she yearned to know.

★ ★ ★ ★ ★

Having learned from the female desk clerk that Shanghai Sal's was a fairly dressy place, Penny took a leisurely bath, then changed into one of her favorite costumes. The vintage dress was the color of bronzy-rust autumn leaves, and its flattering, timeless cut always brought out her most feminine feelings. Beneath the wide cowl neckline the gown fit snugly almost to the knee. Then it flared out into a rustling swirl of fabric.

Strappy evening slippers and understated makeup completed the ensemble. About to reach for the perfume she currently favored, Penny changed her mind at the last minute and opted instead to sprinkle on the last few drops she possessed of an old-timey cologne. Both the light, flowery scent and the black velvet evening cloak she draped over her shoulders had been gifts from Ethan on the occasion of her high-school prom.

Tonight's date was like a retrospective, she thought sentimentally. Old friends, vintage clothing, a classic fragrance. She hoped Matt was in the mood for nostalgia.

Matt Devlin felt confused. He remembered Penny Lasko as a skinny, freckle-faced carrot top who'd counted on him to defend her from bullies. Yet earlier today he'd found himself thinking of her as attractive. Stranger still, the Penny who'd stepped out of the elevator to meet him this evening was neither that Ugly Duckling from the Home nor the composed young female who spoke so confidently of establishing her own business.

This Penny made him wish he'd stopped by the florist's for a corsage, though where such an obsolete idea came from he had no idea. And what could he have been thinking of to choose a restaurant that lampooned the Barbary

Coast's raunchy history as an appropriate spot for their celebration dinner?

The red velvet hangings came as a surprise. So did the waitresses, who were dressed like a brassy bunch of dance-hall hussies, complete with fishnet stockings and beauty patches. Penny's perplexity deepened after a glance at the menu.

"With a name like 'Shanghai Sal's,' I was expecting Chinese food," she confessed. "Not entrees labeled 'Marlinspike Halibut' or 'Two Years Before the Mast T-Bone,' or a vegetarian plate called the 'Scurvy Standoff.'"

Matt laughed in spite of his embarrassment. "This place is patterned on a palace of sin from Gold Rush days," he admitted rather sheepishly. "Prospectors used to come in with their pockets full of nuggets looking for a wild good time as an antidote to the wearying boredom of pick-and-shovel mining."

"I'll bet they found it."

"Some of them got more than they bargained for," Matt told her. "Nobody will ever know how many men lost not only their fortunes but their freedom as well in places like Sal's. In those days, whenever a sailing vessel put into the harbor its master could count on having at least half his crew jump ship. Who wanted to swab decks or rig sail when there were huge fortunes in gold lying around the foothills?"

"I can see the sailors' point," Penny admitted. "How did the ships manage to return to their home ports with the scanty crews they had left?"

"Their captains made an under-the-table arrangement with places like this to have a quota of stalwart young fellows 'shanghaied' the day they were ready to sail."

Matt nodded toward the stage in the center of the room.

There, a siren in a gaudy red dress was beckoning a drunken buffoon toward a half-open trapdoor.

"Today that's just part of the floorshow. But it wasn't an act 150 years ago. The victims were drugged, bundled down a hatch to an underground tunnel leading straight to the docks, then hauled aboard ship. When the effects of the knockout drops wore off, they found they had been 're-cruited' for a long voyage. Sometimes to a destination as remote as Shanghai, China."

"So that's where the term 'shanghaied' came from!" Penny exclaimed. "Wouldn't you have thought that after a few of their friends disappeared, those miners would have learned to be more careful about where they spent their evenings?"

"If it had been me, I'd certainly have watched my step. Listen," Matt added, turning a bit red in the face, "how about going someplace else to eat? Chinese would be great with me. Or Italian? Whatever you'd like, Penny. It's your celebration."

She gaped at him. "What's wrong with this place?"

"It just doesn't seem—well, quite suitable. Considering your age, I mean."

It dawned on Penny what the matter must be. Having tripped over the same stumbling block herself, she recognized the symptoms.

"Matt," she said gently, "remember last night in the hotel lobby? You said something like, 'here we are, all grown up,' didn't you?"

"Sure. I was referring to the fact that I had become an adult even though no family had ever wanted to adopt me."

The confession pulled at her heartstrings. "How old are you, Matt?"

"Twenty-seven," he answered without hesitation. "I

turn twenty-eight in August."

"Now, take a wild guess. How old would you say I am?"

The question caught him by surprise. "You were just a tiny kid—"

"Doggone you, Matt Devlin, I was seven years old when Ethan adopted me. You were ten!" Penny exploded in exasperation. "That makes me just three years younger than you are."

Matt juggled dates in disbelief. She was right, he thought. Come summer it would be eighteen years since he had pleaded with her not to forget him. He had left her locked in time back there in his memory.

"Can you forgive me?" he asked sheepishly. "I can see now that I've spent the entire day waiting for someone to pull your pigtails so I could punch him out."

Great, Penny thought, thoroughly disgruntled. To him, she was still little Penny Lasko. The timid weakling who relied on him for protection!

CHAPTER SIX

Griff Hazelton had twiddled his thumbs in long-suffering silence while Penny read the lease word for word. Now he baited her with a lazy smile.

"You could save yourself a pile of money by nailing down your office space for five years instead of for a measly three months."

They were getting along much better this morning, Penny reflected. He hadn't once called her "honey-chile" or "little lady." Nevertheless, she vetoed his suggestion.

"By the end of ninety days I hope to be able to make a long-term commitment. But first I need to prove that working for myself is really a sound business idea."

She was well aware that the odds were against her. Statistics showed that the great majority of small businesses failed within their first year. This dive into the deep waters of entrepreneurship was a shaky one, indeed.

"It isn't that I don't believe in myself. I do." Penny emphasized the point by picking up a pen and signing both copies of the lease. "Unfortunately, it takes more than self-confidence to keep a new little business afloat."

"Any kind of business." Sounding faintly rueful, her landlord scrawled his signature beneath hers. "If keeping your head out of the red ink was an easy matter, commercial space wouldn't be a glut on the market right now. But don't look for the same conditions to hold true three months from now."

"Do you think the economy will rebound that quickly?"

Diamonds flashed in the Super Bowl ring he wore as Griff Hazelton wiggled his hand back and forth. The gesture seemed to say that while it was hard to pinpoint the exact day a flood of would-be renters would be lining up at his door with deposit checks in hand, things were bound to be back to normal soon.

"The important point to remember is that recessions are only temporary setbacks. All you have to do is ride them out." He leaned back in his oversize swivel chair, regarding her with interest. "You in the microchip game?"

Penny shook her head. "My field is people, not technology. I intend to launch a travel escort service for children."

"To where?"

"To anywhere they need to go."

"And you expect someone to pay you to tag along for the ride?"

His flabbergasted tone revealed exactly what he thought of her chances for success. Penny wished she had fewer doubts on this score, herself. "I wouldn't exactly express it in those terms," she answered. "But yes, I suppose you might say that's the whole idea."

"Why the dickens should the kid's parents get stuck with the expense of an extra fare when there are all those flight attendants on every plane?"

"Because airline personnel have important jobs of their own. Where are they supposed to find the time to baby-sit, on top of their other duties?"

He seemed stuck for an answer, so she went on. "During the summer or around the holidays, as many as twenty children might travel unescorted on a single commercial aircraft. Once the flight attendants make sure their seat belts are fastened and provide refreshments, those youngsters are on their own."

"So, what's the problem? The kid eats his peanuts, reads a comic book, has himself a nap. It can't take more than a few hours by jet no matter where they're headed."

"Right," Penny agreed. "Provided it's a nonstop flight. Even so, what about the child who's diabetic and must take his medicine at a certain time? Supposing he gets confused as to what time it actually is, since the state he's headed for may be three time zones ahead or behind the state he just left?"

"Well, that's a special case, of course," Hazelton backpedaled.

"If there isn't a direct flight to his destination, he'll have to change planes." She gave the developer a challenging look. "When you were a third-grader, could you have found your way through a huge airport in a strange city? What if you missed your connection, and it was the last plane out that night?"

A scowl had furrowed his wide brow. "Would a little kid really be expected to cope with complications like that?"

"All the time. When marriages break up, the divorced couple often moves as far away from each other as they can get. Many former spouses wind up living on opposite sides of the nation." Penny thought of Bethany Kehoe's parents. "If they're sharing their children's custody, it's the youngsters who commute back and forth, not mom or dad.

"It gets really complicated if kids are being sent out of the country," she added soberly. "Then they have to cope with foreign customs and passport control, and people who don't speak their language. Until last week I worked in a big international airport. I saw plenty of kids heading off to Tokyo or the Persian Gulf, or Caracas, Venezuela because their fathers had new jobs overseas."

Hazelton swung his head toward the gleaming trophy cases on the wall. "I never got to travel at all until I started playing professional football," he reminisced. "Then I was on the go every week during the season. I'll bet I suited up in every city in the country with a league franchise."

"Was there time to do much sight-seeing?"

"Nah. We'd come in on the team plane and head for the practice field. Postseason was different, though," he remembered, brightening. "In my day, being invited to play in the Pro Bowl meant a trip to Hawaii. That was always the last game of the season, so there was plenty of time afterwards to chase the wahines around Waikiki Beach."

Penny swallowed a smile. Wahine, she knew, was the Hawaiian word for "woman."

"Some of the preseason exhibition games were more play than work, too." He pointed with pride to a three-foot-high statuette in the trophy case. "I got that one for being chosen MVP at the Kangaroo Bowl."

"MVP?"

"Most Valuable Player. I had three touchdowns and was headed for my fourth when someone slammed me into the ground and gave me a concussion." For some reason this recollection triggered a wide grin. "The doctors wouldn't let me fly home until they were sure my head was okay. I got to spend ten days going to the races and drinking that great Aussie beer, and, uh, meeting every sheila from Sydney to Perth."

Ask him about a famous landmark and he'd probably quote some girl's measurements, Penny thought. She glanced at her watch and stood up. "Let's go take another look at the units you have available in my price range. I'm anxious to pick out my space and start getting settled in."

"No hurry. I figured we'd seal our bargain with lunch out at the Wharf."

"Thank you, but I have a personal rule against socializing with business associates."

Penny picked up her copy of the contract, feeling there was no need to add that the rule was precisely thirty seconds old. Placidly, she waited for Griff Hazelton to hoist his formidable bulk out of the chair. "Have you keys to the empty offices, or are they left unlocked?"

He gave up trying to play Wolf to her Red Riding Hood, and pulled open a desk drawer. "Think I'm crazy? Leave a place unlocked these days, and you'll find someone making himself at home there next time you turn around."

Sorting through several large, jingling bunches of keys, he brought out a ring labeled "700's" and stood up. "You're welcome to take your pick of the empty units," he said, in a brusquer tone than she had heard him use before. "All offices the size you'll be paying for are exactly alike."

Units with the least square footage were located at the rear of the complex. Keeping up with Hazelton's long strides, Penny reflected that an awful lot had happened in the twenty-four hours since she'd caught her first glimpse of the business park.

Along with revising her standards about a suitable workspace, she had also managed to convince Matt Devlin that little Penny Lasko had grown up. Last night at Shanghai Sal's she'd taken out her driver's license and pointed to her date of birth as proof that she had come of age several years back.

Matt had eyed this incontrovertible evidence of her maturity with a dazed expression. Having struggled to overcome the same mind block herself, Penny could understand his confusion.

It was almost like losing a dear old friend to realize that he or she had grown up while you weren't around to watch it happening.

Still sounding miffed that she had turned down his invitation to lunch, Griff Hazelton broke into her thoughts with a gruff comment. "This is the building. Except for two empty offices at the far end, all the ground level space is already rented. But you can pretty much take your choice of the units on the upper floor."

After inspecting several offices, each with an identical large window, small closet, cream paint, fluorescent light and smoke alarm, Penny settled on a second-story location directly across from Matt's warehouse. Her new landlord removed the key marked "763" from the jingling ring, and handed it over.

"I always advise tenants to have their locks changed before storing any valuables on the premises," he said. "Better to be safe than sorry."

During her years in security, Penny had encountered many dexterous crooks. It would have been no problem, she thought, for a light-fingered visitor to lift a ring of keys from Hazelton's desk, quickly take wax impressions, and return them with no one being the wiser. Once the offices those keys fit were rented, the possessions of their occupants would be easy prey.

"Thanks for the warning," she said. "I'll call a locksmith right away."

The first thing she needed was a phone of her own. Penny smiled. The necessity of its installation made a perfect excuse for a visit to Matt Devlin.

With the key to unit 763 tucked in her pocket, she crossed the driveway to rap at his warehouse door.

Matt was delighted to find Penny standing outside on his step. After his blunder of the night before he'd been none too certain she would ever speak to him again. It had taken a date embossed on a driver's license to rout the sentimental image of her as a little kid that he'd carried with him for so many years. After she'd shoved it under his nose he had apologized, of course. But he still wasn't sure she'd understood what the hang-up was.

How could she, when it had taken him half the night to figure out the problem himself?

After much soul-searching he'd come to the conclusion that, subconsciously, he hadn't wanted to think of his childhood friend as being all grown up. Those years they'd spent together at the children's Home had been the best period of his life. Back then, Penny had depended on him. Trusted him unconditionally. Because of that, he had never once let her down.

No one, before or since, had ever made him feel as needed as Penny Lasko had. He'd have battled Darth Vader and all the critters in Jurassic Park for that loyal little girl, Matt thought with a lump in his throat.

Because Penny had believed in him, he'd begun to believe in himself. Even the terrible drama he'd become caught up in several years after they'd said goodbye hadn't managed to erase the self-confidence she had helped him build. Because of her, he could hold up his head today and feel satisfied with the way his life was turning out.

Matt swallowed hard. Was she here to let him know they were still friends? Or to say goodbye again, this time forever?

He widened the door. "Good to see you. Come on in."

Penny thought he sounded distracted. Stepping inside the warehouse, she felt a stab of guilt. She really shouldn't have bothered Matt during business hours. But it was too late now to turn around and leave.

"Good morning." With determination, she forced a cheerful lilt into her voice. "Back in Texas, new neighbors always ran next door to borrow a cup of sugar as a way of getting acquainted. The best excuse I could think of was to ask to use your phone."

"Neighbors?"

It did Penny's heart good to spot the sparkle in those vivid blue eyes as Matt pounced on the word. She tugged the brand-new key out of her pocket and held it up for his inspection. "That's right. For the next ninety days, at least, you're looking at the proprietor of unit number seven sixty-three."

Matt felt as though he'd just felt the sun break through a fog bank. With a massive effort he restrained the clown-sized grin stretching at his mouth.

"That's terrific. Uh, did you say something about wanting to use the phone?"

Penny nodded. "I need to arrange to have one of my own installed so prospective clients can get in touch with me. If there are any prospective clients out there, that is. Our landlord seems to have his doubts about a business like mine ever succeeding."

From impressions he'd gathered during the past couple of days, Matt believed that Penny had outgrown much of her childhood timidity. Even so, he wished that Hazelton had kept his skeptical comments to himself.

"What does he know? Never let other people's doubts challenge your faith in yourself," he advised encouragingly.

"Do that and you're a goner."

Sometimes Matt sounded exactly like Ethan, Penny thought. While she agreed with the outlook he recommended, she had no desire to lapse into their old relationship of strong, confident male propping up small, scaredy-cat female. Still, it felt good to be back on an easygoing footing with him, so she refrained from saying she had learned that lesson long ago.

Instead, she gave his hand a squeeze to let him know she appreciated his moral support. Then, walking over to the office nook, she sat down behind his efficiently arranged desk and arranged an appointment to have a telephone installer come by on Monday to set up a line of her own in unit 763.

No sooner had she hung up than the phone buzzed. Instead of changing places with her, Matt stretched across from the other side of the desk to answer. A surge of awareness bubbled through Penny as the close-fitting jersey he wore strained against the strong, lean musculature of his arms and shoulders.

Matt listened for a moment, face impassive. "All right. I'll pass on the message," he said noncommittally and glanced at Penny as he hung up.

"Russell Kehoe would like to take you to lunch. I didn't want to put you on the spot by admitting you were sitting right here, but you're welcome to use the phone and call him back if you like."

"Well thanks, but no thanks. Yesterday he practically accused me of being a con artist."

Penny's annoyance was clearly detectable in her voice. Matt agreed that the other man could be aggravating at times. On the other hand, he figured it would be unjust to let the incident rankle.

"I gather he wants to offer you an apology. He mentioned having called your former supervisor in San Antonio."

The occasional flare of temper that matched her red hair brimmed up in Penny. "What a nerve! Did he say why he went to the trouble of checking up on me?"

"No, but I imagine he'd tell you if you asked." Matt jotted a phone number onto a small sheet of scratch paper, then handed it across the desk to her. "That's the number for Diversions if you decide to get in touch with him."

Penny remembered that Kehoe's goodwill was important to Matt. A bit reluctantly she decided that for her friend's sake it would be a diplomatic move to return the call. Later, though. Not now.

"Actually, lunch sounds like a great idea," Matt said as she stood up. "If I didn't have an appointment in Sausalito this morning, I'd suggest ordering a pizza sent in for us to share."

"We'll do that another day. Right now my top priority is to track down a place that sells office furniture. I'll just need a few essentials to start with. Like a desk and a couple of chairs, and a telephone, of course, so the installer will have something to install."

At her request, he lent her the phone book so she could check out ads in the Yellow Pages. "Got time to give me a tour of your new quarters?"

"Absolutely." In amusement, she glanced around the echoing warehouse. "If you think you've got lots and lots of nothing in here, wait until you see my place."

Stepping outside while he held the door for her, Penny felt pleased that Matt would bother to take an interest in the little cubbyhole she had just rented. She was glad, though, that he hadn't volunteered to come along and help pick out the office equipment. Having lived at the children's Home, then with Ethan and Arletta, later in a college dorm and most recently in a duplex furnished by its absentee owner, she was eager to experience the novelty of choosing her own furnishings.

Hardware clattered as Matt pulled the door firmly closed. Then, even though the task of looking over her tiny upstairs office could not possibly consume more than a minute and a half at most, he stopped to turn the key in the dead bolt and snap both padlocks.

Security minded as she was, these precautions for a brief absence in broad daylight seemed like overkill to Penny. But maybe not, she thought, remembering Griff Hazelton's warning to have the lock of her office changed.

"Is security a major problem around here, Matt?"

He hesitated. "Nothing's been stolen from me so far," he answered enigmatically. "What makes you ask?"

"Noticing that you've got everything here except a moat and a drawbridge made me wonder, that's all. Are two padlocks and a dead bolt really necessary?"

He glanced back at them over his shoulder. "To be honest, I really don't know. There are times when I suspect a 'Beware of Dog' sign would be equally effective."

Though the bewilderment she felt must have shown on her face, he made no effort to elaborate until they had climbed the concrete steps to the upper story of the office building on the opposite side of the pavement. Only then, closeted securely inside her no-frills little unit, did he turn and meet her eyes.

"I didn't start out with the padlocks," he said. "They were added one at a time, after each of the break-ins."

"Break-ins!"

His jaw clenched. "Yeah, that's what I said."

Penny wished she could offer Matt a chair or a cup of coffee—anything to ease the spring-coiled tension she could sense pulsing through him. Lacking any other source of comfort, she reached up and curled her fingers around his forearm. She knew it was far too little, that simple gesture, but at the moment it was the only solace she was able to provide.

"I'm listening," she said. "Tell me what happened."

His scowl mirrored the frustration in his words. "That's the worst of it, Penny. Nothing actually happened. Nothing I can put my finger on, at least."

The situation had been driving him crazy for weeks. It was so impossibly nebulous that he'd been reluctant to mention it to anyone, even Ben, for fear of being thought paranoid. But when he felt the encouraging warmth of Penny's hand on his arm, and experienced the flow of trust and confidence that had been between them from the beginning, he knew she wouldn't laugh or suggest he see a shrink.

"Someone broke into my warehouse," he said simply. "I haven't any evidence to back up what I'm telling you, Penny, but I know it happened. Not just once, either. Twice."

This was beginning to sound decidedly ominous. "Earlier, though, you said nothing had been stolen?"

How could he make her understand what even to him was still just a whisper of suspicion?

"Not so much as a paperclip," he admitted. "But my stuff had been gone through."

Penny considered the precise orderliness of everything she had seen in his compact warehouse office. Matt would know if any of his possessions had been tampered with, she thought.

Griff Hazelton had told her that empty offices were never left unlocked because of the possibility of squatters moving in. "Matt," she said speculatively, "do you suppose your intruder could have been someone who was too honest to steal, but simply desperate for a dry, safe place to sleep?"

"One of the street people?" He shook his head. "The first time it happened I considered that possibility. It wouldn't have surprised me to see marks in the dust where a sleeping bag had been rolled out, or to have found empty food wrappers tossed in a corner. But there was no trace of another human being having set foot in that warehouse. In fact, it was downright—"

"Downright what?"

"Downright spooky."

Matt looked rather abashed at having said the word aloud, but he didn't take it back. "No kidding, Penny, I half considered the possibility that the place might be haunted. But with hundreds of historic old buildings in this city, I doubt that any self-respecting ghost would hang out in a warehouse that's barely a year old. Still, the thought did cross my mind when the locks showed no sign of having been jimmied. If there was any reason a spook would be interested in invoices and ship schedules and bills of lading. . . ."

Penny kept her mind on the practical aspects of the puzzle. "There has to be a reason why this happened. Matt, you need a decent security system. It wouldn't be a bad idea to install a camera up in the rafters, too. There are some excellent motion-activated devices—"

"For Pete's sake, Penny, I'm running a one-man operation on a shoestring budget," Matt cut in, exasperated. "The kind of equipment you're talking about probably costs thousands of dollars."

"That's true. But Matt, this is exactly the sort of thing Ethel Farnsworth's legacy could help with. It would make me so happy to lend a hand. . . ."

"No way!" Face thunderous, he took a distancing step backwards. "I'm not about to let you float me a loan to protect an empty warehouse!"

His flat rejection hurt. More painful still was the way he had pulled away, as though being too close to her might corrupt him into accepting a favor. If his pig-headed obstinacy ever locked horns with her stubborn pride over a really vital issue, Penny thought, the fallout was likely to destroy them both.

Showing that she didn't need him to hold onto, she jammed her fists into her pockets. "Empty warehouse or not, that place must have some bizarre attraction or these mysterious incidents wouldn't happen. But by all means, handle the problem your own way. Maybe the 'Beware of Dog' sign will work just fine. Or how about piping a recording of ghostly noises through the place every night?"

Being on the receiving end of a scathing put-down instead of the worshipful trust she had bestowed on him in the past was an unpleasant experience for Matt. He hated the icy sense of aloneness her anger stirred deep inside him.

"I'll keep your advice in mind," he said stiffly.

He wanted to stomp away, kicking the steps as he went. But before he could turn toward the door, it occurred to him that he'd been so wrapped up in his own aggravating problems that he hadn't even given her office the courtesy of a glance. His expression softened as he took the time to gaze around the bare little unit.

"This is going to be fine, Penny," he said. "I know it isn't the prestigious location you hoped to have. But people won't let that influence them once they've had a chance to meet and talk with you. All they'll care about is that their children couldn't be in better hands."

Penny gulped down a rush of emotion. "Thanks, Matt. I'll try to make a success of the business to justify your faith in me."

Determined to keep their discussion from turning maudlin, she made a show of glancing at her watch. "My gosh, where has the time gone? You'll be late for your appointment if you don't get going."

Matt checked his own watch and saw that she was right. Damn it, he thought, feeling almost as frustrated as he had the night before, why did feelings always get in the way when he and Penny tried to have a commonsense discussion? And why was there never enough time to resolve anything?

"Come with me," he invited impulsively. "It's a beautiful day for a trip across the bridge. Seeing my client won't take long, and afterward we can have lunch somewhere. Talk. Spend the rest of the day together."

Penny came within a gasp of accepting the tempting invitation. Then, remembering Griff Hazelton's skepticism about her ability to attract clients, she gave herself a mental shake. If she expected her enterprise to succeed, she'd better start making the minutes count.

"Sorry," she said, with a wave at the empty space surrounding them. "As you can see, I have an office to furnish."

CHAPTER SEVEN

Darn that man, anyway! Why couldn't he break down and accept a gift?

Staring after Matt Devlin's retreating back, Penny felt a cauldron of emotions seething within her. Resentment crowded its way to the top of the list. Many times, when they were children, Matt had snatched her out of harm's way. Now it was he who could use some help. But like a stubborn mule he refused to let her pay him back.

What sort of one-sided friendship was that?

Her conscience gave a sudden jab. Why was she standing around fretting about settling an old debt when it was really Matt's safety that lay at the heart of her distress?

It sounded as if something very strange was going on across the way at his warehouse. Something potentially dangerous. Next time—

Apprehensively, she moved closer to the window, hoping to catch a reassuring glimpse of him. But Matt's long strides had already carried him out of sight.

The weight of the phone book she had continued to hold—there was, after all, no place to put it down—reminded her that worrying wasn't getting her office furnished or the locksmith called.

For lack of anywhere else to sit, she walked outside and dropped down onto the top step. Then, flipping quickly through the Yellow Pages, she began jotting a list of the more accessibly located office supply companies into her notebook. She'd start with the closest one first, she decided.

Dusting off the seat of her pants, she set the phone book inside on the floor of her empty office. After tucking the key into her shoulder bag, she pulled the door shut, rattling the knob to make certain the spring lock had caught.

Its reassuring solidity reminded her again of the nerve-wracking problem plaguing Matt. Heading down the short flight of stairs to ground level, Penny appraised the sturdily built warehouse across the way. It certainly appeared inaccessible. Both the front door and the high, wide freight entrance at the rear of the building were protected by formidable bolts and double padlocks.

Even an ordinary lock would keep most people out. But Matt wasn't a fanciful sort of person. If he claimed someone had broken in leaving no trace of evidence behind, she believed him. She could only pray that his refusal to let her help beef up the warehouse's security never resulted in burglary or vandalism.

No bus was in sight when she reached the street running past the business park. What did catch her eye was a telephone kiosk. It occurred to her that, whether he liked it or not, there was something she could do for her obstinate friend. While the two men might disagree on points like delivery schedules and exclusive rights, Russell Kehoe's patronage was vital to Matt's fledgling import company. Even though she had no intention of having lunch with him, returning his call would confirm that Matt had passed on the message.

When the toy shop owner came on the line, she noticed a warmth in his voice that had been missing the previous day.

"Bethany and I had quite a discussion about you last

night," he confided. "And this morning I called San Antonio International. Mr. Noriega gave a glowing report on your qualifications."

While she would have expected nothing less, she wondered what had prompted the call in the first place. "I hope the Chief of Airport Security was able to reassure you about my integrity?"

"He did indeed." Tactfully, Russell Kehoe ignored her stiff tone. "In fact, he considers you one of the most reliable people who ever worked for him. Even though he was sorry to lose you, he feels you will be a natural for this specialized agency you intend to launch."

"It was good of him to say so." Penny caught sight of her bus approaching. "I have a busy day planned, Mr. Kehoe. Thank you for the luncheon invitation, but—"

"I hoped you would have time to discuss the possibility of escorting Bethany back to Philadelphia next week," he cut in smoothly.

Surprise at this turnabout echoed in her voice. "You wanted to offer me a job?"

"Yes, provided we can come to terms about the various arrangements. There are a number of questions I need to ask. I thought it would be more convenient for us both if we ate while we talked. Can you meet me here at twelve o'clock?"

A new light having been thrown on the invitation, Penny realized it would be foolish not to accept. Russell Kehoe was exactly the type of client she had been hoping to attract.

"Twelve o'clock will be fine," she capitulated, hastily revising her plans, and hung up to run for the bus.

There was time before the noon appointment to return to her hotel and change from the casual outfit she had worn to start the day into more businesslike attire. She was pleased at her choice of a softly fitting Delft blue suit worn with a white silk blouse when she entered Diversions and saw the dozen or so well-dressed people browsing among the shelves of toys.

It occurred to her that Russell Kehoe was in a perfect position to recommend her to plenty of affluent parents, should he approve of how she handled his daughter.

One step at a time, she cautioned herself. That little girl was likely to be the fly in the ointment. If Beth still refused to accept anyone but her father as a traveling companion, this job would literally never get off the ground.

Arriving with a few minutes to spare proved to have been worth the hurry. Approval registered on Russell Kehoe's face when he looked up from the sale he had been supervising and saw her walk through the door. With a minimum of fuss he turned the transaction over to an assistant to complete, and came to meet her.

"Glad you could make it," he said. "I made reservations at a new café in the financial district that my customers have been raving about."

During the two-block walk to the restaurant he kept the conversation light, obviously preferring to wait until they were seated before getting down to business.

The menu at the trendy Kearney Street café featured Pacific Rim cuisine. Penny was fond of this combination of California-style cookery with recipes from the Far East. She chose a light entrée of shrimp stir-fried with ginger and lemongrass, and iced tea to drink.

Though her host seemed to appreciate the café's cutting-edge atmosphere, the menu didn't appear to excite him. Almost at random he chose a Thai dish, chicken topped with a tangy peanut sauce. A nostalgic expression crossed his face when the waiter had departed.

"I try to keep up with the 'in' places so I can discuss them intelligently with my clients. To tell the truth, though, I'd give a lot for a good cheese steak."

Penny squashed a smile. You could take the man out of Philadelphia, she thought. But apparently it was harder to take Philadelphia out of the man.

While awaiting their order, Russell Kehoe drew her out at length. Penny willingly outlined her education and work experience for him. She quailed inwardly, though, when he inquired about her business address. This was the acid test, she thought. If he balked at hiring her because of an unfashionable location, she could probably expect a similar reaction from other potential clients.

"I'm renting a small office in the same commercial complex that houses Matt Devlin's warehouse," she responded in an even tone.

A sandy eyebrow lifted. "A bit out of the way, isn't it?"

"It's not Union Square," Penny admitted frankly. "Does that really matter? I'm just getting established, after all, and that's only a base of operations. What really counts is how I handle my job. If you hire me it will be to guarantee that your little girl arrives safely at her destination without any upsets along the way. An elaborate office would just be window dressing."

This outlook appeared to make good sense, for he nodded thoughtfully. "Tell me about your fees."

Ethan had taught Penny never to undervalue her own worth. She quoted a rate that she believed to be fair, considering the service she was offering and the heavy responsibility involved.

Kehoe's expression remained impassive. "Plus expenses, I assume?"

"Yes, of course. I've been trained in tae kwon do and have a black belt," Penny went on quietly. "And I qualified as an expert at weapons handling. Should anyone attempt to harm a child placed in my care, he would literally have to do so over my dead body."

"Mr. Noriega told me much the same thing. He also mentioned your kindness, intelligence, and swift reaction time." Russell Kehoe regarded her soberly. "Bethany means more to me than anything else in the world. I want her to have the best. You're hired, Ms. Farnsworth."

The suddenness of his decision surprised Penny. "I appreciate your confidence in me," she said. "But it's important that your little girl accept me, too. She must be willing to obey me without argument in case of an emergency."

"My daughter and I have already hammered that out." Kehoe shifted his gaze away from hers, but not before Penny caught sight of the deep unhappiness shimmering in the depths of his brown eyes. "I have finally made her understand that I simply cannot fly home with her at this time. She has agreed to accept you as her escort."

The waiter placed an artfully arranged plate in front of her. Though the savory aroma hinted that the food would taste as delicious as it looked, Penny felt too overwhelmed at having plunged so suddenly into the depths of commerce to be able to swallow even a single grain of rice at that moment.

To calm herself, she focused on details. Bringing out a purse-sized calendar and a ballpoint pen, she asked Russell Kehoe if he had settled on a date for his daughter's eastbound flight.

The man across the table produced a small pocket diary of his own. "Pamela and I have agreed that Thursday the twenty-fourth would suit us both."

"Pamela?" Penny echoed, caught off guard.

"Bethany's mother." Kehoe firmly squared his jaw. "She will be waiting for you at the Philadelphia airport when you arrive."

Carefully recording the date, Penny decided that Bethany's father was having just as hard a time adjusting to the aftermath of divorce as his little girl was. While they both had her sympathy, she knew she must stick to business and let the family work out its own problems.

She wouldn't have Dear Abby's job for anything.

"Do you want to arrange for the tickets, or shall I?" she inquired, getting the discussion back on track.

Her new employer seemed to appreciate the noninvolvement pact she had just made with herself. "You go ahead," he said briskly. "First class. Be sure to keep the time difference in mind."

Three hours later in Philadelphia than it was on the West Coast, Penny reminded herself. On the spot, she decided to use first-out-in-the-morning departures whenever possible, and mentioned this aloud.

"That way, if mechanical difficulties delay a flight, there's plenty of time to catch the next one," she explained. "Also, by arriving in mid-afternoon, Bethany will have time to calm down and visit with her mother before bedtime."

"Fine." Russell Kehoe took out a business card and jotted his home number beneath the toy shop exchange. "Have the travel agent call me for a credit card authorization to settle the cost of the tickets."

Next, he wrote out a sizable check to serve as a deposit on her fee and expected expenses, then passed it across the table. "Please keep a record of what you spend on hotels, meals and ground transportation. I'll see that you're reimbursed for the balance as soon as you return."

Penny made a mental note to open a business account at a local bank that afternoon. A small zippered case to fit in her purse would be a good way to keep track of receipts.

"I haven't had time to have contracts printed yet," she apologized. "Along with having you sign one of those, I'll also need a notarized letter formally authorizing me to travel with your child."

He looked nonplussed. "Is so much red tape really necessary?"

"Notarized permission is not a legal requirement for a trip within the United States," she admitted. "Still, the business lawyer I consulted before leaving San Antonio recommended the precaution. Such a document would serve as a safeguard for both parties should any misunderstanding arise en route. And formal paperwork would be mandatory if I were hired to escort a youngster out of the country."

Penny explained that the rash of disappearances of American children in recent years had caused many neighboring governments to tighten their immigration requirements. Along with a passport, any minor crossing an international border now had to carry written proof that his parents or guardians had authorized the trip.

"Canada and most South and Central American nations require a notarized statement from both parents," she added seriously. "Custody disputes are so common these days that even kids traveling with their own mother or father aren't allowed to enter those countries without written consent from the second parent."

Russell Kehoe's face turned ashen at the thought of Bethany vanishing forever. His quick mind took in other devastating possibilities as well.

"Without proper precautions, you could find yourself in a hideous legal mess," he ruminated. "If I were you, I'd bring that notarized permission slip along and have the second parent endorse it at the far end of the trip as proof that the child has been safely delivered."

"That's an excellent idea." Resolving to follow his advice, Penny tucked the check and her notes safely away and did her best to swallow some of the delicious food.

While waiting to sign the charge slip, her new client gave her a curious look. "I must remember to thank Matt Devlin for introducing us. He referred to you as his oldest friend. Are the two of you involved in a relationship?"

A rather private person, Penny resented blunt personal questions. This query was especially unwelcome because it forced her to think of Matt in terms of intimacy, something she had never done. Having been apart for most of their lives, they had nostalgically considered each other as boy and girl long after becoming adults in reality.

She had always loved Matt, Penny realized. But it had been a child's uncomplicated devotion she had felt for him all those years. Now Kehoe's question caused her to wonder how it would be to share an even deeper bond.

"As children, Matt and I were good friends," she replied, with as much composure as she could muster. "Then circumstances separated us. We were reunited this week after having been apart for nearly eighteen years."

She decided to follow through on the impromptu "rule" vetoing any socializing with business contacts which she had plucked out of the air for Griff Hazelton's benefit that morning. Russell Kehoe's inquiry about her private life was probably motivated by his concern to make sure she would be a proper traveling companion for his daughter. On the other hand, it might have signified a different type of interest.

Whatever the case, she had no wish to become involved

with him or any other new acquaintance. Not until she'd had a chance to analyze her grown-up feelings for the grown-up Matt.

Besides, she reflected, people to whom Monopoly was more than a game made her nervous. She had no intention of being picked up like the deed to Park Place or Board-walk, or any other valuable property.

Though visiting a travel agent and opening a commercial bank account headed her "to do" list, Penny impulsively decided to postpone those errands when she passed a large office-supply firm just a block down from Diversions.

"I have very little space with which to work," she warned the friendly clerk who came forward to offer assistance.

Helpfully, he led her to an area featuring a line of scaled-down furnishings. These fit Penny's budget as well as her limited square footage. She chose a work center cleverly de-signed to serve as desk, computer station and file cabinet combined into one compact unit. After picking out a com-fortable steno chair for herself, she added two well-made armchairs for clients.

"Have you thought about floor covering?" the clerk asked, after helping her select a speakerphone and a reliable answering machine.

With only a short lease on her brand new office, Penny wasn't about to invest in wall-to-wall carpet. Still, she liked the idea of an area rug to add beauty, warmth and comfort to her sparse grouping. She settled on a subdued pattern in blues and beiges but was uncertain about which of two sizes would work best.

"If you're able to take measurements and let me know by closing time, I can arrange for a Tuesday delivery," the clerk said.

Penny was anxious to be all settled in before her departure for Philadelphia. "That sounds doable. May I use your phone to call a locksmith while you make up my invoice?"

Though this detail was speedily arranged, Penny realized that she was running out of time. She couldn't visit a travel agent personally if she was to get her floor measured before the store closed at six. Yet it was essential to nail down airline reservations without delay.

She compromised by turning to the Yellow Pages and phoning a travel agent located in a neighborhood shopping center near her office.

Thanks to computerized equipment, the owner of Roberta's Tickets N Tours was able to confirm two first-class seats on a direct flight the following Thursday morning while Penny held the line.

"Wonderful! Please arrange the payment details with my client," she requested, passing along Russell Kehoe's name and business number. "I'll collect the tickets at your office myself, first thing tomorrow morning."

It was fully dark by the time the cab dropped her off in front of her office building forty minutes later. Penny found it disconcerting to see the meager number of cars remaining in the parking lot. Only a few isolated patches of illumination glowed here and there in the complex.

Hurrying up the concrete steps, she unlocked room 763. The flip of a switch brought a spill of fluorescent light from overhead.

Hollow echoes resounded as she paced back and forth across the empty unit, taking measurements with the retractable tape she had purchased at the office supply store. She was pleased to find the room could accommodate the larger of the two rugs she and the sales clerk had discussed, with very little space left over.

Neither of them had given a thought to window coverings, however. Penny disliked the notion that anyone would be able to peer in at her from the dark, open passageway outside. Spotlighted within the bright room, she would be clearly visible to anyone walking by.

Years of working security had taught her that personal safety was often a matter of taking sensible precautions to avoid trouble. And besides protecting her privacy, Penny thought practically, blinds would also enhance the office décor and ward off the strong rays of the setting sun on hot afternoons.

She marched decisively over to the window. After noting its horizontal measurement, she stretched on tiptoe, extending the tape to measure the glass from a vertical direction.

It was then that she saw the narrow band of light glimmering through a crack in the siding of Matt's warehouse.

CHAPTER EIGHT

Penny froze. At any other time she would have found nothing disturbing about a sliver of light gleaming through a crack in the wall. But now, with the complex dark and almost deserted, she recalled the tale Matt had told her that morning. Twice in the past, he'd insisted, someone had mysteriously gained access to his warehouse.

Had the intruder returned this evening for a third illicit visit?

The notion left her so uneasy she stepped back from the window. As abruptly as it had appeared, the slit of light vanished. Puzzled, she moved forward again. There it was, a pale glimmer visible only from a certain angle. She had to be within inches of the glass before her eye could discern it.

Though security-conscious, she wasn't an alarmist. The obvious explanation, Penny told herself, was that Matt had returned from his business appointment, switched on the light himself, and was over there working late.

But it was also possible that he was still miles away.

She hesitated, earnestly regretting the lack of a handy phone. One quick call would either establish her friend's presence in the warehouse across the way or confirm her fears that an intruder had made his way inside. If the latter were the case, it could be too late to do any good by the time she got clear out to the pay phone near the bus stop.

The mischief might be done, the miscreant gone.

She couldn't let that happen. Not when the future success of Matt's business depended on those precious imported toys.

A sharp jab of pain made Penny realize she'd been clutching the metal tape measure so tightly it was biting into her flesh. Setting it down, she picked up her notebook and purse from the floor. Then, switching off her own light before stepping out onto the concrete walkway, she pulled the door of her office silently closed behind her.

No trace of the light she'd spotted could be seen from this vantage point. But that didn't mean whoever had been inside the warehouse had already left.

Common sense was mixed with caution in her approach to the sprawling structure across the way. Penny reasoned that if Matt were there, he would open the door to her knock. On the other hand, if the light had been turned on by someone who had no business in the warehouse and was counting on keeping his presence a secret, she might be able to scare him off before he accomplished his purpose in being there.

She wasn't concerned that any harm would come to her. A trespasser would hardly risk answering someone else's door.

Swiftly, she crossed the driveway. In the gloom she climbed the four steps to the warehouse entrance, and lifted her fist to rap.

Just as her knuckles grazed the wood, the door jerked open. Penny jumped back with a yelp of surprise. One heel slipped; her balance wobbled.

Matt Devlin grabbed her wrist just in time to keep her from tumbling backwards down the steps.

"Watch out, Penny! You'll hurt yourself!"

It felt wonderful to be drawn back to safety and the strong, protective circle of his arms. For the space of a dozen heartbeats, Penny was content to simply nestle there.

"Gosh, you scared me," she murmured, lifting her head to look up at him. "I wasn't expecting—"

His answer sounded slightly amused. "This is my place, after all. Who else did you think would be here?"

For a moment, the stunning closeness of her oldest, dearest, most trustworthy friend scattered Penny's wits. The urge to twine more closely into his warm embrace, to tilt her head and touch his lips with hers, was almost irresistible. But his laid-back manner cautioned her that friendship and the long habit of protectiveness were all that had motivated Matt to wrap her close.

Drawing a reinforcing breath, she tried to furnish a sensible explanation of what had brought her to his door.

"I'd been taking some measurements in my office when I looked down and saw a glimmer of light over here. It worried me, since almost everyone else in the complex seems to have left some time ago."

"You were worried about me?" An electric tingle vibrated deep within Matt as he smoothed his hands down the delicate curves of her arms. "Why?"

"Because this morning you told me about the mysterious intruder who has already broken into the warehouse twice. I figured that if he had managed a third illegal entry, I might be able to scare him away by beating on your door."

It unnerved Matt to think that Penny—small, delicate, trouble-dodging Penny—might have jeopardized her own safety for his sake. What if the door had been opened by a sneak thief or vandal who had found some clever way to gain entry and didn't care whom he had to attack in order to get out again unseen?

With a gulp he pictured the harm that might have befallen her. He wanted to shake her until he was sure he'd gotten her attention, then preach a whole sermon about fools rushing in where angels feared to tread. Then he wanted to kiss her until she was too limp to argue that she was able to take care of herself. Obviously, she couldn't.

Just in time, a rational inner voice protesting that friends didn't treat friends that way got through to him. He reached back, flipped on the light switch he'd snapped off when preparing to leave for the evening, and drew her inside.

"Penny, please promise me you'll never take such a foolhardy risk again," he begged. "What are you doing back here, anyway? I thought you meant to spend the day looking for office furniture."

"I found exactly what I wanted at the first place I visited. Which reminds me," she added, shooting a hasty glance at her watch, "I need to call and confirm something, if it isn't already too late."

Luckily, the helpful sales clerk hadn't yet gone home for the day. Penny let him know that the nine-foot-by-twelve-foot rug would be a perfect fit for her office.

"By Tuesday afternoon, unit seven sixty-three will be the proud possessor of a phone, a new lock, and a nice little assortment of furniture," she crowed to Matt after hanging up. "How did your appointment go today?"

"I guess you could say that there's good news and bad news." He turned out the light for the second time that evening as they left, then paused to snap both padlocks and turn the key in the dead bolt. "I still have the car I rented this morning for the trip to Marin County. Want to come grocery shopping with me? We can have dinner on my boat while I tell you all about it."

She agreed with pleasure. At the big supermarket near

the waterfront they bought halibut steaks, a quick-fix box of rice and noodles, and greens for a tossed salad.

Matt's cabin cruiser, *Gypsy*, was moored at the small craft harbor off Marina Green. Showing her around once they climbed aboard, he remarked that the vessel's name had been bestowed upon her by a previous owner.

"It's a handy place to live," he added, "but mighty cramped after eight years aboard an aircraft carrier."

Down in the compact galley, he rubbed the fish with butter and lemon juice, wrapped it in foil, and carried it back up on deck to grill it on the portable barbecue. Working together in quarters that made a sports car seem roomy by comparison, they produced the rest of the meal.

Topside, they set up a table and chairs in the open air. For a few minutes, Penny was held spellbound by the wrap-around view of bay and bridges and twinkling city skyline. But as they ate, her attention seldom wandered far from the man who lived in this fabulous setting.

"This has been a wonderful dinner," she sighed, after savoring the last flaky morsel of fish. "Now, what was that about 'good news and bad news'?"

The retailer he'd contacted that morning had placed an immediate order, Matt said. "But he complained that I'm offering too little variety. He's right, unfortunately. I've been so busy setting up the warehouse and learning the mechanics of being an importer that I haven't had much chance to expand my line. It's time for me to head back Down Under and search out another batch of creative toy makers."

The trip couldn't be postponed if he hoped to have extra stock ready for holiday distribution, Matt added.

"That light you spotted in the warehouse was me poring over projected figures and setting up arrangements to leave for Sydney as soon as possible. I'm booked to fly out on Qantas week after next. While I'm there, I hope to help Neville Baker solve his production problems."

"Sounds like you need to make that a top priority," Penny said, remembering Russell Kehoe's annoyance at the delivery delay of the Billabong Babies.

Still, the news of Matt's upcoming departure left her feeling dejected. Before they'd scarcely had a chance to get reacquainted after years of separation, they were getting ready to fly off in opposite directions.

That thought reminded her that she hadn't shared her own news with him.

"I'll soon be off on a business trip myself," she confided. "Come next Thursday I'll be on my way to Philadelphia with Bethany Kehoe."

Matt looked thunderstruck. "How did that happen?"

"Remember the phone message you took for me? I gather that after we left his shop yesterday, Mr. Kehoe and his daughter continued to go round and round. Finally, she agreed to travel without him provided I escort her instead.

"He called my old boss at San Antonio International, checked out my credentials, then asked me to come down at noon for a personal interview."

"I see. Well, uh—congratulations." Matt knew he would sound like a jealous fool if he voiced his misgivings. Maybe he was. But Penny was extra special. He hated the thought of her becoming involved with a suave, older man who was still hung up on his wife.

Misinterpreting his less than enthusiastic response, Penny hastily assured him that she had never set out to trespass on his business relationship with Russell Kehoe.

"He just adores his daughter, Matt, and I was lucky enough to show up at the right time to help them work out a compromise on their dispute. It seemed to me that if this first job went well, he'd be in a good position to refer me to other parents with children who traveled. But if it's going to make it awkward. . . ."

"No reason why it should."

Matt hoped his disclaimer sounded convincing. Penny was right, of course. Kehoe's recommendations could give her travel escort business a great boost. Unfortunately, she already thought of himself as an overprotective big brother. That impression would only be intensified if he tried pointing out that her new client had wife trouble as well as daughter trouble.

On the other hand, she'd probably laugh herself silly if he mentioned his suspicions that Kehoe might have been responsible for the break-ins at the warehouse. He had no proof that it was the shop owner who'd raided his files. But the motive was there. The toys he imported had proven to be enormously popular—all the more so since the supply was so limited.

Kehoe wanted them all for Diversions. Matt didn't think the man would balk at snooping through private business papers. Not if doing so would give him a pipeline to the overseas artisans who produced those popular toys. He might be hoping to make a separate deal with them and cut out the middleman entirely.

Fortunately, Neville Baker, Meg Limmons and the others had already signed exclusive contracts with Matt. The legal documents were tucked away in a safe-deposit box. If whoever engineered the break-ins had been after those papers, he must have been extremely disappointed.

But would he be back?

Tickets N Tours was located in a tree-shaded outdoor

mall anchored by a branch bank at one end and a grocery store at the other. A score of smaller businesses ranged between the two majors. Faded For Lease signs in three of the empty shop windows reminded her of Griff Hazelton's problems in attracting permanent tenants for the business park. Nor were there many Help Wanted signs on display. The current recession seemed to be having far-reaching effects on the economy.

Roberta Wickersham had done an efficient job of reserving and ticketing the requested air space. Pleased that seat assignments had been confirmed in advance and details about in-flight meal service supplied, Penny concluded that she could not have done better dealing with one of the large international travel agencies.

"Everything looks great," she complimented the other woman. "I have just launched a travel escort service for young children. My office is located in that big business park near the docks. It'll be much more convenient for me to pick up tickets here in the neighborhood than having to travel clear downtown."

A smile lit up Roberta's plump features. Between the after-effects of the East Coast terrorist attacks, nose-diving commissions, and so many people making their own airline reservations via the Internet these days, small agencies like hers had a struggle keeping afloat.

"More than once I've had people in here buying tickets for their kids," she said. "Lots of times they're reluctant to send their little ones off alone. They also resent having to pay full adult fare for a youngster who's traveling by himself, even though he might only be five years old. And that extra fee for each connection is a bit of highway robbery, if you ask me."

It was common knowledge that most airlines tacked a

surcharge onto the cost of a young traveler's ticket for each change of planes he made along the route. "Especially when the extra money carries no guarantee that the child will have help in making the transfer," Penny agreed indignantly.

Roberta tucked the tickets into a long envelope and handed them across the counter. "Leave a few of your business cards with me," she suggested. "Next time someone asks where they can find a traveling companion for their kindergartner, I'll pass along your name."

"How nice of you. As soon as they're made up I'll bring some by," Penny promised. "Could you recommend a printer who does good, speedy work?"

"Sure, be glad to." Roberta flipped through the Yellow Pages, then copied information onto a scratch-pad sheet. "These people are reliable, and they're located within easy walking distance."

"Perfect."

From Tickets N Tours, Penny headed toward the corner bank. It gave her a glow of pride to open a commercial account with the first fee she had earned as an independent businesswoman. This accomplished, she walked two blocks north to the center where Ink, Inc. was located.

Following dinner with Matt the previous evening, she had spent hours back in her hotel room blocking out a sample contract to be signed by herself and her clients. Afterward, she laid out the wording for the authorization letter. Now she presented these pages to the owner of the print shop.

They carried on a shouted conversation over the clanking, ka-thumping presses. Learning that her order would be ready on Monday afternoon, Penny arranged to pick up the supply of forms by five o'clock.

"By then I'll know my office phone number and can place an order for business cards, too," she told the printer. "My new business is to be called Wing Away. Would it be possible to have a small drawing on the cards along with the lettering?"

"No problem." He pointed to a display tacked to a bulletin board on the shop's side wall. "My wife is a commercial artist. Take a look at some of the customized designs Joan has produced. I'm sure she'll be able to work up a suitable sketch to suit you."

The logo Penny had in mind would show the silhouette of a woman and child, each carrying a small suitcase, approaching a jetliner ready for takeoff. It was a relief to find eye-catching concepts presented here in a few crisp strokes of the pen. Joan, she decided, was just the artist she needed to design her business cards.

A second bulletin board seemed to serve as an unofficial community forum. A poster for a high school play was pinned up between a blurb for a Friends of the Library book sale and a flyer describing an Easter egg hunt being sponsored by a local church. Next to them, a forest of 3x5 cards advertised items for sale, baby-sitting services, and rewards for lost dogs. Penny also spotted several cards describing apartments for rent or to share.

Oddly enough, it had been a similar notice that had led to her sharing the duplex in San Antonio with Dinah and Charmaine. The circumstances were quite different, however. That ad had been posted in the employees' lounge at the airport, and she and her two future housemates were already acquainted.

Common sense warned Penny that it would be risky to share lodgings with strangers in a city where she knew practically no one. Besides, she would welcome the chance to try living alone for a change.

It was urgent that she find a place to rent in a hurry. Staying at a hotel and eating in restaurants three times a day was like camping out in a taxi with the meter running. She couldn't afford it for long.

One good thing about neighborhood bulletin boards, she mused, was that all the ads displayed on them were strictly local. Everything here would doubtless be found within a few blocks' radius. Chances were, she'd be able to walk back and forth to work from any apartment listed on this board. Time enough to start plowing through newspaper ads that covered the whole city if none of these panned out.

Pulling her notebook out of her purse, Penny jotted down a few details and a phone number for each of several ads offering a studio or a one-bedroom apartment for rent. As an afterthought, she added the specifics about a sublet being offered for a limited time.

Two of the contact numbers she tried went unanswered. She arranged to stop by and inspect the other five apartments on her list as soon as possible.

The first address turned out to be a shabby old firetrap of a building. The second was a luxuriously appointed flat perched on the side of Telegraph Hill. It also had luxury-flat rates that were far beyond her budget. Noisy neighbors, shoddy maintenance, and a bedroom window that looked down on a fire station caused her to reject the next three apartments.

That left only the sublet. Penny had saved it for last because the notion of having to move again within a few months seemed like such a hassle. On further consideration, though, she decided there might be advantages as well as drawbacks to opting for temporary lodgings.

For starters, it would give her time to look around and

decide what she really wanted in the way of permanent quarters. She could also check out the neighborhood at leisure. Besides, there was always the possibility that she'd decide not to stay on at the business park once her ninety-day lease expired. If prospective clients shied away from visiting her present office and she was locked into a long-term housing situation, she might well wind up with a lengthy commute to work.

The sublet was located in a pleasant cul-de-sac only a block from a pocket-sized park. Penny liked the well-maintained, cream-colored building on sight. Three stories high, the squarish, art deco style house had an air of enduring permanence about it. After she was buzzed in from upstairs, the solid front door swung promptly shut behind her, relocking itself with a no-nonsense "thock" of the latch.

Matt, she thought, would undoubtedly approve of this safety feature.

Naomi Thibault awaited her in the doorway of the third-floor unit. Snow-white hair contrasted dramatically with the woman's café au lait skin. After studying her visitor for a moment, Mrs. Thibault made a gesture of welcome.

"Come in, do."

The soft voice carried a hint of Jamaica in its lilting cadences. Inside, the cane and mahogany furniture and the vivid primitive oil paintings decorating the walls also suggested an island ambience.

But what Penny noticed first were the houseplants. Lush greenery cascaded from hanging pots and shimmered like baskets of emeralds on counters and tabletops. She turned to the older woman in surprise.

"Aren't you reluctant to entrust all this gorgeous foliage to someone who mightn't have a green thumb?"

"It's in the voice, not the thumbs," Naomi said seriously. "Lots of people have called me about that ad on the bulletin board. Most of 'em talk quick and sharp. Tells me they got no time for anyone but themselves. You sound different. Got any objection to having a few words with ivy and ferns and *ficus benjamina* from time to time?"

Penny laughed. "None at all. One of my housemates back in San Antonio used to come home from work every day and tell her plants all about the aggravating customers she had to deal with at the airport car rental agency she managed. Dinah insisted the chats kept the greenery healthy as well as saving her the cost of a psychiatrist."

"I can see how it would. Though it's best to sing 'em a cheery little song once in a time, along with unloading the woes. Helps boost everyone's spirits. Yours included."

A look of wistful nostalgia crossed her face. "My husband took sick last year. Nothin' the doctors tried could make him well. Those last few months would have been mighty dreary without a song now and again."

Penny recalled how low she had felt during Ethan's last illness. Maybe a song would have helped. Swallowing hard, she said, "I'd be pleased to keep your plants company. How long will you be away?"

"Half a year. T'isn't a vacation," Naomi quickly explained. "My Armand was a fine carpenter. All his life he built houses for folks who could afford to pay for them. But he had a dream that had been growin' on him for years."

With the tenderness of a mother feeding a newborn, she picked up a spray bottle and sent a fine film of moisture misting across the leaves of a spreading arborecola plant.

"A volunteer group at our church builds homes for the needy all across America. Armand planned to spend some time helpin' them out. God saw fit to take him before he had a chance."

"You're going in his place? Going to build houses?"

"That's it, girl." A look of determination crossed the woman's face. "For thirty years I worked for the same company, handling files and insurance policies. My supervisor helped me apply for a six months' leave of absence. I've been going to trade school at night, learnin' how to hammer nails and saw a straight line through a two-by-four. Haven't done too bad, either."

Setting down the spray bottle, she turned toward the phone. "Got some references I can check? If they're as good as I expect, the apartment is yours until the first of October. Yours and the plants."

Early the following Thursday morning, Penny made her way through SFO's main terminal. The vast international airport swarmed with travelers bound for all points of the globe. A warm coat was draped over her arm, as defense against freezing March temperatures on the other side of the country. Carrying a soft-sided overnight bag, she headed toward the airline check-in counter where she had arranged to meet Mr. Kehoe and his daughter.

She found herself looking forward to a few hours' enforced idleness in the comfortable surroundings of a big jet's first-class cabin. For the past ten days her life seemed to have been moving with the speed of a Texas twister.

It was hard to believe she had arrived in San Francisco only the previous week. Following a dream, Penny thought with a nostalgic smile. No, two dreams. By then, the yearning to find Matt Devlin again had overshadowed even the hope of launching her own small business.

Both these aspirations had now been realized, and yesterday she'd become the live-in companion to thirty-seven attention-loving houseplants. Today, she was set to escort her first young charge on a long journey by air.

It didn't seem that life could get any fuller. Or better.

Then suddenly, it did. Only a few yards short of the check-in counter, Penny paused as she heard someone call her name. She swing around, a great rush of gladness filling her heart when she spotted the man striding across the terminal in her direction.

"Matt!"

CHAPTER NINE

Single-mindedly, Matt Devlin forged a path through the bustling airport. He paid no heed to interested glances cast his way by women intrigued by his dark, rather dangerous looks. Had he noticed them at all, he would still have continued on without pause. In all that crowd there was only one person he had come to find.

Anxiety clutched at him. The cell phone which provided a communications link between his boat and the outside world had gone on the blink sometime during the past week without his noticing the defect until last night. By then it was too late to call Penny. Worse, if she had tried to contact him to say that her plans had changed, she wouldn't have been able to get through.

A camera-laden group of tourists veered aside. Ahead, he caught a glimpse of a petite figure, short auburn curls bouncing as she walked.

As always at the sight of Penny, he had the urge to jump out in front and clear the way for her. Make sure there was nothing in her path she could trip over. No one lurking who might do her harm. Matt couldn't explain this reaction. She'd had the same astonishing effect on him when they were little kids. The moment she popped back into his life, the urge to safeguard her had also returned, stronger than ever.

This time around, though, it seemed to be more than

mere protectiveness. For the first few days following their reunion, Matt had resisted the evidence of his own eyes. He kept telling himself it wasn't possible that the pig-tailed child he remembered so vividly was halfway through her twenties. It had taken a date on a driver's license to jolt him into facing reality.

But even knowing full well that Penny was an adult, he couldn't break the resurging habit of springing to her defense. He'd had a nearly overpowering urge to punch his landlord in the jaw when he caught Griff Hazelton leering at her. And when Russell Kehoe called with a message for her, Matt's first impulse had been to hang up in the other man's ear.

If a buddy had been acting this way, he'd have assumed the guy had fallen hard for the lady and was nervous about losing her to the competition. But this was he, himself, who was acting so weirdly—and over Penny, of all people. Could it really be jealousy that ailed him?

As a neglected toddler, Matt Devlin figured he must not deserve anybody's love. That conviction grew after he was sent to a group home for orphaned children. Only once, thanks to Penny and the devoted childhood bond they had forged, had he known any true affection.

Looking back, Matt realized their first adult meeting had rekindled the lingering warmth of that connection into a small, bright flame. Now, little more than a week later, it was threatening to flare into a bonfire.

It concerned him that other men could offer her far more in the way of material resources. Worse, since he was going to be out of the country for at least a month, they'd have a clear field with her.

Annoyed, he shook off these hangdog thoughts and reminded himself that only an exceptionally strong friendship could have survived years of separation. The next few weeks would soon pass. Once home again in San Francisco—

Unfortunately, no brilliant plan for demonstrating to Penny that the pugilistic little orphan she'd known had grown up solid and reliable had yet occurred to him. But he'd work it out before he got back. Meanwhile, he couldn't wait even one more second to see her.

"Penny!"

The woman ahead of him swung around at his call. Her face lit up like the beacon of a lighthouse when her gaze homed in on him.

Matt Devlin gulped in a steadying breath. That radiant glow was meant for him. All the shadows he'd been living with vanished.

"Matt! How wonderful to see you!"

The glad words poured out as naturally as water bubbling up from the depths of a spring. Jammed with travelers and airline staff, the vast terminal reverberated with hastening footsteps, loudspeaker announcements, and the muffled roar of jet engines outside on the runways. But all the hubbub faded into insignificance when Penny swung around and saw Matt hurrying in her direction.

Vaguely, she felt her overnight bag drop. The coat over her arm slipped, landing on the floor at her feet. In a warm, welcoming gesture she held out her hands.

Matt didn't stop until they were toe to toe. His fingers caught hers, lacing through. They stood there, looking at each other, oblivious to the sea of travelers eddying around them.

Penny was the first to find her voice. "I can't believe you're here. Bucking that rush-hour freeway traffic was pushing friendship to its limits."

"Not our friendship."

For more than a week, Penny had been hovering on the brink of falling in love. Matt's uncompromising words sent the guardrail flying. It was dizzying to realize that he'd felt this unbreakable link between them, too.

"I tried calling you last night after Mrs. Thibault finally finished saying goodbye to her beloved houseplants. But by the time she left, it was too late to catch you at the warehouse, and I couldn't get through to you on the boat." She let the words pour out in a stream while holding tight to his warm grip. "I was resigned to not talking to you again until I'd returned from Philadelphia."

Matt grimaced painfully. "Tomorrow would have been too late. I—"

"There you are, Penny!"

Small heels drummed across the floor as Bethany Kehoe ran toward them with a shrill cry. "You're late! You were s'posed to meet us at seven o'clock. Daddy and I thought you prob'ly weren't even coming."

"Beth!" From his exasperated tone as he caught up with his daughter, Russell Kehoe's patience was on its third trip through the recycler.

Penny suspected that the little girl's outburst was a case of wishful thinking. Beth must have hoped that if her hired traveling companion failed to arrive, her father would break down and accompany her on the trip after all.

Matt intervened before she could attempt to defuse the situation. Stooping down to place himself on a level with the distraught child, he looked her squarely in the eye.

"It's not fair to be mad at Penny," he said in a reasonable tone. "She was right on time until I delayed her."

A flicker of interest wavered across the six-year-old's sulky expression. "Why did you do that?"

"Because Penny's my friend. I came to see her off. But it

isn't easy to say goodbye to someone you like a lot."

"Yes." Sniffling, Beth shot a longing glance at her father. "I know."

There had been times lately when Penny found herself resenting Matt's overprotective attitude. Now, his gentle approach triggered a rush of emotion. Unlike so many men who thought tenderness wasn't macho, he hadn't hesitated to show the softer side of himself to a little girl. From the look on the child's face, he had said exactly the right thing.

In another minute both she and Beth were apt to dissolve in tears. Briskly gathering up her things, she held out her hand to the little girl. "Come on, non-stranger. Let's go pick up our boarding passes."

As they completed the check-in procedure, Penny was uncomfortably aware that how well she handled the next few hours could either jump start her new career or leave it laying in the dust. If Beth wound up resenting her authority, Russell Kehoe wouldn't hire her a second time. Nor would he be likely to furnish her with a good reference. Yet neither could she let the willful youngster gain the upper hand.

Much as the difficulty of maintaining a delicate balance concerned her, she found her thoughts reverting again and again to the unfinished conversation with Matt. When the four of them turned down the long corridor leading to the departure gates, she lagged slightly behind, allowing Russell Kehoe and his daughter to take the lead by a few steps.

Taking advantage of this modicum of privacy, she looked up at the man who walked beside her. "Matt, what did you mean about tomorrow being too late? If you aren't leaving for Australia until next week—"

An almost savage shake of his head let her know that her information was outdated. "Qantas had a cancellation.

Since I'd asked for an earlier flight to begin with, they slotted me into the space. This time tomorrow I'll be aboard a flight for Sydney."

She wouldn't see him again for a month!

Once, rehearsing for a school play, Penny had misjudged the width of the stage and stepped off into thin air. Matt's blunt announcement gave her the same horrid sensation of having the floor yanked right out from underneath her.

Matt jammed his hands in his pockets, angry at himself for viewing his upcoming trip with such reluctance. He should have been jubilant at having his flight pushed forward. If he expected his toy-import business to continue to thrive, he couldn't afford to let it stagnate. It was essential for him to make new contacts. Widen the variety of merchandise he could offer to retailers.

And he also needed to touch base with the toy makers whose work he already carried. Neville, especially. Perhaps by spending some time in the Outback himself, he could help find a solution to the persistent production problems that plagued the Billabong Babies.

But he didn't want to go. Not this week, or next. Not if it meant leaving Penny.

Penny swallowed, holding in her distress. Thinking of himself as her brotherly buddy, Matt couldn't possibly understand how devastating she found the notion of another long separation from him. But he was waiting for her to say something.

"Well, the sooner you go, the sooner you'll be back," she produced an upbeat response after a struggle. "And while you're away I know you'll discover all sorts of wonderful new toys. It won't be long before your warehouse is overflowing."

She knew exactly how to boost his morale, Matt thought

gratefully. He managed a grin. "That would be a welcome change."

"And don't worry about the place while you're away," Penny added reassuringly. "So far, this trip to Philadelphia with Beth is the only assignment I have. The rest of the time I'll be around to keep an eye out for burglars."

Matt had just begun to relax. Penny's blithe offer brought tension crackling through his system again.

"Don't you dare!"

"What?"

Hearing the note of outrage in her voice, Matt wished he could retract those last three words, or at least soften that thunderous tone.

"Honest, Penny, I don't mean to sound domineering," he apologized. "But if you go looking for danger, you just might find it."

"And you think I couldn't handle it?"

"That's not the point," Matt lied, hoping to cool her indignation. "Why anyone should have wanted to break into my warehouse, or how he managed the trick, is beyond me. But I don't want you finding out the hard way. Believe me, Penny, if you don't promise to give that warehouse a wide berth until I get back, I'll cancel my trip this instant."

He would, too. Penny had no doubt that Matt meant every word he said.

"And to think I considered Bethany obstinate! But coping with that headstrong little girl is sure to be a Sunday stroll compared to trying to get someone as mulish as you to see reason!"

Penny shook her head. "All I was suggesting was something like a neighborhood crime watch," she added defensively. "After all, my office is right across the way. But if the notion upsets you so much, I'll forget the whole thing."

"Thank you." Matt's solemn tone of voice implied that she had just given her word of honor, and that he now considered the pledge etched in granite.

Penny found it impossible to stay mad at a man who only wanted to keep her out of harm's way. She doubted that she would ever be able to convince him that she was capable of defending herself. But life would certainly run more smoothly if he could at least just get it through his head that everyone needed an occasional helping hand.

"Would you do one thing for me in return?"

Matt's jaw relaxed. "Of course. Name it."

"Talk to the landlord about security," she urged. "Maybe some of his other tenants have concerns, too. In any case, it's management's responsibility to keep the business park safe. Insist that he hire some on-site protection."

"Put our rent dollars to work on our behalf? Good idea," Matt said approvingly. "I'll tackle Hazelton on the subject as soon as I get back to the city."

Up ahead, ten or twelve people had halted, awaiting their turns to pass through the security checkpoint. The scene was a familiar one to Penny. Carry-on luggage was being x-rayed as it passed along a sophisticated conveyor belt. Uniformed airport personnel ushered ticketed passengers one at a time through the metal-detector gate, while firmly discouraging people there to see them off from proceeding any further.

Penny saw Russell Kehoe give his daughter a farewell hug. In another minute the little girl would be her responsibility. Yet much as she had looked forward to this moment, she could hardly bring herself to walk away. There was so much more she wanted to say to Matt.

"Keep your coat buttoned when you land," he said

gruffly. "The weather back east can be miserable this time of year."

"So I've heard. Thanks for the reminder."

It was heartwarming to know she had a friend who cared whether or not she caught cold. "It'll be autumn where you're going, won't it?" Penny felt suddenly shy. "Maybe you could drop me a note? Tell me about Australia's fall colors, and how the toy search is going?"

The notion that she might be interested in hearing from him made Matt a trifle light-headed.

"Sure. I'll send it to your office. Number seven sixty-three, right? It'll be something to read when you run out of junk mail." Awkwardly, he cleared his throat. "I'll be staying with Neville Baker toward the end of my stay. If I gave you his address, do you think? . . ." Eyes glowing, Penny looked up at him. "You wouldn't mind hearing how the houseplants and I are doing?"

"That's it," Matt confirmed, managing a grin. "You and the houseplants."

"I can manage that. Well . . . goodbye."

Penny set her possessions on the conveyor belt, then stepped slowly through the metal detector. Bethany was waiting for her on the other side of the arch. Hand in hand, she and the little girl continued on to the departure gate.

As it turned out, Penny realized later, it was a good thing Matt had vetoed her offer to keep an eye on the warehouse during his absence. He was away much longer than either of them had expected, and she was gone too often herself to make a reliable sentry.

The week following her return from Philadelphia, Penny received an urgent call from Roberta Wickersham.

"Would you be able to escort a ten-year-old boy in a

wheelchair to Atlanta?" the owner of Tickets N Tours asked. "Chad Walsh is the son of clients of mine. A few days ago he was shaken up pretty thoroughly and had both legs broken in a bad freeway accident."

"Poor kid!"

"Poor family," Roberta echoed. "Mr. and Mrs. Walsh were even more seriously injured. I gather they'll both be all right eventually, but until they are discharged from the hospital and strong enough to care for their son again, they want to send him back to his grandparents in Georgia. I went out on a limb and mentioned that I knew someone who might be able to take on the job of escorting him there. Could you? Please?"

Penny's sympathies had already been aroused; she had no need of coaxing. "Of course. How could I say no?" She thought for a moment, considering ways to make the trip as unstressful as possible for the injured child.

"Get us on a nonstop flight if at all possible, Roberta. It would be best if Chad could be delivered to the plane by hospital ambulance," she decided. "But if the grandparents are able to bring a van to meet our flight on arrival in Atlanta, it would save the family a considerable expense at the other end of the trip."

A flurry of preparations followed. Penny had had the wording of Wing Away's contracts checked and approved by an attorney during her trip to the East Coast. Now she had the necessary forms messengered to Chad's parents at Mt. Zion Hospital. They were returned, signed and notarized, within hours. With them came formal permission for Chad to travel, granted by his doctor.

Before the next day's mid-morning departure, Penny found time to run over to Ink, Inc. The business cards Joan designed had turned out even better than she'd hoped. She paid for them, then for luck tacked the first one up on the print shop's bulletin board.

Beneath the liberal sprinkling of freckles across his pug nose, Chad Walsh's skin had no more color than a roll of adhesive tape. Still, despite heavy casts immobilizing both legs, he seemed determined to enjoy his first cross-country flight. Settled as comfortably as possible into the spacious forward cabin of the jet, he tucked into his lunch with gusto. Afterwards, he trounced Penny at rummy.

Glimpsing a haunted expression behind his too-bright eyes, she had a hunch that beneath his air of bravado lurked panic. But not until they were within minutes of touchdown did he reveal the fears he'd been carrying on his slim, young shoulders.

"I'm awfully worried about my dad," he confessed. "A pickup truck plowed right into his side of the car, Penny. The guy must have been drunk or asleep, or something. Dad's a great driver, but he just couldn't get out of the way."

Penny reached out to comfort him. Matt had been just Chad's age when he battled bullies on her behalf, she remembered. To her young eyes he had seemed fearless and invincible.

But inside, had he been as scared as Chad was now?

She offered a meager drop of solace. "Grown-ups don't heal as fast as children do, but I was assured that your parents are going to be okay. Would it make you feel better to know that before the orderly wheeled you up to say goodbye to them, both your mom and your dad signed a letter giving me permission to bring you on this trip?"

"They did?"

"Word of honor."

Penny suspected that the boy might have heard a lot of

well-meaning platitudes from nurses and neighbors and wasn't sure what to believe any more.

As convincing proof she reached into her handbag, brought out the authorization letter, and handed it to him.

Chad's small shoulders slumped in relief when he saw the signatures. "That's my dad's writing, all right. Mom's, too. Maybe they weren't hurt as bad as I'd thought." He knuckled a small fist across his eyes. "Thanks, Penny."

"No problem, pal." She tucked the letter back into her purse and surreptitiously reached for a tissue.

With Chad safely delivered to his grandparents, Penny concentrated on seeking out a karate studio where she could practice her *katas*. She had missed the discipline of this intensely emotional training that had been part of her life since age seven. She chose a *dojo* with a well-regarded *sensei* (teacher) and flexible hours, and welcomed the chance to lose herself in the ancient art several times a week.

She had just returned from a second invigorating session at the *dojo* when Russell Kehoe contacted her by telephone. "I want to thank you for taking such excellent care of my daughter," he said warmly.

"My pleasure."

"Her mother was most impressed, too. The other night on the phone Pamela told me she hopes you'll be able to fly out to Philadelphia and escort Bethany back to San Francisco at the end of her visit."

"Why, yes. I'd be delighted."

Jotting a note on her calendar, Penny marveled at the Kehoes' ability to keep their priorities separate. Though fierce business competitors, the divorced pair appeared to have a smooth working relationship when it came to their child.

She had liked Pamela Kehoe on sight. At first, the lovely blonde woman who gave her a lift into downtown Philadelphia from the airport had carefully excluded her former husband from the conversation. But Bethany chattered about him nonstop. By the time they reached Penny's hotel, the little girl's mother had given up trying to avoid the subject.

"How *is* Russ?" she asked, in a tone that wouldn't have deceived an infant.

Now, from the awkward pause from the other end of the line, Penny deduced that her client was trying to think of a way to pose a similar question about his ex-wife. Her sympathies went out to these two hurt people. Prudently, she kept silent.

"Incidentally," Kehoe got the conversation going again, "my friend Lon Templeton is interested in meeting you. There's a possibility he may ask you to accompany his twin girls to Massachusetts when school lets out for the summer."

Penny caught her breath. So, as she had fervently hoped he would, her first client had decided to recommend her!

"That shouldn't present a problem. How old are the girls?" she asked.

"Seven or eight. Lon can give you all the particulars. His schedule is even more hectic than mine, but we have breakfast together now and then. Join us tomorrow in the coffee shop at the Mark Hopkins, and I'll introduce you. Eight-thirty all right?"

The views were world-famous at that prestigious hotel atop Nob Hill. But Penny doubted she would have much time for gazing out the window.

"Eight-thirty at the Mark it is," she repeated. "I'll see you both there."

★ ★ ★ ★ ★

A widower, Lon Templeton proved to be a balding man in his forties who practically crackled with kinetic energy. He mentioned that his firm manufactured deep-water scuba gear for the U.S. Navy.

"This summer we'll be testing a new breathing apparatus in the Bering Sea, off the coast of Alaska," he added. "My sister has offered to look after my daughters while I'm away, but with three youngsters of her own, she can't fly out to pick them up."

He directed a character-assessing gaze at Penny. "Russ tells me that you are a highly reliable young woman. Would you be willing to fly to Boston with Teri and Tina, then island-hop them over to Nantucket?"

"Willing? I'd be delighted," Penny replied with an exuberant smile. "I've never been anywhere near that part of the country."

"As long as you're there, why not take a little vacation? Stay over for a few days and explore the island. It's well worth a visit," Mr. Templeton assured her. "I spent my boyhood summers there. Now I'm anxious for my girls to enjoy the same experience."

Penny hoped she didn't look as wistful as she felt. Only the thought that she had a long way to go before her fledgling agency had survived its crucial first year kept her from seizing on his suggestion with delight.

"Someday I hope to linger awhile in all sorts of fascinating places," she answered. "But I've just launched a new business. I'm afraid vacations will have to wait until it has been more firmly established."

"How well I remember those brave, shaky days of start-up with a new enterprise." Mr. Templeton's restlessly drumming fingertips stilled momentarily against the tablecloth. "Our first designs were produced in my father-in-law's garage. We tested them in the pool at the YMCA."

"And now you have a major government contract and an entire sea as your test site," Penny marveled.

"Sounds like a real success story, doesn't it?" The twins' father gave a short bark of laughter. "It is, in a way. Yet when my wife died suddenly last year, I realized that we had let ambition crowd all the fun out of our lives. Frankly, I'd much rather be spending the summer at the Cape with my family."

As though embarrassed by this nostalgic look into the past, Mr. Templeton swiftly reverted to the purpose of the meeting. Within five minutes a definite assignment had been inked in on Penny's calendar, and the hyperactive Mr. Templeton had left the restaurant without taking time for a second cup of coffee.

A short time later, riding down the steep hill clinging to the outside pole of a cable car, Penny reflected that while the loss of his wife must have been a severe blow, her newest client had made no effort to change his workaholic habits after her death. Had he really wanted to, he could have delegated a trusted employee to oversee the testing of the new gear while he spent a few weeks' quality time with his daughters.

Soberly, she warned herself that once time sped past, you could never get it back. Career success was important. Years from now, though, she didn't want to look back and realize that she had allowed ambition to gobble up her life, leaving only bank deposits to show for it. Ethan had taught her that each day was a gift. Those gifts, Penny realized, would be even more precious if they could be shared with someone for whom she cared very deeply.

She and Matt had been given the sort of second chance

that very few people were lucky enough to receive. Having been reunited to find their friendship still intact after such a long separation was truly miraculous. Was it selfish to yearn for more?

Closing her eyes, Penny wished with all her heart that she could persuade Matt to see her as more than a mere friend. "If that day ever arrives," she told herself, "nothing in the world would ever be able to come between us again."

She had no idea how wrong this complacent assumption would turn out to be.

CHAPTER TEN

Had she not been on the lookout for a letter from Australia, Penny might never have encountered the security guard.

Matt had dropped her a note on his arrival in Sydney. Two weeks later, a card postmarked Brisbane showed up in her mail. More than a month had passed since then, with still no word as to when he might be coming home.

May's temperatures soared into the eighties, an unusual occurrence for San Francisco. Heeding dire warnings about rolling blackouts and a statewide energy crisis, Penny firmly resisted the temptation to buy an air conditioner to cool her office. Instead, she fell into the habit of leaving her door partway open after lunch. That way she could take advantage of the refreshing breeze wafting in across the Bay, and watch for the mail at the same time.

But the man who paused on her threshold on the last Friday of the month wasn't from the post office. Hearing someone clear his throat in what was obviously meant to be an attention-getting sound, Penny looked up in surprise from the contract spread across her desk.

Her eyes met those of a soldierly looking individual with a bristly white moustache, wearing a khaki uniform and peaked cap. The legend "Golden State Security Patrol" was stitched in a tight circle around his blue and gold arm patch. Though he carried no firearm, loops on his wide Sam Browne belt held a businesslike truncheon and a two-way radio.

"Something the matter, officer?"

"When I saw your door ajar, I thought I'd better check that nothing was wrong here."

"It isn't. I was just getting a little air."

As if it would take more than words to convince him, he shot a sharp glance around the small, pleasantly decorated space. Keen eyes took in the slim vase of daisies atop the file cabinet and the framed print of soaring birds displayed on the opposite wall. Clearly, all was well here, but his stern expression didn't soften.

"The person who leases the warehouse across the way mentioned a concern about break-ins to the owner of this property," he explained in a gruff tone. "Mr. Hazelton hired our company to patrol the grounds and make certain the business park remains a secure environment for his tenants."

Penny was touched that Matt had managed to follow up on her suggestion before his rushed departure for Australia. "It's reassuring to know that you're keeping an eye on everything," she told the guard. "Has anyone else reported a security problem?"

"No, ma'am. That's the way we want to keep it. Everybody safe and sound."

His words sounded like a pointed warning. Penny got the message. "From now on, then, I guess I'd better leave the window open on hot days instead of inviting the breeze in through the door," she decided.

The guard nodded approval. "Better than courting trouble, I always say."

Impulsively, meaning to express her appreciation for the

increased security he had arranged, Penny stopped by Griff Hazelton's office before heading home that afternoon. A few days earlier she had posted a check to cover her second month's rent. But this was the first time since the day she'd signed her lease that she had actually spoken with her landlord.

The former football star was glowering at a sheaf of legal-sized papers when she tapped at his door. The sight of the slim, auburn-haired young woman standing on his threshold in her summery flowered dress had an instant effect for the better on his black mood. He swept the papers into his briefcase with an out-of-sight, out-of-mind gesture, and gave her a grin Red Riding Hood would have recognized at once.

"Hi there, little lady," he greeted her jovially. "How's everything been going?"

Even that detested phrase couldn't ruffle her calm today. "Fine and dandy," Penny told him serenely. "So well, in fact, that when my lease expires next month I'm almost sure I'll be renewing it for a much longer period."

"Glad to hear it." His grin turned teasing. "Guess that must mean your fancy clients didn't turn up their noses at this unritzy neighborhood after all."

That was exactly what Penny had feared might happen, particularly after the receptionist for a company on the lower level of her building told her about the unsavory old Barbary Coast connections this near-waterfront location had once boasted. During the days of the original Forty-Niners, Vanessa had said, the property where their building now stood was occupied by one of the most notorious gambling palaces in San Francisco.

With a slight blush, she apologetically admitted that her fears had been baseless. "The clients I work for are more interested in my references than my business address, thank goodness."

His heavy eyebrows shot up. "No kiddin', people are actually hiring you to schlep their kids around the country?"

"No kiddin'," Penny confirmed happily. "Already, I'm almost fully booked for June. Once school lets out, children will be heading all over the map."

"Well, I'm glad things are working out." He closed the briefcase with a snap and stood up. "End of a long day," he said, tucking it under his arm. "How about dinner?"

Not a chance, Penny thought. But she softened her refusal with a word of thanks. "I met one of the new security guards this afternoon. He seemed very efficient. I know that Matt Devlin and the other tenants, too, will appreciate your providing us with this extra protection."

Hazelton held the door, then stepped out after her, turning back to jiggle the knob to make certain it was securely locked. Aware that she'd noticed the precaution, he shrugged a bit sheepishly.

"Hate to have anyone walk off with my trophies. Not that there's much danger of that. Personally, I think your friend Devlin has been imagining things. But as long as I'm paying for security, I might as well follow their advice."

Making her rounds with the sprinkling can that weekend, Penny carried on cheery one-sided conversations with the thriving foliage that brightened every room of Mrs. Thibault's apartment.

"We had another postcard from Naomi today," she told the Norfolk Island pine in the corner of the living room. "She misses everyone here at home. But," she added, turning to the lacy asparagus fern on the coffee table, "it's uplifting her spirits to be able to assist folks who need a helping hand."

Penny wondered if the families being aided by the church building program appreciated the efforts of the volunteer carpenters. There were people in this world, she thought grumpily, who were so pig headed they wouldn't let anyone give them a hand.

People like Matt Devlin. Was he never coming home?

As if her thoughts of him had been reciprocated, an airmail envelope sealed with colorful Australian stamps arrived the following week. Reading the eventful account of his sojourn Down Under, Penny began to understand why Matt's return had been delayed.

He had spent the first few weeks searching for promising toy makers, and declared himself more than pleased with the fourteen new craftspeople whose work he'd arranged to import. But the day after his arrival in Brisbane, an electrical short touched off a serious fire at the plant where the Reefies were assembled. Matt had pitched in to help Meg Limmons and her crew salvage the machinery and find a building to replace the structure that had burned.

Then in Cairns, where the Dreamtime game was fabricated, he'd become involved with a group of environmentalists who were waging a last-ditch struggle to keep the cassowary from extinction. Matt had written:

That's a friendly, man-sized bird left from the dinosaur age. Only a few of them remain on the face of the earth. Because I hate the idea of another unique species vanishing, I spent about ten days in a coastal rain forest working with ecologists to design a video game that will teach children about these big birds. The people here will produce the game, and I'll distribute it in America. All the proceeds will go into a fund to preserve the cassowaries and protect their unique environment.

151

A smile curved Penny's lips. What a softie you are, Matt Devlin, she thought. Who else would have come up with the idea of using something as modern as a video game to keep an ancient bird from extinction?

Matt closed his letter by saying that he was at last on his way to visit the inventor of the Billabong Babies.

Neville's Aborigine helpers are still on walkabout. Over the phone he told me that his newspaper ad had drawn applications from two people with toy making experience in South Australia. So far, though, those men haven't shown up. Soon it may be too late because The Wet will have started. Getting around in the Outback can be mighty difficult when winter rains are washing out bridges and causing every stream to flood.

As soon as I do my bit to get the Billabong Babies into high gear, I'll be on my way home. Here is Neville's address in case that takes a while. Write to me if you have a minute. I haven't exactly been having a wonderful time. But I wish you were here.

Matt

Not "Love, Matt." Not even "Affectionately, Matt," Penny noticed with a sigh. Then she brightened. But he wished she was there. That was progress.

Seven times in June Penny traveled to various destinations around the country. Each time she escorted a child, sometimes two. After shepherding the Templeton twins into their aunt's care, she did take a one-day break on Nantucket and resolved to return soon to that charming island. From there, she flew down to Philadelphia. She'd been hired to bring the son of one of Pamela Kehoe's friends out to Seattle for a summer stay with his father.

Davey had recently started martial arts training. His awe knew no bounds when he learned that his escort was not only skilled at karate, but patterned her eating habits and portions of her daily routine on the precepts of the art.

Three other jobs resulted from the small ad she had placed in the travel section of the Sunday newspaper, and Roberta arranged a second connection for her. The last trip of the month came from a contact lined up by the commercial artist who had designed her business cards.

The day following her return from ferrying a hearing-impaired youngster to a special summer camp in Wisconsin, Penny stopped in at Ink, Inc. to thank Joan for the reference.

"Glad to do it." The printer's wife added that she had gone to high school with Alison's mother, a busy CPA who'd been concerned about the ability of a deaf child to travel alone. "Did the two of you get along all right?"

"Having two weeks' advance notice to prepare for the trip made all the difference," Penny told her gratefully. "Before leaving, I took a crash course in American Sign Language. I'm still a beginner at signing, and I had to keep slowing down Alison's flying fingers to catch her meaning. But at least she and I were able to communicate without having to write down every word."

"Good thinking." Joan looked over at the bulletin board where Penny's card was displayed. "There may be another job in the offing," she added. "I noticed a woman copying down your phone number this morning."

When the telephone rang later that afternoon, Penny was prepared to answer a query about her services. Instead, she found that her caller was looking for a job.

Introducing herself as a former stewardess for Pan-American World Airways, Inez Garcia asked if she could come and fill out an application for part-time employment.

"Sorry, but I'm in no position to hire anyone," Penny replied. "My agency was launched only recently. It won't even be listed in the Yellow Pages until the new phone books come out this summer. Meanwhile, most of my jobs are coming by word of mouth."

"When your customers recommend you to their friends, that means they are really satisfied." Inez assured Penny that she wasn't looking for a regular paycheck. "But I did wonder if you might occasionally be able to use a Spanish-speaking assistant with eleven years' flying experience."

The term "Spanish-speaking" silenced the firm refusal hovering on Penny's lips. Like Texas, California had a large Hispanic population. Two queries had already come her way about the possibility of escorting youngsters to Latin America.

"Why don't you stop by my office," she invited cautiously, suggesting a time later that afternoon. "At least we can get acquainted."

Strands of silver frosted Ms. Garcia's glossy black hair. While her movements were brisk, her figure was comfortably mature. To Penny, regarding her from across the desk, she looked like a youthful grandmother.

Inez told Penny that before retiring to care for an elderly parent, she had served on many of Pan-Am's routes criss-crossing Central and South America. Later, she had also been based in Manila, and was familiar with most of the major airports in the Far East.

"My father passed away last February, leaving me a house and a moderate income. I'm enjoying my freedom too much ever to want another full-time job," she added frankly. "But I miss the thrill of hopping on an airplane and flying off to faraway places. When I saw your card I hoped you might have some overflow I could handle."

A strong believer in the value of looking ahead, Penny cogitated that at the rate the business was growing, she might soon find herself in the position of having to either delegate some pressing assignments or turn them down. Inez certainly seemed to be well qualified for the work. Besides, she had liked her at first sight.

"How do you feel about children?" she asked cautiously.

A dimple flared in Inez's rounded cheek. "I am fond of *los ninos* unless they are badly spoiled. Are you?"

Penny laughed at having the tables turned on her. "Usually," she said, and decided to begin checking Inez's references that very afternoon.

The positive feedback she received regarding the woman's character and reliability spurred Penny into giving her a chance when she received two job offers for the Fourth of July weekend. The experiment turned out well. Still, a month or more might have passed before she called on Inez again—if it hadn't been for the cablegram from Matt Devlin.

Fingers trembling with eagerness, Penny ripped open the long-awaited message. Then she groaned. Matt's return coincided with a job she had scheduled!

It was a plum assignment, likely to generate many profitable referrals if the Hillsborough matron whose great-niece she had undertaken to escort to the East Coast was pleased enough to recommend the agency to others in her social set.

Penny wavered, torn. Then Lon Templeton's rueful words popped into her mind. "When my wife died suddenly last year," he had said, "I realized that we had let ambition crowd out the fun things of life."

Without a healthy dose of ambition, her business would never have gotten started. But in twenty years did she want to look back with regret at having chosen one more job over Matt?

It was no contest. She reached for the phone.

"How would you like an all-expenses-paid trip to Newport, Rhode Island?" she asked Inez.

"Newport? You mean that fabulous town where the cream of New York society built their hundred-room 'summer cottages' around the turn of the last century?"

"The very same," Penny assured her. "The trip will be first class all the way. A friend of mine is arriving home on Friday after a long stay in Australia. If you're able to take this assignment for me, I can stay here and meet his plane."

"That must be quite a friend!"

"The best," Penny assured her, thinking of all Matt had meant to her over the years. "I don't think I could wait even one extra day to see him again."

CHAPTER ELEVEN

Matt Devlin reined in his impatience as he exited the jumbo jet and inched toward SFO's international terminal. The flight had been long and tedious, the jet jam-packed. From somewhere nearby a cranky child echoed the fatigue he and several hundred fellow passengers were feeling.

"Didn't want to come," she whined. "Damon promised me a horse for my birthday, and now he'll think I—"

Someone else sneezed, drowning out the rest of the girl's complaint. It didn't quite muffle her father's sharp command to pipe down, however.

Matt clenched his teeth. The pair had been seated four rows behind him on the plane. Just far enough away that he couldn't hear more than the rise and fall of their interminable argument. Plenty close enough to know it hadn't ceased for longer than five minutes at a time all the way across the Pacific.

The stocky man in his late thirties and the nine-year-old girl shared the same straight, fair hair, cleft chin, and washed-out blue eyes. The father's had an arctic gleam in them, though. The sullenness around his mouth looked chronic, as though he'd been holding a grudge forever.

Against the kid? Those were fresh bruises on her arm.

Thirteen years earlier, Matt had vowed that he would

never again interfere in a family dispute. He had kept that promise. These days, he seldom thought of Jimmy, or of the disastrous consequences his meddling had triggered. But occasionally he still awoke shuddering from the nightmare. He knew he would never be able to forget it was his fault the younger boy had died.

Now, Matt found his resolve to mind his own business wavering. When everyone else in line continued to turn a deaf ear to the suppressed violence simmering in the wrangle between father and daughter, his reluctant conscience rebelled.

Hoisting his suitcase onto the counter when his turn finally arrived, he handed the Customs inspector his passport and the form he had filled out aboard the plane.

"Anything to declare?"

"No. But I'm not very happy with—"

"Does this problem concern smuggling?"

Taken aback by the brusque demand, Matt shook his head. "But—"

"Sorry, Sir. You'll have to lodge all other complaints with airline personnel. Next!"

Left speechless, Matt was pushed ahead as a heavyset matron burdened with tote bags, umbrella and several suitcases marked with red pompoms took his place at the counter.

As a teenager he had lost faith in the power of the law to guarantee ordinary people a fair shake. More positive experiences in the Navy hadn't quite managed to curb his natural inclination to bypass authority and handle problems himself. But now, having made up his mind to break his most unbreakable rule, he'd been dismissed with a curt word and a squiggle of chalk.

Neither bullies' fists nor yards of red tape had ever dissuaded Matt Devlin from following through on a course he believed was right. But at the instant he started to turn back for a second attempt to convince the official that something might be amiss, a fluttering hand from the crowded lounge where family and friends had gathered to greet returning passengers snagged his attention.

Everything else vanished from his mind as he stared at the woman doing the waving. When he'd sent that cable, he hadn't imagined that Penny would come to meet him. Each of the friendly little notes she'd sent him in care of Neville Baker made it clear that her schedule grew busier every week.

Yet, miraculously, she was here. "Penny!"

"Matt! Welcome home, Matt!"

Auburn curls bouncing, Penny darted forward. With an enormous exercise of willpower, she managed to keep from flinging her arms around Matt's neck. But she couldn't quell the sheer delight in her smile as she tugged him out of the milling crowd toward an out-of-the-way corner.

"Thank goodness you're back!" she cried. "I've never been so happy to see anyone in my entire life!"

Immediate anxiety clouded the warmth in Matt's deep blue eyes. He dropped his suitcase on the spot. His lean, tanned fingers fanned out across her shoulders in a protective gesture.

"What's the problem, Penny? Tell me, and I'll take care of everything."

"Nothing's wrong, Matt. If there was, I could handle it myself," she declared. "I only meant that I missed you while you were away. I'm awfully glad you've come home at last."

Matt felt a catch in the region of his heart. He was used to being Penny's protector. Her champion. But now he felt like putty in her hands. Silly Putty.

"You're serious?"

Penny felt a forcible impulse to wrap her own fingers around his neck and squeeze. Either that, or to tug his head down and fasten her lips against his to stifle the overly solicitous questions he kept asking.

Instead, she raised her hands and splayed them across his chest. Somewhere, locked inside that strong ribcage, beat a heart filled with warm, loving emotions. She knew it. Somehow, without scaring him off, she had to find a way to bring them out while squelching his worry-bug attitude.

"Very serious," she assured him. "Why else would I be here in this mob scene when I could be home talking to the plants? Why else would I have begged Inez to take that trip to Newport in my place?"

Matt hadn't a clue as to who Inez was. He didn't care. What counted was that Penny seemed almost as glad to see him as he was to be back home with her again.

"You're all I thought about when I was away," he murmured.

Penny knew she'd do something disgracefully mushy if she didn't watch out. "Sure," she said, with a sparkly, lopsided grin. "Me and the cassowaries and the Reefies and the Billabong Babies."

An exuberant family group swarmed past, jostling them while shouting a welcome to someone still trapped back in the Customs line. Grateful to them for reminding him where he was, Matt took a quick step backwards and snatched up his luggage. He'd come mighty close to wrapping Penny in his arms and kissing her until her lipstick melted. But her career demanded circumspect behavior. Suppose one of her strait-laced clients had spotted them making a public spectacle of themselves?

Matt hadn't said he'd been worried about her, Penny mused happily. He said he had thought about her while he was way. There was a world of difference between those two things.

"Are the Reefies back in production yet?" she asked, as they started down the corridor to the main terminal building.

"Almost. That blaze might have been a blessing in disguise," Matt said. "The new plant is larger and a lot safer."

"Great! What about Neville's labor pool woes? Did that pair of applicants with toy-making experience take up the slack left by his vanishing native workers?"

"They never even showed up," Matt replied in disgust. "A few of the Aborigine craftsmen started to trickle back from walkabout while I was there in the Outback. But it wasn't until I was almost set to leave that a couple of Sydneysiders who'd been caravanning around the countryside on holiday had their motor home break down right outside his gate. When Neville learned they were too broke to pay for repairs, he offered them a bonus to stay on through The Wet as his employees. They pitched in enthusiastically and had the assembly line going strong within a day or two."

Matt and Penny sauntered on, happily filling each other in on news that had happened during their separation. They paid no attention to anyone else until the bickering pair from the plane caught up with them.

"You didn't even let Mama know where we were going," they heard the girl sniffle. "She'll be so worried about me!"

"I left her a note when I took your passport out of the drawer."

"Yeah, but Dad, she mightn't find it for days. Puh-leeeese can't I call her? At least let her know I'm okay?"

"Discussion's over, Francie. One more word and you'll be sorry you didn't shut up when I told you to."

With a ruthless jerk of her arm, he propelled her past the strolling couple. Penny looked scandalized when she saw the little girl's short legs churning to keep up with the man's long strides.

Matt glowered after the pair. "They've been going at it like that for hours."

"Then it's high time somebody did something about the situation!"

Francie's father looked about as persuadable as one of the granite faces carved into Mount Rushmore, Matt decided. Neither his daughter's spunky defiance nor the glares sent his way by a planeload of travelers had had the slightest softening effect on the man's rigid attitude.

"It's better not to interfere. Having strangers cause him to lose face by challenging his authority in public is bound to make it even harder on the child in the long run," he cautioned in a troubled tone.

Penny felt a spurt of outrage. "He's kidnapping that little girl! How much harder on her could it get?"

"I agree. It's not right. But he's her father, Penny."

What had happened to her old pal, the champion of the underdog? "Maybe so," she snapped. "But I'll bet anything Francie's mother was granted custody of her."

Within Matt a terrible struggle had been raging. Haunted by the memory of the fate he'd brought down on Jimmy, he had sworn never to intrude on a family quarrel again. Yet by refusing to intervene now he was in danger of losing his self-respect, and probably about to forfeit Penny's good opinion of himself as well.

Ahead of them, the man gave his daughter's arm another cruel jerk.

"A long time ago, I learned a horrible lesson about meddling in other people's affairs," Matt growled. "But this is more than any decent person can tolerate. Run and get a cop, Penny. I'll find some way to keep that brute from hauling his kid out of the building until you return with some official backup."

If only she knew this airport as well as she'd known San Antonio International! There, she could have whistled up help in ten seconds flat. "Be careful," she whispered. "He's packing such a load of hostility he's apt to answer any challenge with his fists."

Penny was on the verge of racing off in search of assistance when Francie pulled a surprise maneuver. Spying restroom signs ahead, she yanked free and bolted toward the door marked with a skirted figure.

"I gotta go!" she howled back over her shoulder.

Penny felt convinced that had the two of them been alone in the corridor, the child's father would have chased her inside without hesitation. Instead, aware that onlookers were viewing him with disapproval, he cut his small quarry a bit of slack. "Three minutes!" he snarled, and strode into the men's room next door.

Quickly, Penny revised their plan. "Matt, that poor kid needs to know that she's not alone. I'll stay with her while you fetch security. Hurry!"

He headed off at a sprint while she pushed open the restroom door. Inside, the quaking youngster whirled around to confront her in panic. "Take it easy," Penny said in a low, placating tone. "My friend has gone to get the police. Are you okay?"

"I won't be after my dad drags me out of here," Francie blubbered. "He'll punch me black and blue, just like he used to do to my mom."

Penny dampened a paper towel, then bent over to dab the hot tears from the little girl's cheeks. "Your parents are divorced?"

"Uh-huh. Mom got married again. I'm s'posed to live with her and Damon all the time. But he tracked us down—"

She broke off with a terrified gasp at the sound of a fist thudding heavily against the outer door.

"Francie! You have five seconds to get out here!"

The child's trembles increased as she peered desperately around for an escape route. But her father blocked the only way into or out of the restroom.

Penny remembered how frightened she used to be when a bully menaced her. As a child, she'd never had a predicament this terrifying to contend with, though. Sucking in a deep, strengthening breath, she forced calm confidence into her voice.

"Everything's going to be all right, Francie. I'll protect you."

"H-h-how are you g-g-gonna do that?"

"Don't worry. I know how." She smoothed the girl's straight fair hair away from her damp cheeks. "I've had lots of training in self-defense."

"Like that cool dude on the Texas Ranger TV show?"

Penny nodded gravely. Karate champion Chuck Norris was a favorite of hers, too. "You got it."

She spun around as the vicious pounding at the door began anew. Foul curses accompanied the intimidating blows.

"Francie," she instructed quietly, "run down to that end cubicle. Lock yourself in, then hop up on the seat so your feet don't show underneath. Be still as a mouse. Maybe we can trick him into believing you got away."

There was no way of telling whether the ruse would have

worked. Francie had scurried no more than halfway down the row of stalls when the outer door burst violently open. Face contorted with fury, the man stalked inside, intent on collaring his small victim.

"Get out!" he snarled at Penny. On the smug assumption that his command would be obeyed, he swaggered past her without a second glance. Advancing menacingly toward his daughter, he jerked his thumb backwards.

Francie had figured the lady with the red hair would run away. Most people couldn't flee fast enough any time her father's temper got out of control. But when she realized that wasn't going to happen this time, she hesitated.

The long mirror above the row of sinks reflected the confrontation in stark, ugly detail. Penny could tell the man was oblivious to everything except the defiant child. Statue-still, she watched the vein at his temple pulse, purpling as his fury threatened to erupt. She prayed that Matt and reinforcements would arrive before that happened.

Her prayers went unanswered. The man's fists tightened. A savage snarl rumbled in his throat as he raised a foot, preparing to lunge at Francie.

The stance betrayed his murderous state of mind. Before he could bring that foot down again, Penny catapulted into action. In a blur of motion she slammed a disabling blow to the back of his neck, then yanked his feet out from under him.

The rampaging bully collapsed chin-first, sending vibrations through the tile floor. A breathless minute ticked by. Still, he didn't move.

"Wow!" Francie lifted a face bright with hero worship. "Wow! You really did it!"

Suddenly, her tears began spurting anew. "You'd better run," she bawled. "He's gonna kill you when he wakes up.

Then he'll kill me cuz I saw it happen. He'd never let anyone tell how a girl knocked him unconscious!"

"Calm down," Penny forestalled the impending hysterics. "He won't have a chance to hurt anyone, honey. Any second now my friend will be back with the police, and they'll haul him off to jail."

"Wh-wh-what about when he gets out? You don't know how mean he can be when somebody makes him mad."

If what she had just witnessed was an example of one of this guy's temper tantrums, Penny hated to think what would happen if he really got riled. There was no question in her mind that Francie's father was seriously deranged. He ought to be institutionalized permanently. But who knew what a judge would decide?

"Suppose," she said thoughtfully, "a girl had nothing to do with it? I doubt if he'll even remember I was still in the room. What if he just, uh, slipped on a puddle?"

Francie's sobs diminished into snuffles. She stared down at the spotless floor. "What puddle?"

Penny turned the faucet on full blast and scooped a cascade of water over rim of the sink. She drizzled a last splash across the soles of the unconscious man's shoes.

"That puddle." She dried her hands and the porcelain with a paper towel. "It's a mystery how it got there."

Mirth danced in Francie's washed-out blue eyes. "Some sloppy washer in a hurry, I'll bet. Cross your heart and hope to die you'll never tell what really happened?"

"Cross my heart," Penny echoed. "Here. Blow."

CHAPTER TWELVE

Several hours later, a taxi deposited a tired couple at the entrance to Penny's apartment building. Upstairs, she heated minestrone and sliced a crusty loaf of Italian bread, both fresh from her favorite deli.

Exhausted from the long trip and its explosive aftermath, Matt slumped into a kitchen chair. "Believe me, if anything could make you glad to be an orphan, it's watching people play tug-of-war with their kids!"

Penny soberly agreed. "Francie is luckier than some," she added, filling a teakettle and setting it on the stove to boil. "Her mom and a stepfather she's fond of are already on their way to bring her home. And between assault and kidnapping charges, her biological father is likely to be locked up for decades."

She wished she could forget the ugly words that had spilled out of him once he had regained consciousness and learned he'd been taken into custody. "The worst part of it is that he doesn't even love his daughter. He only snatched her to revenge himself on his ex-wife for escaping from him."

Matt flexed his shoulders, trying to shrug away a chill of fear that was no less keen for being retroactive. "Lord, Penny, it gives me the shivers to realize you were in as much danger as Francie. Imagine what could have happened if that lunatic hadn't slipped and knocked himself cold!"

Penny opened her mouth. Firmly, then, she closed it again. She had promised. Crossed her heart and hoped to die.

Ladling out two steaming bowls of soup, she set them on the table. "You worry too much, Matt. I keep telling you I can take care of myself."

Unfortunately, she thought, there was about as much chance of convincing him of that as there was of recapturing that exuberant moment at the airport's arrival gate when he'd told her she was all he had thought about while he was away.

As children they'd been nearly inseparable, she mused sentimentally. What they needed to do now was build a future of shared love on the solid cornerstone of friendship that had linked them together earlier in life.

First, though, there were gaps to be filled in. Penny set down her spoon and leaned forward intently.

"Matt, today at the airport you said you once learned a horrible lesson about becoming involved in other people's affairs. What did you mean?"

All these years later it still gave Matt an agonizing stab of guilt to remember how he had played Russian roulette with someone else's life, and lost the game.

He had never discussed that grim incident, not even with Ben, and Ben was part of what had happened that fateful August. But now, maybe because he was so tired or maybe because the day's events had brought back the old aches so vividly, he felt the desperate need to tell Penny about it. He hoped she wouldn't judge him as harshly as he judged himself.

Wearily, he met her eyes. "I tried to help out a friend

once, and wound up getting him killed instead."

"Oh, Matt!"

The blunt force of his statement slammed into Penny like a tidal wave.

Seeing the anguish on his face, she berated herself for having triggered such a painful memory. But it was too late now to pretend the subject had never been mentioned. She could only hope that talking it out might ease the misery of that boyhood tragedy for him.

"Tell me what happened, Matt. Often it helps to share your problems with a sympathetic listener."

It surprised Matt to realize that after keeping all the details bottled up inside for so long, he did want to talk about the part he had played in Jimmy's death. Penny was his friend, the best one he'd ever have. Each time they met, his feelings for her deepened. But he knew he could never achieve the closeness with her he yearned for so long as this shameful incident from his past remained concealed.

"The summer I turned sixteen, my two best buddies were Ben Zimmerman and a kid named Jimmy Ritter, who was a few months younger than either of us." His voice ached with the memory. "Jimmy came to live at the Home after his father died, though he did have an uncle who could have acted as his guardian. But Floyd Ritter didn't want any part of that kind of responsibility. Not then, anyway."

"Later he changed his mind?"

"Not out of the goodness of his heart, I assure you," Matt replied bitterly. "Jimmy had been at the Home for almost a year when Floyd hit on a get-rich-quick scheme. Unfortunately, he needed control over Jimmy to carry it through."

Jimmy's mother, who'd been killed in an accident soon after his birth, had become estranged from her own family when she married. But when the last of her relatives died without leaving a will, the courts decided that her son was legally entitled to inherit a parcel of land which would have come to her had she still been alive.

"That chunk of desert on the outskirts of Las Vegas wasn't worth five cents—until urban sprawl brought the city stretching out in its direction. Then property developers began taking an interest in the acreage. And Floyd suddenly remembered that he had a nephew."

"Let me guess. He decided that Jimmy's rightful place was with him."

"Worse still, the court agreed," Matt confirmed gloomily. "Floyd was an abusive drunk who enjoyed using his fists. The battered women's shelter used to save a spot for his wife every Saturday night. Before she finally left him, Jimmy spent a weekend at their place. He came back covered with bruises."

"Then how on earth—" Penny began.

"Religion." Matt's tone was cynical. "Good old Uncle Floyd swore he'd had a vision of the Lord and been converted into a born-again do-gooder. He convinced the judge that he wanted to make amends for past misdeeds by taking in his brother's orphaned boy. His petition for custody of Jimmy was granted."

"Couldn't Jimmy have refused to go with him?"

"He wasn't given any choice. Even though he begged to stay at the Home, Floyd had been named his legal guardian by a court of law. No contest."

With a flash of insight, Penny guessed what had happened next. Matt Devlin, champion of the underdog, would have gone to the rescue.

"So you stepped in."

"We were friends," Matt said, as though that explained

everything. "I knew darned well that Floyd would treat Jimmy shamefully, then abandon him the minute he got his hands on the cash from the sale of that land. So I urged him to run away."

It had been stupid, Matt told himself for the thousandth time. Really stupid. But from an earnest teenage viewpoint, taking off to escape from Floyd had seemed like Jimmy's best bet.

"Jimmy was too weak and timid to do it on his own, so I said I would go along," he continued, making no excuses for himself. "Ben had been squabbling with his folks about something. At the last minute, he decided to come with us."

They had hitchhiked south, walking part of the way, picking up rides when they could.

"To us, Southern California meant Hollywood. Malibu. Surfboards and gorgeous girls. We sure weren't prepared for the desert."

Their luck had run out at Paso Robles. Trudging through the desolate landscape in 100-degree temperatures was like treading the outskirts of Hell. Cars sped right on past. Local ranchers refused them shelter.

"The last old guy we talked to threatened to call the sheriff if we didn't get off his property pronto. I wish now that he had," Matt lamented. "By then, Ben had had enough of our big adventure, and Jimmy would have agreed to whatever we decided. But they made the mistake of looking to me for leadership."

He gave a bitter laugh. "I pointed out that Jimmy would wind up in Floyd's clutches if we went back. Instead, I talked my friends into heading west across the hills toward the ocean."

After a pause, he finished the sorry tale. "We didn't know about snakes seeking the stored warmth of the pavement after the sun goes down. None of us saw the rattler Jimmy stepped on. He died before we could find anyone to help."

Visualizing the scene, two desperate boys and their dying companion, Penny wanted to bawl. "How horrible for you all," she whispered.

"Yeah," Matt agreed hoarsely. "Afterwards, Ben's parents clapped him into military school to keep him away from 'bad companions.' Namely me. As the instigator of the whole mess, I wound up doing a stretch in Juvenile Hall."

"What a rotten deal, when your only crime was trying to help a friend." Penny stood up and extended her right hand across the table toward him.

"What's this?" Matt sounded gently mocking. "Congratulations?"

"Exactly. I'm proud of you, Matt Devlin. After that experience it must have been incredibly difficult for you to offer assistance to Francie at the airport today."

He dragged in an agonized breath. "I almost didn't. Getting involved meant breaking a solemn oath. When Jimmy died, I swore that would be the last time I ever meddled in anyone else's family problems."

"I'm glad you changed your mind. If you hadn't decided to call security, Francie would surely have been harmed by her father. Instead, thanks to the fact that strangers were willing to interfere, she's on her way back to a happy home."

Matt saw that Penny was still waiting for him to take her hand. He reached out and wrapped his fingers around hers. It was a good hand, soft but solid. The hand of a staunch ally.

He held tight, his spirit feeling lighter than it had in thirteen years.

CHAPTER THIRTEEN

July and early August breezed past in San Francisco's own unique pattern: foggy mornings, glowing afternoons, nights that were downright chilly. Penny, however, was seldom in the city to sympathize with tourists buying coats they had never expected to need.

She counted herself lucky if her path crossed Matt's more than twice a week. With school vacation in full swing, she and Inez averaged four trips a week escorting young charges all over the map. Matt was away frequently, too. Since his return from Australia, much of his time was spent speaking to environmental groups, promoting the video game designed to help save the cassowaries from extinction.

It was a very good cause, she reminded herself. Just as it was absolutely essential that she build up her savings reserve during this high season while job offers were plentiful. When the summer school holidays ended, her business was bound to drop off sharply. Remembering Lon Templeton's wistful remark about how all work and no play had impoverished his life, Penny resolved to share large blocks of quality time with Matt as soon as the pressure eased up.

"Once we're past Labor Day, I probably won't be offered another escort job until Thanksgiving," she remarked on one of their rare get-togethers.

"That wouldn't hurt my feelings a bit."

They were taking advantage of a free Thursday afternoon to look over the latest batch of imports to arrive at the
warehouse from Australia. Matt had been displaying one
delightful toy after another for her admiration. "The way
things have gone all summer, those darned houseplants
have seen more of you than I have," he added. "Which reminds me. Have you done anything about finding another
place to live yet?"

Guiltily, Penny shook her head. "No. But the problem
has been on my mind."

It had been on her mind, all right. Morning, noon, and
night. Naomi's sublet had provided her with a wonderful
short-term home, but her hostess would return before too
much longer, and she had made no definite plans for what
came next.

She kept hoping that Matt would suggest they look for a
place large enough for two. She loved him. Deeply. What's
more, she felt certain that he was extremely fond of her.
Penny had seriously considered the idea of proposing to
him, rather than waiting for him to be the first to speak.

What if she did, though, and Matt said yes? That possibility stopped her every time. He was such a devoted friend,
he might accept simply because he decided that wedlock
was the best way to protect her. She wanted him to marry
her not because they were pals, but because he couldn't live
without her.

Muffling a sigh, she handed back the toy. "I love the new
imports, Matt. But the Billabong Babies are still my favorites. Will you receive a shipment of them in time for holiday
distribution?"

"I sure hope so. Otherwise, we're both likely to be tight-
ening our belts this winter."

Swallowing a groan, he tried not to think about the unavoidable expenses connected with the upcoming conference inspired by his work with the endangered cassowaries. Torn between wanting to support the cause, yet wondering how he'd be able to afford another stint of international travel, he wished that California, rather than Australia, had been chosen as the venue. But the extra distance would have put attendance out of reach of many Third World representatives.

Focused as she was on keeping her fledgling agency afloat during its first crucial year, Penny refused to let any business commitment interfere with Matt's birthday. August tenth fell on a Saturday. Setting aside misgivings about looking gift horses in the mouth, she tactfully declined two different requests to travel as a child's escort that weekend. When a job offer popped up for Sunday the eleventh, she accepted the assignment, but delegated the trip to Inez.

"Matt and I have plans to spend the entire day together on Saturday," she enthused. "This way I won't have to worry about getting to bed early or being up at the crack of dawn to catch the early-bird flight to Montreal."

"Expecting a late night, are you?" the older woman teased.

"I don't know." Penny bent over the calendar and concentrated on inking flight information into the correct square. "Whatever kind of celebration Matt has in mind for his birthday, he hasn't told me the details yet."

In spite of the limited amount of time they'd been able to spare for togetherness since Matt's return from Australia, their friendship had continued to deepen and solidify. Penny's heart grew more deeply involved each time he took her into his arms. He, on the other hand, always seemed to be holding back. His kisses invariably stopped just short of the wild passion she dreamed of rousing in him.

175

Consciously or subconsciously, Penny thought in exasperation, Matt was still watching over her like a devoted big brother.

She felt certain that given the proper setting she could transform his protectiveness into ardor. What they needed was a place to be alone together. A private spot where sweet desire could build, slowly and naturally.

Matt's boat wouldn't work. The deck was open to scrutiny by one and all, and the below-decks cabin was almost claustrophobically small. Down there, intimacy would be forced upon them, like it or not. One hug, and they'd be molded together.

It wasn't want she wanted.

She could tell that he felt no more comfortable in her sublet apartment than she did aboard his boat.

"Did you realize you've almost lost your Texas accent?" Matt asked, the last time she'd invited him over for a spaghetti feed. "Except when you talk to those plants. Watching you go around with the watering can drawling sweet nothings to all that greenery makes me feel as if I have thirty-seven rivals for your attention."

Definitely not the place to coax a fervent declaration of abiding love from the man!

More than once Penny had been tempted to suggest a rendezvous at a hotel. But while she believed Matt was romantically interested in her, she couldn't be positive. There was always the risk that such a bold proposal might endanger their beautiful friendship.

The problem still simmered unresolved when the downstairs bell sounded on Saturday morning. Penny hurried across the room and pressed the buzzer to release the lock on the building's street entrance. Then she opened the apartment door and widened it a few inches so Matt could walk right in when he got upstairs, and hurried back across the room to wind up the telephone conversation his arrival had interrupted.

She sent a blithe wave of welcome in Matt's direction when he stepped inside, but spoke into the receiver.

"I'm sorry you're feeling achy, Inez. Are you positive you'll be all right by tomorrow morning?"

The former stewardess made light of her ailment. "Don't worry about me. I'll survive. I've been coping with this problem once a month since I was a teenager. I'm just one of those women whom PMS always hits hard."

"Isn't there anything you can take to relieve the discomfort?"

"I gave up on the over-the-counter stuff years ago," Inez confessed. "But my sister-in-law just got back from a visit to her family in Mexico City last week, and she brought me a sample of a new medication to ease menstrual cramps that a research lab down there pioneered. Between the pills and a nice bowl of chicken soup, I'll be feeling fine by the time I get to the airport in the morning."

"I hope so. Be sure the Dumonts give you their notarized authorization letter," Penny cautioned. "The Canadian officials are sticklers about refusing to let a minor across the border unless both parents have practically sworn in blood that it's okay for him to leave the States."

Hanging up, she swung around to greet Matt with a hug and a radiant smile. "Happy Birthday! For an old man of twenty-nine, you're looking very fit."

Her spontaneous show of affection provided a giant boost to Matt's morale. He'd been having trouble controlling his emotions where Penny was concerned. Once he'd got it through his thick skull that the timid Ugly Duckling with the carroty hair who'd befriended him at the children's

Home had matured into a lovely young woman, he'd guarded his heart against getting too involved.

A happy bridegroom himself, Ben argued against such restraint. "Trudi agrees with me that you and Penny make a great pair," he said over a deli lunch the day after the two couples had double-dated. "If she was my girl I'd move in fast before some Silicon Valley type dazzles her with his microchips."

"Or a smooth pillar of society like Russell Kehoe captures her affections," Matt agreed gloomily.

During his eight years in the Navy he had avoided long-term commitments on principle. There'd been a girl he was fond of in Pensacola and another stunner he'd dated regularly while his ship was stationed near Brisbane. Until lately, though, he'd never come within a mile of falling in love with anyone.

"Penny is really special," he acknowledged the depth of his feelings. "But I can offer her so little at the moment I'm afraid to plunge into deep water. What if I proposed and she told me she preferred to find someone with better prospects?"

Ben looked up from his hot pastrami, understanding. "That's heartbreak, my friend. Nobody's exempt from the risk."

"Right. It's safer acting the part of her big brother."

Now, much as he'd liked to have followed up her exuberant greeting with an affectionate display of his own, he stuck to his chosen role.

"Darn it, Penny, you're always telling me you know how to take care of yourself. Then you go and do something airheaded like leaving the apartment door open. Anyone could have walked right in."

Penny conceded that he had a point. Even so, she

wished that for once in his life Matt could manage to put aside the image he had of her as a little girl in pigtails who needed a cavalier to keep the bad guys at bay.

"Matt, the only reason I left the door open was that I was expecting you to show up exactly when you did," she offered a reasonable explanation. "I was on the phone when I heard you buzz from downstairs. It would have seemed ridiculous to interrupt the conversation a second time so I could run over to the door to let you in when you got off the elevator."

"Why don't you compromise between safety and convenience by getting an extra-long cord for the phone?" he suggested. "That way you can keep the chain on the door until you peek out to see who is standing in the hall."

Penny threw him a sassy salute. "Aye, aye, Sir. First thing Monday I'll buy the longest cord they have in the telephone store."

Matt didn't miss the underlying exasperation in her tone. He hadn't meant to start out the day by ruffling Penny's feelings. Still, he felt that keeping her safe was worth risking five minutes' worth of annoyance.

"I thought you two had the weekend off," he tactfully changed the subject. "From the sounds of it, Inez will be heading off to Canada in the morning."

"Yes, it's a plummy job that came up at the last minute."

It wasn't in Penny's nature to sulk. She took a jacket and scarf from the closet and tossed them over her arm while explaining about the assignment.

"Louis and Colette Dumont are French Canadian chefs who were hired to create an elegant menu for the dining room at one of the downtown hotels here in San Francisco. Neither can get time off to take their little boy back to Montreal to visit his grandparents, so they called to ask if we could escort Alain."

She checked to make sure the door to the balcony was locked, then picked up her purse. "Actually, I was glad to have the job," she admitted. "Our schedule is jammed for the next few weeks, but after mid-September it will be tighten-the-belt time. The fee from that journey will pay several bills."

Having launched a small business of his own, Matt was familiar with the financial tightrope a proprietor had to walk in trying to nurse a new enterprise through its first crucial year. A significant portion of Penny's small inheritance had been invested in start-up costs. In June, when assignments started coming her way on a regular basis, she had confided her intention of banking as much of the summer profits as possible to provide a safety cushion for the lean winter months.

"Sounds as if we'll soon have more time to spend on our personal lives," he pointed out the silver lining to her anticipated dip in business and the end of his promotional tour on behalf of the cassowaries' video game. "Meanwhile, we have a whole day off right now. Wait until you see the magnificent chariot we'll be riding in today."

"Awesome!" Penny exclaimed, when she caught sight of the Mustang convertible he had rented. The racy car sported a metallic turquoise finish and white leather seats. Its white canvas top was still up because the morning fog hadn't yet burned off. But the weather forecast called for a glorious afternoon.

The need to rent a car seldom arose. When it did, Matt enjoyed choosing something different to suit each particular occasion. Now he gave Penny a look of unrestrained delight as he headed for the approach to the Bay Bridge. "I thought it might be fun to take a run up to the wine country."

Had it been Penny's choice, that was exactly the outing

she would have selected. "I've been dying to go," she confided. "But I thought it would be best to wait until the grapes were ready to be harvested."

"Some of them are at their peak right now," Matt assured her. "Others are just turning purple. The vineyards are sure to be spectacular."

Once on the Oakland side of the Bay, Matt took Interstate 80 north as it arrowed through Berkeley. The sun came out of hiding as soon as the highway turned away from the water to wind through small East Bay communities with a Latino lilt to their names: El Cerrito, Pinole, Benicia, Vallejo. When her companion pulled over for a moment to lower the convertible's white ragtop, Penny rejoiced in the feel of the breeze whipping through her short, fluffy curls.

A short time later she gazed down at the mothballed fleet as they drove across the high toll bridge above the Carquinez Straits. Row after row of silent grey sentinels rode at anchor, hardy ships that had once roved the seven seas and could be reactivated should the need arise.

"Do you ever miss the Navy?" she asked.

Matt met her eyes and smiled. "Not any more."

An attractive flush bloomed in Penny's cheeks. He did care for her, she told herself. People didn't look at mere friends like that.

The fresh air had given them ravenous appetites. They stopped at a charming café in downtown Napa, and soon were enjoying bowls of a cool, creamy fruit gazpacho ladled from an exquisite tureen. This was followed by a sumptuous entrée of chicken cacciatore, served with chewy, buttery breadsticks, redolent of garlic, and glasses of hearty Chianti.

"I won't be able to move for hours!" Penny groaned, when every morsel of the feast had disappeared.

"I'm not anxious to get back into the car until the effects of that wine wear off," Matt admitted.

Overhearing, their waitress suggested that they might enjoy a first-hand look at several of the town's famous bed-and-breakfast inns. She added that a guided walking tour sponsored by the Chamber of Commerce, located across the street, was scheduled to start in just a few minutes.

The idea appealed to Penny. Several of her friends were enthusiastic fans of B&Bs, as the mini-hotels were called, but she had never stayed in one.

"Want to give it a try, Matt?" she asked uncertainly. "After all, it's your birthday."

"Sure," he answered with an amiable shrug. "Why not?"

Driving into town he had noticed a number of restored mansions that looked as if they could easily qualify for inclusion on the National Register of Historic Places. Nice, he supposed, but hardly his style. He had always lived in spaces barely large enough to contain the basic necessities. Huge old nineteenth-century residences cluttered with stiff, fussy furniture weren't the sorts of living quarters that appealed to him.

But he didn't care where he spent his birthday so long as Penny was with him.

While the interiors of the Victorian guesthouses turned out to be every bit as opulent as Matt had envisioned, they proved to be comfortable and homey as well. The antiques furnishing the high-ceilinged rooms had been chosen to harmonize with their surroundings. He found himself noticing the tinkle of a pianoforte, the yeasty aroma of freshly baked bread, the sumptuousness of a Persian carpet underfoot. Close your eyes, he thought, and you could easily imagine yourself back in a time of hourglass figures and handlebar mustaches.

In the fourth stately home they toured, they ascended a spiral staircase and stepped into the most perfect room Matt had ever seen. It was spacious, luxurious, lavishly wallpapered. Everything, in fact, that his own Spartan cabin aboard *Gypsy* was not.

A canopy, hung with sheer silk curtains, draped the vast round bed strewn with embroidered cushions. On the dresser, chocolates in fluted papers filled a hand-painted candy dish. Logs were laid in the white brick fireplace; candles glowed in crystal sconces. Fresh flowers, glossy magazines, gilt-framed pictures all promised prodigal pampering for the overnight guest.

With a murmur of appreciation, Penny moved through the doorway into the adjoining bathroom. Matt followed. Here, he saw, there was no cozy clutter, only frank sensuality. The towels were huge. Plush. Vibrantly colored. A clear glass enclosure allowed an unimpeded view of a marvelous corner shower. Niches for scented soaps and body oils had been carved into the sparkling, midnight-blue tile, and benches to invite lounging in the rain-soft spray were built in beneath the lavish gold-plated fixtures.

Into Matt's and Penny's head popped the simultaneous thought that the shower was quite large enough for two. Had, in fact, been built for two.

Exchanging stunned glances, they quickly looked elsewhere. But their images were trapped by floor-to-ceiling mirrors wrapping the walls. Wherever their eyes moved, they found reflections of each other.

Matt saw a ragged throb hammer against Penny's pulse points.

Penny stopped wondering whether Matt wanted her. In the glass, his aching desire was evident.

"It's beautiful," she gulped. "This, I mean. All of it.

Whoever decorated this place had an incredible amount of imagination."

Betrayed by his tumescent body, Matt could have groaned that that was exactly his problem. His imagination kept picturing Penny in that shower. With him. Penny nestled in front of the fireplace. Against him. Penny in that cushion-strewn bed. Beneath him.

A testy voice called from the stairway. "You guys coming? Anyone who wants to stay any longer will have to rent the room. The tour is ready to leave."

Matt and Penny fled.

After that, their tour of the wineries proved to be a distinct anticlimax. Pinching herself, Penny forced her mind to focus on an earnest vintner's claim that the history of wine-making could be traced back to the time of the ancient Egyptians.

Matt managed to concentrate long enough to grasp the difference between still and sparkling wines. But when he slid an arm around Penny's shoulders, he didn't give a rap about the contrast between light and fortified wines, or what differentiated them from the aromatized varietals.

Their thoughts kept regressing to that perfect room. If they had stayed. . . .

At last, the afternoon thinned into evening. The tasting rooms closed. With bright determination they discussed places to eat.

But it wasn't food they were hungry for. Top still down, the turquoise convertible returned to Napa by a now-familiar route. Matt drew the car to a halt at the curb of a beautifully landscaped address on Brown Street. Then he inclined his head toward the house's front window.

"The vacancy sign is still up."

Penny's heart slammed against her ribs. For five solid

hours, a question had been burning holes in her brain. "Matt," she asked it of him, "would it be possible, do you think, to stay best friends if we were also lovers?"

"I'd die before I did anything to spoil our friendship." Fingers trembling, he stroked a soft caress across her cheek. "My blood is on fire for you, Penny. Will you share a night with me in that perfect room?"

She had loved him forever, it seemed. Now, that love was about to transform their whole relationship.

"I will," she promised solemnly. One small drawback occurred to her. "I don't even have a toothbrush in my purse."

"Me neither. I wasn't prepared—"

It wasn't the rosy twilight that added such sudden deep color to his face, Penny realized. Being Matt, he was as usual thinking about protecting her. In a totally new context, now.

Having been orphaned, he knew what it was like to grow up alone and unloved. Never would he allow a child to be conceived because he hadn't taken the proper precautions. Nor would she. She resolved to make an appointment with a doctor first thing on Monday and obtain a prescription for birth-control pills.

"We passed a drugstore a few blocks back," he remembered. "They'll have everything we need."

As Matt swung the car into a U-turn, Penny remembered that there had been no phone in that perfect room. "I should call home from the drugstore to check my messages," she said. "That way, I'll be able to relax completely."

But relaxation wasn't slated for their agenda, after all. Five minutes later, Penny hung up the receiver with fingers that trembled.

Seeing her stricken expression, Matt wrapped both arms around her, drawing her close. "Tell me. Whatever's the matter, you can tell me."

"Inez suffered a severe allergic reaction to a new medicine she tried," Penny said shakily. "She managed to call 911 and get to the hospital in time to save her life. That was her nurse, relaying the message at Inez's request. She says her patient is off the critical list, but she'll still have to stay in the hospital for quite some time. There's no question of her being able to take that flight to Canada tomorrow."

"How awful!"

And not just for Inez, Matt thought. Then he pushed the unworthy reflection aside and urged Penny toward the car. "Come on. I'll get you home so you can pack. You and the Dumont kid have an early flight to make in the morning."

CHAPTER FOURTEEN

Inez's condition had improved slightly by the time Penny returned from Montreal. But the ordeal had left her looking thin and wan, and dangling IV tubes restricted her movements.

"Believe me," the former stewardess vowed, "I will never again take a medication that hasn't been prescribed specifically for me. No matter who recommends it or how well it works for them. I've learned my lesson."

"Thank goodness," Penny murmured. "Oh, Inez, I've been so worried about you!"

Tears glistened on the older woman's cheeks. "I feel like such a traitor for letting you down. You had me scheduled to handle half a dozen trips before Labor Day. How can you cope by yourself with the calendar so jammed?"

That question had already caused Penny considerable inner turmoil. "Some of the jobs you would have handled had to be forfeited," she admitted. "But Roberta is a genius at reshuffling air reservations. Thanks to her, I'll be able to shoehorn your other assignments into my own schedule."

Tactfully, Penny neglected to mention that this had been achieved by booking red-eye flights directly home following deliveries of children to distant eastern cities instead of her usual practice of resting overnight at hotels before returning to San Francisco. But she would manage—somehow.

Forcing a smile, she patted the other woman's listless hand, and rose to leave. "Mind the doctors and nurses, now, and eat up your pudding like a good patient. Come the Christmas holidays, I'm depending on you to be back up to weight—and pulling your own!"

Bethany Kehoe's parents had agreed that their daughter should live with her mother during the upcoming school year. Penny's next-to-last scheduled job of the busy summer season was to escort the little girl back to Philadelphia.

Parting from either parent was always a miserable wrench for Beth. "I won't be seeing my daddy again for months and months and months!" the six-year-old sobbed during takeoff.

She continued to mope as the jet winged its way above California's eastern border, then crossed vast, empty stretches of Nevada and Utah. Eventually, Penny took a break from the child's morose company to stroll down the aisle of the first-class cabin.

Sandra Shroeder, one of the flight attendants, had become acquainted with Penny on a previous flight. She shot a concerned glance at the dispirited child occupying a window seat on the right side, two rows behind the cockpit.

"Is your young charge sick?"

"No, just down in the dumps. Not even my best efforts to cheer her have worked today," Penny said with a tired sigh. "Beth will perk up once we reach Philadelphia, but right now she's in the throes of missing her father. If we were headed for San Francisco, she'd be shedding tears because she missed her mother. Her parents share custody of her, and she wants them both full time."

"Poor baby." The woman in the jaunty blue uniform

glanced at her wristwatch. "Better not dilly-dally if you were headed for the lavatory. Captain says we'll soon be encountering some heavy turbulence. There's a widespread system of thunderstorms ahead."

Penny gazed in concern at the high peaks of the Rockies passing slowly beneath the aircraft's wing. Even after a long, hot summer many of them were still snow-capped. The mountains looked cold and jagged, and very inhospitable.

Of all the places to run into trouble!

By the time she regained her seat the "Fasten Seatbelts" sign was already lit. Outside, the sky had grown perceptibly darker. Hastily, she cinched up her belt and reached across to tighten Beth's. She was locking the tray tables back into place when the first jagged streaks of lightning electrified the sky. As if these pyrotechnics were some sort of signal, the plane went into roller coaster mode. Up, down, and sideways it jolted while ferocious gusts of wind hammered the fuselage and wrenched at the wings.

Beth shrieked in terror as a sharp clap of thunder exploded in their ears. Bolt after bolt of lightning sizzled past their windows. Abruptly, the jet began to lose altitude. Earlier, the captain had announced that they were flying at 33,000 feet. Now it appeared he was attempting to dive beneath the bad weather front.

A few minutes later the bumpiness abated as the plane leveled off. The PA system crackled to life. "From back there, it must have felt like you were riding a shooting star," the pilot remarked, with a strained attempt at humor. "We have descended to an altitude of 11,000 feet, well below the worst of the storm, but still about 5,000 feet above the terrain we are currently flying over.

"Nevertheless," he went on, "for the safety of passengers

and crew we have decided to divert to Denver. The tower there has given us the OK to set down and wait out this system on the ground before continuing our flight to Philadelphia."

As he started a gradual descent to the mile-high city's huge international airport, Penny heard the familiar thump of landing gear being locked into place. Their airspeed slackened still more as flaps were lowered in preparation for the unscheduled landing.

Beth's lip wobbled mutinously. "I don't like this place," she protested. "Look! It's all stormy up ahead."

Peering past her small companion, Penny saw rain streaking down out of the sky. At least the clouds were above them now, she thought, and gave thanks when through the deluge she caught sight of runway lights glimmering in the distance. Before she could call Beth's attention to this reassuring sight, however, the plane took a sudden upwards swoop, then dipped dizzily earthward again.

Words jammed in her throat. Her stomach lurched. Instinctively, she slung out an arm to shield the small girl beside her, pulling her away from the window and into the protective curve of the seatback ahead of them.

From behind the cockpit's reinforced door a computerized voice that seemed to belong to the plane itself blared a sudden warning.

"Windshear! Windshear!"

Instantly, the pilots throttled up to maximum power. Penny learned later that they had elevated the jet's nose to 20 degrees above the horizon in their fight to keep from being forced down by the microburst, a catastrophic downdraft that creates winds in excess of 100 miles an hour.

The plane shuddered, vibrating violently, locked in a battle between the forces of nature and the powerful thrust of its engines. The urgent tones of a second computerized warning resonated into the first-class cabin from beyond the cockpit door:

"Terrain! Terrain! Pull up!"

In vain, the jet struggled to pull free of the Earth's powerful gravity. Only skillful maneuvering by its experienced crew plus the fact that the landing gear had locked into place instants earlier kept the hard landing that followed from becoming a full-fledged crash.

With a deafening clamor the aircraft slammed down onto the end of a runway. Twice it bounced, a giant bird attempting to recapture the freedom of the sky. Twice it was wrenched back onto the unyielding tarmac. Sparks flared, trailing out behind the juggernauting machine like the tail of a comet.

Above Beth's whimpers and the accelerated thud of her own heartbeat, Penny could hear shrieks of alarm from her fellow passengers. An infant howled; cries of pain rose from several sections of the plane. But the human sounds were overwhelmed by the tumult of the plane's wild forward motion. It sounded as though speed and brakes were locked in a desperate, life-or-death conflict.

As their velocity slowed at last and the furor of clanking, scraping, tormented metal ebbed to an almost tolerable din, a new sound pierced Penny's consciousness. The wail of sirens, distant at first, built to a strident crescendo as a pair of fire trucks roared down the field toward the battered plane.

CHAPTER FIFTEEN

Matt Devlin was heading out the door on his way to lunch when the news bulletin interrupted the easy-listening music that had been thrumming through the warehouse. He spun around, attention riveted on the staccato report.

Penny!

Knuckles straining white, he gripped the corner of the desk. The racing beat of his heart quieted somewhat at the announcer's assurance that no fatalities had been reported among the passengers and crew of the downed aircraft.

But the news brief had mentioned injuries. Who knew—

He reached for the phone to dial the airport, then changed his mind. Instead, he tapped out the number for the Sutter Street toy store.

"As a relative of someone aboard that plane, you'll have a better chance of getting accurate, up-to-the-minute information than I would," he said, after filling in Russell Kehoe on what little he knew so far.

The other man sounded as if he were reeling from shock. "You say they went down in C-Colorado?"

His voice broke on the last word. All too aware of the horrible possibilities that must be flashing through Kehoe's mind, Matt felt a kinship with his client that previously would have been inconceivable.

"The plane set down on a runway at Denver International." Matt spoke quietly, hoping to dispel panic-stricken visions of jagged peaks and high, lonely mesas that must be spiraling through the other man's mind. "Apparently, the plane encountered such a fierce storm that the flight crew decided to divert to the closest major airport and sit out the bad weather on the ground. They were almost down when a rogue wind caught the plane and slammed it into the runway with the force of a pile driver."

"My God! Do you know . . . ?"

"No." Matt didn't intend to sit there speculating. "Try to get more details, will you? Meanwhile, I'll contact the travel agent Penny uses. I intend to be on the next flight to Denver."

"Reserve a seat for me, too." As the first shock wore off slightly, the retailer began to sound more like his old, take-charge self. "If there's nothing immediately available, we'll see about chartering a private jet."

That option proved unnecessary. Roberta managed to book reservations for them both aboard a flight departing SFO at 1:45.

Cutting it close, Matt thought edgily, glancing at his watch as he headed toward the door and the taxi waiting in the street. In his rush to be on his way, he almost didn't stop to pick up the shrilling phone. At the last instant he paused and grabbed for the instrument, thinking the call might be important.

It was.

There was a moment of stunned silence as the battered aircraft, miraculously still in one piece, came to a shuddering halt. Before anyone had a chance to unbuckle their seatbelts, the loudspeaker crackled with orders from the captain.

"Stay seated!" he commanded in a terse tone destined to squelch arguments before they began. "And stay calm."

He added that the fast-approaching fire trucks would spray the plane and the runway beneath it with a special solution to smother any sparks that might possibly touch off a blaze.

"If at all possible, we hope to avoid an emergency evacuation," the captain went on. "People inevitably get hurt going down the slides. So unless there is some potential danger our instruments haven't told us about, we're going to sit tight until steps can be towed out here from the terminal. Once they are in place, EMTs will come aboard to care for those who were shaken up during the landing."

The injured would be deplaned first, he emphasized, and assisted into ambulances. "Meanwhile, I suggest the rest of you relax while the airport personnel round up buses to transport you and your luggage into the terminal."

While Penny thought the notion of being able to relax was somewhat optimistic, she and Beth watched with interest as firemen swiftly unrolled hoses and set to work. The windows soon became splattered with foam, cutting off their view. At this point Penny removed a couple of bananas and a new storybook from her oversized travel purse. Food and the humorous tale kept the child entertained for another half hour before she fell into a fretful doze.

Penny closed her eyes and leaned back in her own seat. Unlike Beth, she didn't nap. Instead, she reflected on how close everyone aboard this plane had come to death that morning and whispered a prayer of thanksgiving at having been spared. The more she thought about the narrow escape, the more inclined she was to view the incident as a dramatic wake-up call.

What if the plane had crashed, and she had been killed?

She would have gone to her death with aching regrets at joys left undiscovered, life's possibilities gone unexplored. Having survived, she had no intention of continuing to neglect those important aspects of life. Her first priority, Penny resolved, would be to deepen her long, platonic friendship with Matt into a close, intimate union.

Since the evening in Napa when they were forced to turn their backs on that perfect room, they'd had the opportunity to spend very little time together. But Matt's speaking tour was scheduled to end this week. And she had only one more assignment on the books.

Mulling over the destination to which that job would take her provided the germ of an idea. Ethel Farnsworth's will had specified that her beneficiary use the bequest for a purpose that would make her happy. The career Penny had launched with part of that money had already brought her great satisfaction. She knew, however, that nothing in this world could make her happier than winning Matt Devlin's love.

She began to plan exactly how and where to spend the rest of her legacy.

Several hours later, a redheaded young woman accompanied by a cranky six-year-old was among the rumpled contingent that stumbled into the arrivals lounge at Denver International. Rounding up buses to provide ground transportation for passengers of the crippled plane had seemed to take forever. Another interminable delay accompanied their wait at baggage claim to collect Beth's suitcases.

A complimentary night's stay at a nearby hotel had been arranged as a courtesy to the stranded travelers. Wearily loading the luggage onto a cart, Penny admitted that she would be glad to accept the airline's hospitality. "But first I need to find a telephone and try to call your parents. They must be frantic with worry about you."

Tired, hungry and thoroughly bored, Beth looked up to reply. But before she could respond, a face in the crowd of newcomers just approaching the baggage carousel caught her eye. She darted forward with a shriek of joy.

"My Daddy's here!"

Penny wheeled to call back the exuberant child, then halted to stare in glad amazement at the man who had seen them off from SFO that morning. She was still trying to take in the fact of Russell Kehoe's presence when she received an even greater shock. Glimpsing the tall, dark-haired man who was pushing his way toward her, Penny realized that the toy store owner had not come alone.

"Matt! Oh, Matt!" She threw her arms around him and burst into tears of joy. "I had hoped you wouldn't hear about what happened until I had a chance to call and assure you we were all right."

"You look just fine to me," he murmured, holding her close.

Before either of them could say more they were joined by the little girl and her father. Beth was literally jumping up and down with excitement.

"My mommy's coming, too!" she squealed. "We'll all be together!"

Russell Kehoe's haggard expression still mirrored the terror he had felt at learning his child was in danger. Greeting Penny, he explained that neither he nor his ex-wife could bear the prospect of waiting a moment longer than absolutely necessary to see with their own eyes that their daughter was safe.

"Pamela's plane is due in at 6:35," he added. "The whole family will stay here tonight, then continue on to

Philadelphia together in the morning."

"Good plan," Penny approved, exhilarated by this turn of events but too tired to say more.

Next morning, she watched a sleek, privately chartered Lear jet lift off, bound for Philadelphia with the Kehoe family aboard. All three of them had been wearing smiles when they turned to wave at her.

"Looks as if Beth's parents might have reshuffled their priorities," she remarked to Matt, who had just arrived from the hotel where he had spent the night. "I hope they decide to make their reunion permanent."

"Careful. You'll wish yourself right out of business."

His words were light, but Penny caught a somber undertone to his voice. Swinging around to eye him in surprise, she thought he looked drawn, as though he hadn't slept well.

A little anxiously, she reached for his hand.

"Is something the matter, Matt?"

The notion suddenly came to her that perhaps she had been taking too much for granted. Once again he had shown up just when she needed him most. Nothing strange about that. In the past he'd seemed to take great delight in coming to her rescue. Yet this morning a casual observer would have gained the impression that Matt had just lost his best friend instead of having been safely reunited with her.

"Whatever's wrong, you can tell me about it," she assured him quietly. "If we can't fix the problem, we can at least stand shoulder-to-shoulder against it, like we used to do in the old days."

Matt gave a mirthless laugh. "Ah, Penny, you can't know how much I wish that was possible. With my speaking tour due to end at about the same time your business slacked off for the season, I was looking forward to our having some solid time together. Maybe . . . maybe even getting some things settled between us, once and for all. But now—"

Penny felt her breath stop. When it came to spending solid time together, Matt might have been reading her mind. But what could he mean about "getting some things settled"? And why did he sound like none of that was going to happen, after all?

"But now?" Her choked repetition of his words sounded like a death rattle. The wild thought came to her that maybe that was exactly what it was. The demise of a lifetime's worth of dreams.

"Now," Matt groaned, "I have to turn right around and leave again. Which reminds me," he added, shooting a glance at his watch and swinging toward the departure gates, "I called Roberta last night and had her re-book your return to SFO from here instead of from Philadelphia. Our plane leaves in less than an hour."

The rigorous pre-boarding security checks were almost complete when the two of them stepped forward to collect their boarding passes. "That makes a full load," the gate guard declared, scrawling numbers on long white stubs and stapling them to their tickets. "Seats three-A and twenty-seven-C. Enjoy your trip."

Fat chance, Penny thought, turning left into the first class compartment. She watched in frustration as Matt paced through the economy class cabin to the seat which had been the only other space available on such short notice. Now she would have to wait until they landed at SFO to find out what the problem was.

But there was no chance for a private conversation in the crowded airport limo that shuttled them into the city in company with a number of other travelers. By mutual consent, they continued on by taxi to the business park.

After being closed up for thirty-six hours in the sultry September weather, Penny's small office was sweltering. Outside, however, a cooling breeze wafted in from the Bay. Gratefully, she and Matt moved her two clients' chairs out to a shady spot on the concrete walkway and sat down at last for their long-delayed talk.

"The video game idea to teach kids about a vanishing species has caught on like wildfire," Matt remarked. "At least partly because of it, people from countries as widely separated as Zaire and India and Brazil have jumped on the ecological bandwagon. They're hoping a similar approach might be a way to start reversing the damage that's already been done to their own precious natural resources, and help them save what's left."

"Like the rain forests?" Penny asked.

He nodded. "Yes, and elephants, and the Bengal tigers. People have come to realize how much their children and grandchildren will be missing if those priceless natural wonders are allowed to vanish."

She touched his sleeve. "Matt, I'm so proud of you. You're the one who woke people up to the dangers by designing that terrific game. Have they set a date and place for the international conference yet?"

"Well, that's the bad news."

He explained that the group's chairman, an esteemed ecologist largely responsible for Costa Rica's success in harnessing volcanoes to generate much of his nation's output of electrical power, had just been diagnosed with an illness from which he was not likely to recover. Reluctantly, his doctors had agreed to let him attend the international conference on designing and marketing games and software to benefit the environment—but only if the meeting's timetable were accelerated so he could travel while he still had the strength.

"So instead of being held next January, the conference has been scheduled to begin next Friday, in Cairns, Australia," Matt finished. "Since I designed the game that spotlighted the plight of the cassowaries, the ecologists feel it's vital for me to be on hand as a resource person. I was on my way out the door heading for Denver yesterday when the Brazilian ambassador phoned and more or less commandeered my services."

He added that the conference's sponsors would cover his travel expenses. "My conscience wouldn't let me refuse."

"Of course not. You couldn't turn down an honor like that. Besides, they need you. They'd never find a better consultant anywhere," Penny said loyally.

"I hope it turns out to be worthwhile. To tell the truth, I had been looking forward to using the time to relax rather than tackling another responsibility just now."

Penny knew exactly what he meant. "Because of Inez's sudden illness I feel like I've been running in place for weeks. The unfiled paperwork is inches thick by now, and I still have the final long escort trip of the season to handle personally."

She glanced down at the hands clenched in her lap, then back up at Matt. "While we were waiting to leave that stranded airplane yesterday, I gave that upcoming assignment a lot of thought. But at that time, of course, I didn't know anything about the new dates for your conference."

She paused, swallowing hard. After a moment, Matt reached over and took her hands, unclasping the rigidly laced fingers and wrapping them inside his own warm grip.

"Tell me what's troubling you," he urged. "You know there's nothing you can't tell me, Penny."

Wordlessly, she nodded. He was right. She could tell Matt anything. It was how he might react to what she had to say that worried her. Still, dubious as she felt, she couldn't go back on her decision. Not without feeling like a coward. Not without wondering for the rest of her life what might have happened if she'd had the courage to follow through.

She inhaled deeply. "Before you told me about the conference, I had decided to invite you to come along on the trip. My treat," she added, her tone implying that she had no intention of arguing the point. "The expenses would come out of the legacy Ethel Farnsworth left."

Matt was familiar with the terms of the woman's will. "She instructed you to spend the money on something that would really make you happy," he murmured. "Will this trip accomplish that purpose?"

"I think it might."

"Then I'll go."

The simple generosity of his statement touched her heart more deeply than any pontificating about loyalty and support could have done. "Thank you, Matt, but I won't let you pass up that conference on my account. It's too important."

Even as she spoke, though, a new possibility was taking shape in Penny's mind. Abruptly, she hopped up and hurried inside her office. When she returned she was carrying a globe. "There might be a different way to solve the dilemma," she said. "When do you expect the conference to end?"

Matt pulled out a pocket calendar and checked the dates. "September sixteenth," he said, glancing curiously at the globe. "Cairns is located clear up in northeastern Australia, near the Great Barrier Reef. The travel itinerary they've set up includes an extra day for me to make my way down to Sydney. I fly home from there on the eighteenth."

"That's absolutely perfect!" In more ways than one, Penny added to herself. Aloud, she explained, "I leave Los Angeles bound for Tahiti that same day. If you were to re-route your return journey to include a stopover in French Polynesia, we could meet at the airport in Papeete, Tahiti's capital, and continue on together from there."

Matt looked a trifle dazed. "Continue on to where?"

"To Bora Bora. It's part of the same island group, only about an hour further on by air."

She twirled the globe on its axis, letting her fingers trail lightly over land masses raised in bas-relief from the flat blue of the surrounding oceans. Tilting it to display the Southern Hemisphere, she thought what an apt nickname for Australia and New Zealand "Down Under" was. Like the southern half of Africa and most of South America, those lands lay beneath the equator, with their seasons reversed to those of the northern half of the world.

"The stopover would be directly on your way home," she said, pointing to a cluster of islands lying several thousand miles east of Australia in the South Pacific.

"I can see that." Matt still looked a bit bewildered as he traced the route with his finger. "And you're traveling clear out there on a job?"

Penny nodded. "That's right. Remember Alain Dumont, the son of the two chefs I escorted up to Montreal the day after Inez landed in the hospital?"

That wasn't an occasion Matt was ever likely to forget. "You're taking him someplace else now?"

"Not Alain. His cousin. The Dumonts recommended me for the job."

Penny explained that Mme. Dumont's brother, Claude

Villiard, managed a vanilla plantation in French Polynesia. "When Claude was widowed year before last, he sent his son, Jean-Paul, to live with his parents in Montreal. He and the boy have missed each other terribly. Now Claude intends to remarry, and he wants his son home. I brought Jean-Paul as far as San Francisco with Alain the other day. He'll be staying with the Dumonts until our departure for the South Pacific."

"Is he too young to fly by himself?"

"Not really. Being bilingual and awfully bright, I believe he could manage very well in spite of the distance if it weren't for the problem of changing planes in Los Angeles."

Penny explained that the daily flight of UTA, a branch of Air France, out of LAX was currently the only connection between California and Tahiti. "And by U.S. law, children under eight aren't allowed to travel alone if it's necessary for them to change planes en route. Jean-Paul is seven."

Matt realized that Penny's plane fare would be covered by her contract with M. Villiard. But the stopover she had mentioned would be made at her own expense. He considered the invitation for him to join her incredibly generous.

"Bora Bora is one of the Society Islands, isn't it?" he asked, stalling for time while he tried to decide what to do. "Part of the group Paul Gauguin made famous with his paintings? During my eight years in the Navy I visited a lot of tropical places in the South Pacific, but not that one."

If Penny had been a nail-biter, both index fingers would have been thoroughly nibbled by now. She wished he would give her a definite answer, yes or no, before she keeled over from the strain.

"They say it's the most beautiful island in the world. Remember Bali Ha'i, in Michener's *Tales of the South Pacific*? That fictional island was patterned on Bora Bora," she babbled. Then, shyly, she looked away. "I hoped that maybe . . . maybe finding a perfect island might make up for missing out on that perfect room we discovered on your birthday."

Matt remembered the crushing disappointment he had felt when Penny hung up the phone that night and relayed to him the news about Inez's sudden illness. Earlier that day, the attraction simmering just beneath the surface of their outward relationship had come close to reaching the boiling point. As if playing a cruel game with them, fate had dangled a glimpse of what might have been before their eyes, then snatched it away.

The bittersweet incident would haunt him for years to come, Matt knew. But he'd had no inkling that Penny had ever given it another thought. Now her remark made it clear that she, too, looked back on the occasion with regret.

Their emotions had taken a lot of battering lately. He decided that they could both do with some well-deserved happiness for a change. Blessings on Ethel Farnsworth and her legacy.

"A visit to Bora Bora sounds like an awesome getaway," he said. "Unless you had your heart set on a long stay in the tropics, I'd be delighted to meet you there and keep you company."

"Terrific!" Penny reminded herself that the plush sensuality of the perfect room had enchanted their senses. The chance of achieving the same magical spark again in another place at a different time was remote.

"I couldn't spare more than a few days myself," she answered, steadied by the thought that in Bora Bora she would keep both feet on the ground. "Will you be starting to gear up for the holidays as soon as you return to California?"

Matt nodded. "Believe it or not, a shipment of Billabong Babies is finally on its way. I've had a cable from Neville. The freighter carrying the toys is due to dock in San Francisco around the end of this month. I'll need to be back by then to guide the crates safely through Customs."

"Your retailers will be overjoyed," Penny predicted. "Do you suppose Russell Kehoe will keep right on trying to corner the entire lot for Diversions?"

"I think he'll give up the day Lucifer needs ice skates," Matt muttered darkly. "He's been trying to monopolize those imports for months. Even if he and Pamela reconcile, I doubt he'd change his attitude."

Catching sight of a jeep slowly patrolling the grounds, Matt felt glad that Penny had nudged him into reporting the warehouse break-ins to their landlord. Though Griff Hazelton had scoffed at the notion of intruders being able to open locks and bolts without leaving a trace, he had grouchily agreed to hire some reliable security for the tenants of his business park.

The whisper of suspicion he'd felt each time he discovered traces of a trespasser having prowled about the warehouse had prompted him to believe that Russell Kehoe was to blame. But the summer had passed without further incident. Maybe the security patrols had done the job, Matt thought. Or maybe Hazelton was right, and the break-ins had been a figment of his own imagination.

Either way, the problem appeared to have been solved.

Standing up to replace the pocket calendar in his wallet, Matt realized how close he was to the edge of exhaustion. He needed to get home to his boat, shower and change into fresh clothing, and get some rest. Nightmares about

Penny's close brush with death had shredded his sleep every time he closed his eyes the previous night. The glum realization that he would have to leave her again almost immediately had only intensified his distress.

"I have to get home before I fall asleep right where I'm standing," he said, muffling a yawn. "Go ahead and make those reservations for Bora Bora if you're convinced the trip will make you happy. I'm agreeable to whatever you plan. Just be sure to let me know if you should change your mind."

He hadn't understood, Penny thought in distress as she watched him jog lightly down the steps and head for the bus stop. When she'd talked about spending Ethel Farnsworth's money on something that was sure to make her happy, he'd assumed she meant that visiting Bora Bora would provide that joy. It hadn't dawned on him that it was his company she longed for.

Hopefully, they could straighten out the misunderstanding when the moment arrived. When they weren't both so weary and rushed. When they could relax and enjoy being with each other. Scandalous as it sounded, she had no qualms about spending a big chunk of her legacy to buy some high-quality time with him.

"Don't worry," she called softly after her oldest friend. "I have no intention of changing my mind."

CHAPTER SIXTEEN

Having been almost frantically active all summer, Penny would have found the week following Matt's departure for the conference in Cairns unbearably dull had it not been for practice sessions at the *dojo*. Since the age of seven, karate had been a vital part of her life. Now she apologized to her *sensei* for neglecting the ancient arts, and spent part of each day practicing her *katas*. Honing her skills. Calming her soul.

Still, she worried. What if she had shocked Matt by suggesting that they share a vacation?

She hadn't seen much of him the past month. What if he'd met someone else and fallen in love with her?

What if agreeing to join her for a few days in Bora Bora was just kindness on his part, a concession because of their long friendship?

What if he decided not to come, after all?

Then an awful lot of money was going to be wasted, Penny told herself firmly. Because she had already given Roberta instructions to make the reservations for their stay.

She blessed the impulse that had led her to see a doctor following their visit to Napa on Matt's birthday, and to immediately begin taking the birth-control pills he'd prescribed. Having by now completed a full cycle, it was good to know that she could count on their effectiveness in Bora Bora—if the need arose.

Being a woman bound for an exotic destination, she shopped for lovely, lightweight, islandy clothes. Being a woman in love, she also bought a wardrobe of lacy next-to-nothings.

Upon arriving in Papeete with her young charge, the collection of filmy lingerie caused a stir of interest at the Immigration counter. The official who searched her suitcase for possible contraband raised his brows in appreciation. Seeing that she wore no wedding or engagement ring, he groomed his slim mustache with his little finger.

"Magnifique, mademoiselle!" he remarked sincerely. "You will be remaining for some weeks with us here on Tahiti, I most sincerely hope?"

Penny concealed her amusement with difficulty. By local time it was the middle of the night. The garishly lit terminal was sticky-hot. Furthermore, it reeked from the foul, pungent odor of Gauloise cigarettes. Yet the young official was representing French machismo halfway around the world from gay Paree.

After all her uncertainties about Matt's reactions, her feminine pride rejoiced at the inspector's uncomplicated admiration.

"Not this time," she answered demurely. "I will be continuing on to Bora Bora in a few hours, as soon as my friend's plane arrives from Australia."

Further back in the line, a lovely green-eyed blonde was sauntering along. Speedily, one eye on the newcomer, the Frenchman stamped Penny's passport. After making certain she possessed a valid air ticket to carry her out of French Polynesia when her vacation was over, he issued her with a visa for a brief stay.

"Bonne chance!" he called, motioning the next tourist forward.

She and her young charge had been separated during the Customs inspection, he having passed without challenge through the gate assigned the local citizenry. Joining up with Jean-Paul again, she took him by the hand and stepped past the barrier and into a cheerful throng waiting to greet incoming travelers.

Jean-Paul was claimed at once by his fond papa. Joyful tears ran down Claude Villiard's face as he embraced his small son. Then he led him across the room and presented him to a sweet-faced, dark-haired woman whom Penny assumed would be the little boy's new mama.

The woman held out her arms. After a shy hesitation, Jean-Paul cuddled into the soft embrace. Moments later, the formalities of handing over the youngster complete and a generous sheaf of francs pressed into her hand by the boy's grateful parent, Penny turned away brushing tears from her own eyes.

She tried telling herself that her emotional overload was strictly due to fatigue. The previous day she had been up at dawn, tidying the apartment before Inez's arrival. Her assistant had promised to pamper Naomi's houseplants, even to the point of singing them lullabies in Spanish.

Then Penny recorded a "gone on vacation" message for her office answering machine, and collected Jean-Paul for the trip to Los Angeles. The jet with its French-speaking crew had taken off from LAX at midnight. The eight-hour, south-by-southwest flight pushed back the night as it soared across time zones.

But Penny knew her weepiness was triggered by more than exhaustion and jet lag. Her conscience had been plaguing her. It kept reminding her that this trip was being taken under false pretenses.

It was all a lure. Bait. An attempt to mousetrap her oldest friend into falling in love with her.

Planning it hadn't been fair to Matt. Not fair at all!

Matt Devlin had never been so bushed in all his life. Though exhilarating, the eighteen-hour days of the conference, coming on top of a strenuous speaking tour and a flight that carried him nearly halfway around the world, had his energy supply running on empty.

But Matt's resilience had been challenged before. He could have paced himself. Could have adjusted to the time change. Could have been feeling fit and capable again by now—if it hadn't been for Neville Baker.

On the fourth day of the conference he'd finally found time to give the toy maker a call. The other man had sounded weak with relief at the sound of his voice.

"You're in Cairns? No wonder I haven't been able to get hold of you," Neville exclaimed. "I've been frantically telephoning you in San Francisco!"

"What's gone wrong?" Matt broke in, alarmed. "I thought the shipment was already on its way."

"There's a lot you don't know," the Australian hinted darkly. "But nothing I dare talk about over the phone. Where are you staying in Cairns—the Coral Reef? Sit tight. I'll be on the first plane headed your way."

Which was how Matt came to be making two wearisome air journeys back-to-back. Instead of having a spare day to travel to Sydney, stay overnight at a hotel and shop for a special gift for Penny, he'd spent most of that twenty-four-hour stretch in an anxious confab with the creator of the Billabong Babies. At the end, he'd boarded the last possible plane out of Cairns, caught the connecting flight in Sydney with minutes to spare, and was all but walking in his sleep when the jumbo jet disgorged him at Papeete in the first light of dawn.

Matt's watch had been reset so often recently that he'd lost track of time. He felt himself reeling with fatigue as he made his way across the tarmac toward the terminal, and hoped he'd have a chance to splash his face with cold water before dealing with the finicky French bureaucracy.

No such luck. He presented his travel documents to a smartly uniformed official, who compared his face to that of his passport photo and stamped the page without comment.

Lord, Matt ruminated; did he look that bad? Tucking the small booklet with its dark blue cover away in an inner pocket, he struggled to keep his eyes open.

Penny was likely to take him for an idiot unless he could manage to perk up and take notice of the tropical paradise she'd been so set on visiting.

Penny. She had seldom been out of his thoughts since they parted. Again and again he'd found himself mentally replaying that brief conversation on the walkway outside her office, and wondering. She had talked about spending Ethel Farnsworth's legacy in a way that would make her happy. But he couldn't quite make up his mind what it was she felt convinced would bring her joy.

Visiting an exotic South Seas island? Sharing the experience with him?

Gaining official permission to set foot in French Polynesia was complicated by yards of red tape. Finally, Matt was allowed to proceed into the terminal.

Immediately, a petite redheaded hurricane whirled up beside him, seized his hand, and began tugging him toward a door on the other side of the low, rectangular building.

"Hurry, Matt!" Penny urged, seeming oddly reluctant to

meet his eyes as they emerged into the open. "We have exactly six minutes to catch the plane for Bora Bora!"

They sprinted downfield toward an Air Tahiti turboprop vibrating noisily at the end of a runway. The plane, designed to carry about two dozen passengers, looked Lilliputian compared to the behemoth 747 which had just deposited Matt on this tropical French protectorate. He could only pray that it would prove to be airworthy.

Clattering aboard, they boosted their luggage into bulging overhead bins, then looked around to find that seating was apparently a matter of first come, first served. Both remaining seats were on the aisle. One was directly behind the cockpit, the other at the rear, in the last row opposite the cubbyhole where soft drinks in paper cups were being handed out.

Penny's morale slipped another notch. "Oh, Matt, what a disappointment! I had wanted you by my side when I caught my first glimpse of Bora Bora."

They were still standing in the aisle. From the increased pitch of the engines, it was clear to Matt that the pilot of the small craft was ready to take off. Clearly, they needed to sit down and buckle up without delay.

"There's no time to try and persuade anyone to change places with us now," he said. "Would you rather sit up front beside the large lady with the twins on her lap, or back here next to the refreshments?"

"Up front. Maybe I can rock one of the babies to sleep. That way only one of them will be screaming," Penny added, and turned left to trudge up the aisle with a sigh of resignation.

An hour later they glimpsed an exquisite tropical island encircled almost entirely by a coral reef. Bora Bora's mountainous interior was crowned by a distinctive craggy peak.

Beaches as pale and smooth as butterscotch pudding stretched out from beneath the shade of coconut palms to fringe a lagoon of heart-stopping beauty. On sheltered water that ranged in color from deepest indigo to a clear, translucent aquamarine, numerous small bits of land known as motus floated like sugar cookies. With reef and lagoon, these tiny islets formed the main island's barrier against the vast, deep Pacific and its pounding surf.

Rather than landing on Bora Bora itself, the plane dropped to an altitude of about ten feet above the waves, then swooped smoothly down onto a long, flat ribbon of coral and sand.

"First time here? This islet is called Motu Mute," Matt's seatmate remarked informatively. He added that like the road encircling the island of Bora Bora itself, the airstrip had been built by U.S. Seabees during World War II. "Durable piece of construction. Been in use ever since."

They stepped off the plane into an open-air perfumery. The sweet, potent fragrance of flowers drifted across the water from the tropical paradise in the center of the lagoon. Penny set her suitcase down on the pebbled ground and clasped her hands in awe. It was like suddenly finding herself in Oz.

"Oh, Matt!" she breathed ecstatically. "Have you ever seen anything like this?"

He gazed not around at the exotic landscape, but at Penny herself. "No," he murmured, thinking how lovely her eyes were. "I never have."

They squeezed onto the launch that arrived to take them across to Bora Bora proper, then crowded to the rail, anxious not to miss a single vista. Quickly arriving at the other side of the lagoon, the boat deposited passengers onto various docks. One group piled off at the jolly-looking Club

Med resort, where guests were greeted with music and leis draped ceremonially over their heads.

Island residents returning from their travels disembarked at the village of Viatape. Along with a half-dozen other couples, Penny and Matt rode as far as Matira Beach, at the foot of the island.

Several small hotels shared this prime location. These bore little resemblance to mainland-style lodgings. Guests were accommodated either in individual villas set among beautiful gardens, or in *fares*, picturesque bungalows with thatched, A-frame roofs cantilevered out over the crystal-clear water.

A friendly Polynesian girl guided them to the *fare* that had been reserved for their use for the next five days. Making their way along a private plank deck, they proceeded through an entry hall with a bathroom off to one side, then into a large airy bed-sitting room.

The far wall of the bungalow formed a huge picture window. Through it, a sliding glass door opened onto a secluded verandah built out over the lagoon.

Penny was struck by the contrast between the magnificent open-air view and the plainness of their room. The *fare* was furnished with extreme simplicity. Mats woven of some natural fiber covered the floor. The few pieces of furniture were made of rattan. Unadorned grass cloth served as wall coverings. A batik coverlet in restful shades of brown, ivory and rust was spread across the bed.

Against the image of another room, that perfect room which she remembered in every detail, these premises seemed almost Spartan. Fighting a sense of disappointment, Penny reminded herself that in this balmy climate feathery comforters, velvet draperies and a fireplace would be redundant, to say the least.

Still, these surroundings with their lack of color and absence of small, luxurious touches, appeared almost humble.

The realization stole over Penny that her feeling of disillusionment had less to do with the room than with herself. As children at the Home, she and Matt had always played square with each other. But this time she had gone behind his back. Set up a lavish trap to influence his emotions.

Now, here they were. Trap sprung, emotions ripe for plundering. Though too tired to exactly recall that old saying about victory turning to ashes in one's mouth, she suspected it would probably suit this occasion. Even had the room not seemed so drab, her conscience would have balked at allowing her to appreciate its fine points. The shabby trick she had played on her best friend was bound to taint this entire experience.

It was a bitter lesson. A terrible waste of Ethel Farnsworth's legacy. Penny hoped that when she wasn't quite so exhausted she could find a way to confess her perfidy to Matt and win his forgiveness.

With an effort, she shoved a smile into her voice. "Shall we change and go for a walk on the beach?"

"What? Oh, sure. Good idea."

Matt had been hovering on the threshold, clutching his flight bag. With a pang, she realized there had been a definite lack of enthusiasm in his manner ever since he'd gotten off the jet from Australia. Hopefully, some exercise would perk up their spirits and help her deal with her own chicanery.

Unzipping her suitcase, Penny removed a pair of sandals and one of the lightweight outfits she had bought especially for this trip, then retreated to the bathroom. Like the outer room, this section of the *fare* was almost austere in appearance. The walls and fixtures were plain white. Far from

215

being supplied with benches to encourage lounging under the spray, the shower bore a neat sign printed in four languages emphasizing the island's chronic shortage of fresh water. Guests were asked to use this precious resource sparingly.

Penny sighed. Served her right.

Slipping out of her traveling clothes, she pulled on crisp cotton shorts and a coordinating sleeveless blue and white top. While September was San Francisco's warmest month and a relatively cool time in the South Sea Islands, the two climates were hardly comparable. Bora Bora's tropical humidity was going to take some getting used to.

Finding herself yawning uncontrollably as she fumbled with the strap of her sandal, Penny thought in annoyance that she seemed to be moving in slow motion. "Be right out," she called to Matt through the door.

She heard no answer. Emerging moments later, the reason was clear. He too had changed into walking shorts and a lightweight shirt. But his deck shoes were placed neatly alongside the bed, while Matt himself was stretched out atop the batik coverlet, eyes closed in sleep.

Tears of remorse stung Penny's eyes as for the first time she noticed the black hair curling about his ears. As a rule, he wore it cropped almost militarily short. What sort of harrowing schedule had kept him too busy to visit the barber?

Look who's talking, she thought groggily. Over the past few weeks, her own stamina had been pushed far beyond sensible limits.

Without further hesitation, Penny tiptoed around to the other side of the bed, slipped off her sandals, and swung up her feet.

When Matt Devlin finally opened his eyes it took him a

few disoriented blinks to recollect where he was. Then the seductive scent of frangipani and ginger wafting through the screen brought memory flooding sharply back.

Bora Bora!

He wanted to die of embarrassment. The most beautiful island on earth, and he hadn't been able to stay awake long enough to so much as admire a palm tree. What a way to treat paradise.

What a way to treat Penny!

A soft sound interrupted his muffled groan. Penny was curled up on the other side of the bed, sound asleep.

It had been mid-morning when they'd arrived, Matt remembered. Now, judging from the slanting shadows, it must be fairly late in the afternoon. However, he felt much, much better. And if Penny had been asleep all this time, a solid rest must have been exactly what she needed, too. Silently, he slipped off the bed.

Half an hour later he heard the whisper of her footsteps crossing the room. Turning away from the rail at the side of the verandah, Matt smiled and held out his hand.

"Come and look," he invited, in a voice hushed with wonder.

Quietly, Penny walked across the open, sunlit deck to join him. A gasp of delight escaped her lips. The lagoon was a natural aquarium, habitat to angelfish, clown fish, damselfish—fish of all sizes and shapes and colors of the rainbow!

And not just fish. Sharing this tropical, undersea paradise was a fabulous variety of other living sea creatures. Peering through water that resembled pale liquid jade, Penny glimpsed a large, exquisite triton shell, brilliant scallops and speckled cowries, and a breathtaking cone that might have been a rare Glory of the Seas.

Matt slipped an arm around her shoulders. With his

other hand he pointed to what appeared to be an ordinary grey stone a foot or so in diameter.

"Keep your eye on that rock for a minute and watch what happens." Penny felt herself relaxing against him. Why, she wondered, had she tried to push their beautiful friendship into the deep waters of love and commitment when the shallows of camaraderie had contented them for so long? It was enough merely to be here with Matt, enjoying simple pleasures together as they had done for years.

Unexpected movement interrupted this rueful thought. Tentacles, their undersides tinted an exquisite shade of blue, gradually unfurled as the dainty octopus Penny had mistaken for a stone ruffled the water.

Stunned, she looked up at the man standing beside her. "Matt, so help me I feel just like Dorothy. There's nothing like this in Kansas—nor in Texas or San Francisco either, for that matter."

"No, it's unique. And how wonderful that we're seeing it together."

She laced her fingers through his and gave his hand an affectionate squeeze. "Thank you for coming with me. Bora Bora is the sort of place that needs to be shared with a dear friend."

A letdown jolt of regret throbbed through Matt's veins. Until ten days ago he'd been unaware of how deeply feelings for Penny permeated his being. Until then he had never believed he would be fortunate enough to experience true, unconditionally committed love. The bond of devotion that lasts a lifetime.

But at that moment in the Denver airport when he caught sight of her safe and sound, he realized that love had found him long ago. Without recognizing Cupid's arrow for the binding tie it was, he had succumbed to its wallop the first time he'd put up his fists in defense of a pigtailed Ugly Duckling.

Unfortunately, Matt thought in chagrin, the lovely woman that little girl had become still thought of herself only as his very dear friend.

Forcing a swallow down his clogged throat, he suggested setting out on their long-delayed walk. "Now that we're rested, let's get our shoes on and see what paradise looks like up close. And also find out where we can get something to eat in the very near future."

Penny laughed, quieting the ache of regret that came of appeasing her conscience. "I'm starved, too. Maybe we'll come across a coconut on the beach to tide us over."

Later, they took brief turns in the shower, then changed into clothing suitable for a meal in the hotel dining room. Eating at such an unfashionably early hour left them with plenty of daylight to saunter through gardens aglow with hibiscus and bougainvillea before enjoying a spectacular sunset from the verandah of their *fare*.

"I finally figured out why our room is decorated with such classic simplicity." Thoughtfully, Penny glanced over her shoulder at their starkly furnished quarters, then back at the brilliant hues traced across the western sky. "Outside, everything is in glorious, intensely vivid Technicolor. Inside, the muted colors provide a relaxing contrast. Guests have a chance to rest their eyes while they absorb Bora Bora's radiant natural beauty."

"The strategy sure worked on me," Matt admitted with a chuckle. "All I had to do was sit down in that undemanding room this morning to go out like a light. I'm sorry if I spoiled your first day in Bali Ha'i, Penny."

"Oh, no!" She had been leaning back, enjoying the panorama of sky and sea at sunset. Now she sat up and reached toward him across the small caned table separating their individual chaise lounges. "Truly, the day wasn't spoiled. But if it had been, I would have been the one to blame."

She closed her eyes, ashamed of the admission she felt compelled to make. "Matt, I—I lured you here under false pretenses."

"What!" He might have thought she was joking if her face hadn't reflected such inner turmoil. "Penny, dear, what are you talking about? What false pretenses?"

There was no way to skirt the issue. Her conscience demanded that the truth be told. Confession, Penny thought, was the only way to assuage the miserable burden of guilt that had blighted her existence the past few days.

"I could tell, the day we went on the winery tour and saw the perfect room, that you—that you desired me." Wretchedly embarrassed, she ducked her head. "I wanted you, too. After all, we're young and healthy, and around each other a lot. . . ."

Not enough, Matt thought, wondering where her rambling tale was leading. Not nearly enough.

She gulped, chattered on. "Remember, I even asked you if we could go on being best friends if we became. . . ."

"Lovers? Uh-huh. But as it turned out, we didn't have the opportunity to put that question to the test."

"I know. That was one of the main reasons I felt cheated when the plane Bethany and I were on went out of control in Colorado, I feared I had postponed reaching out and grabbing real happiness a little too long, and that—that I was about to die before the chance came my way again."

Matt swung to a sitting position and reached a placating hand toward her.

"Penny—sweetheart—there's no need to say any more."

"But there is!" she insisted. "My conscience will never

leave me in peace unless I level with you." Penny gulped, blundering on with eyes brimming because she didn't dare stop now that she had finally embarked on the truth.

"After that miraculous safe landing, I realized that I had been granted a heaven-sent opportunity to try again. Much as I prized our friendship, I was greedy for more. I—I decided to invite you to a place so romantic that you simply couldn't help falling in love with me."

One of the tears spilled over and trickled down her cheek. "Please forgive me, Matt. It was a miserably dishonorable sort of ruse to pull on my best friend."

"Penny," Matt croaked. Overcome with emotion, he found it necessary to swallow hard and start again. "Penny, sweetheart, are you saying you love me? That happiness for you is wrapped up in my loving you in return?"

Composure hanging by a thread, she bobbed her head. If she tried to speak, Penny thought, she would disgrace herself further by bawling.

Matt shoved the table out from between them, then stood up and gently pulled Penny to her feet. His crisscrossed arms cradled her against his chest.

"I've been in love with you for years," he said in a tremulous tone. "I just didn't recognize the symptoms until I heard the news flash about your plane being downed. In that instant I knew that you were more important to me than anything else in the world."

Heedless of her own tears, Penny reached up to smooth the black hair out of his eyes. "Why didn't you tell me?"

"I didn't know how. Honest to God, Penny, I didn't know how to say words like 'I love you.' I'd never said them to anyone, and nobody had ever said them to me, either. But that's how I felt. Now I'm just blurting it out. Penny, you're my life. Without you, I'm miserable. We both owe

Ethel Farnsworth an awful lot for helping us discover what happiness is really all about."

Matt kissed her, gently at first, then deeper, then with a foretaste of the passion he felt flickering through his soul. He swung Penny into his arms and carried her back inside. Reaching over his shoulder, she pulled the screen closed when they passed, but left the glass door open to the elements.

The fragrant night air left its perfumed scent on skin quickly bared. The satin waters of the lagoon rippled softly. A tiki torch wedged in the sand a few yards down the beach limned their bodies with its flickering glow.

Penny loved the burnished bronze of Matt's hands and arms against the pallor of her own lightly freckled skin. And the contrast of his smooth, hard chest against her soft, pink-tipped breast. And the sinewy masculine length of leg and thigh and lean, hard hip against her petite, more rounded dimensions.

Matt loved her eyes, luminous and large, with lashes that quivered at his caresses. And the sharp nip of her small white teeth catching his tongue. And her supple, pliant, peach-fuzz skin.

They stroked and kissed and, trembling, stroked again.

"Darling Penny," Matt whispered, the strong male responsible for his woman's safety, "do we need. . . ."

"No. I planned ahead." In the near darkness, Penny smiled. "Haven't I told you all along that I can take care of myself? Don't worry about anything, Matt, my love. Just come here."

CHAPTER SEVENTEEN

Penny discovered there was something positive to be said for jet lag. Awaking in the hushed hour before dawn, she found Matt propped on his elbow, watching her.

"I love you," he said. "I need you."

"I love you. And we most definitely need each other."

After gliding her fingers appreciatively across the hard swell of Matt's biceps, Penny trailed them along his chin. Overnight, whiskers had sprouted. Their sharp prickle against her skin was a tantalizing memento of locked bodies and fierce, stinging pleasure. She tried to make the sensation last this time, to spin it out. But with passion drumming a tumult through their blood, there was no holding back.

Lit only by the pearly glow of moonset, the *fare* swayed gently on its moorings in time to their sighs.

Much later, Penny tried on the *pareu* she had bought in Papeete the previous day while waiting for Matt's plane to arrive. The modest sarong, which left one shoulder bare, was standard wear for females in French Polynesia. As children, island women learned the knack of draping the long rectangular length of cloth in graceful folds about their torso, then fastening it securely. Penny, however, found wrapping herself in the garment a tricky affair.

Matt had an enjoyable time pretending to be of assistance. Finally, suspecting that if she did not call a halt to this activity soon they would wind up back in bed, Penny tugged the fabric into place, skewered it with a safety pin, and led him outside by the hand.

Over a light lunch of broiled mahi-mahi on the terrace, they watched windsurfers clinging with dogged tenacity to the frames of their bright sails while the breeze swirled them about. The sport looked challenging. Much too strenuous for people recovering from the frantic pace they had been setting of late. They opted instead to snorkel lazily through the shallows, enjoying the sea life but giving a wide berth to fire coral and the shellfish called cones, whose venomous sting had been known to prove lethal.

That night they dined at Bloody Mary's. Before departing for the restaurant, they arranged with the manager of their hotel to borrow two bicycles on the following day.

"You'll enjoy touring our island," the pleasant fellow told them. "It's not much more than twenty miles around the perimeter. A nice flat ride all the way. At about the halfway point there's a charming little café where you can have lunch."

"What about detouring inland to the mountains?" Matt asked.

The manager shook his head. "Away from the coast, Bora Bora's interior is scrub jungle, very wild and rugged. Even those who manage to beat their way to the base of Mt. Otemanu by jeep see at once that it cannot be climbed." An uneasy expression crossed his face. "It is better to follow the natives' example and stay away. Sacred altars and shrines called *maraes* are left up there from ancient times. Venturing near them is *kapu*. Forbidden."

Understanding that this was a matter of cultural pride, Penny nodded gravely. "Thank you for telling us the reason the interior is off-limits. We wouldn't want to violate any taboos."

With only one road on the island they found it impossible to get lost. The coral track rimming Bora Bora's coastline was shaded by tall, graceful coconut palms, stately banyan trees, and a profusion of blossoming shrubbery. Matt and Penny pedaled slowly past exquisite bays where men fished and dark-eyed children played. They exclaimed in delight at the sight of Outrigger canoes tucked into floating thatched shelters. They paused often to touch, to kiss. Tangles of lush, impenetrable foliage stood guard over the secrets of the stern black mountains dominating the island's rugged center.

"I can sure understand why people prefer to live along the water than up there, *kapu* or no *kapu*," Matt commented. "Think of the trek up and down to go fishing!"

Bicycling appeared to be the islanders' favorite mode of transportation. Penny smiled at the colorfully dressed youngsters and their equally brightly dressed grandparents pedaling past. She thought they looked as cheerful as the pastel houses they lived in.

Among her favorite sights along the way were small structures placed outside each home. In another country, this was the location a mailbox might occupy. But on Bora Bora, these tiny houses were built to hold the long, crusty loaves of French bread that were delivered fresh by the baker's boy each day.

At Chen Lee's, the general store in Viatape, Penny bought a hardbound book with lovely flowers brightening the cover. "What are you going to do with this?" Matt asked, flipping through the book's thick, blank pages.

"Use it as a journal." She slipped her arm around his waist and hugged. "I don't want to forget any of our time here. Not a single detail. I'm storing up memories to treasure all my life."

On their last afternoon in Bora Bora, Penny carried the journal along to the beach. Her redhead's complexion could not tolerate large doses of the sun's strong rays. She stayed in the water only a short time, then waded out to dab more sunscreen on her nose and don a wide-brimmed hat woven from palm fronds. After slipping a cool cotton cover-up over her shoulders, she opened her journal and started to write.

She filled one page, looking up often to wave at Matt swimming vigorously past, then another. But when she turned to the third page, she caught her breath. The pen slipped from her suddenly limp fingers.

Words already filled the page.

"I love you, Penny," Matt had written. "More each day. Will you marry me? Be my wife and let me take care of you forever?"

For a long, sun-dazzled moment all Penny could do was stare down at the heartfelt proposal. Every letter of every word seemed filled to the brim with love for her. Then a shadow fell across the page. The man she adored dropped down beside her, still wet from the sea.

"Will you, Penny?" he asked, sounding a trifle anxious. "Hearing you say you'll be my wife is the only thing in the world that could make me happier than I am right now."

Penny fished her pen out of the sand and turned to a fresh page of the journal. "Yes, Yes, Yes!" she wrote. "I love you, Matt Devlin. Will you be my husband and let me take care of you forever?"

Matt's joyous laugh could be heard clear down the beach. He took the pen out of her hand and reached for the book. "Yes, Yes, Yes!" he wrote.

That night they celebrated their engagement with a lobster and spaghetti dinner at the Bora Bora Yacht Club. A *fete* was in progress. Penny knew she could never hope to adequately describe the haunting voices of the singers or the stunning grace of the dancers in their plumeria leis and long grass skirts and lovely flower crowns. But she wouldn't need her journal to help her remember this night. For as long as she lived, she would never forget a moment of it.

When the entertainment had ended, Matt laid a small, tissue-wrapped packet on the table. He asked Penny to open it. "As soon as I saw these, I thought they might make a beautiful ring," he said. "But if you'd rather have a diamond. . . ."

Penny's fingers shook as she peeled back the wrappings and found three luminous jade-green Tahitian pearls inside. "Matt, they're magnificent!" she cried. "I can't think of anything that would make a more beautiful ring. No diamond could possibly compare!"

On this wave of euphoria they went to bed. But very late that night Penny awoke to find herself alone. Reaching sleepily for her robe, she walked barefoot out to the verandah. Flickering tiki torches down the beach cast dark troubled shadows across Matt's face as he leaned against the railing.

"Something's wrong, isn't it?" Penny felt a sudden stab of fear. "Please, Matt, share whatever it is with me."

"Quit worrying. I guess it was just an advance touch of the jet lag we're sure to be facing this time tomorrow." Silencing her with a kiss, Matt swung her up in his arms.

Not until they landed in Los Angeles and had run the gauntlet of Customs and Immigration inspections did Penny learn the truth. While awaiting the departure of their connecting flight home to San Francisco, Matt absentmindedly mentioned having seen Neville Baker in Australia.

Penny glanced up in surprise. "I didn't realize you'd had time for a visit to the Outback on this trip."

"I didn't." Though he had hoped to shield her from unpleasantness, Matt couldn't bring himself to tell Penny an outright lie. Anyway, he thought, it was better to level with her. After all, it would be important for her to stay away from the warehouse until he had coped with the ugly problem that had arisen.

He met his fiancée's eyes, knowing that Penny was the one person in the world he could depend on for unqualified support.

"Toward the end of the conference I telephoned Neville from the hotel in Cairns to say hello," he explained. "That's when I learned he had been frantically calling the States trying to reach me. But he refused to tell me over the phone what the crisis involved."

Frowning, Penny said, "I thought he had solved the production problems with the Billabong Babies, at least for a while. Didn't he hire some temporary workers who managed to help him put together that huge order of toys? The shipment that's on its way across the Pacific to you right now?"

"Right," Matt said grimly. "However, it turns out there's a slight problem." He began to tell her what it involved.

Normally, it took an act of God to pry Neville Baker away from his beloved Outback and into a big city. But this time he was on his way to Cairns within twenty minutes of the time he had finished speaking to Matt on the phone.

Not even waiting to shake hands, he came directly to the point. "Remember those two blokes who showed up outside my place at the beginning of The Wet, claiming their caravan had broken down?"

"Voss and Brightey?" Matt nodded. "What about them?"

Nervously, as if he were a caged animal looking for escape, the Australian paced back and forth across the hotel room. "There was nothing wrong with their rig at all," he spat out. "Soon as that cargo ship sailed with the toys on board, they tinkered with the engine for five minutes, then up and left."

Impolite not to say goodbye, Matt thought, but hardly cause for hysteria. After all, the Aborigines went on walkabout without notice all the time.

"Nev, you knew they never meant to stay on permanently," he reasoned with the inventor. "They fulfilled their agreement—worked for you until the rains tapered off and the roads were passable again."

"If the roads had been passable, they wouldn't have drowned a week later trying to ford a branch of the Darling River." Gloomily, the toy maker dropped into a chair. "The current's wicked in that spot. It capsized the vehicle and swept their bodies eight miles downstream before washing them ashore."

"Good Lord! How did you find out about it?"

Neville groaned. "Turns out they were wanted by the police for being involved in a sensational robbery last March. Five mine-ratters hijacked a cache of opals from Coober Pedy down in South Australia, where the gems are found. The papers raked the whole scandal up again when Voss and Brightey washed ashore. By then, the police had managed to identify all five members of the gang. Two others had been picked up weeks earlier, headed north to my part of the country."

Matt was beginning to get a very bad feeling about where this tale was leading. " 'Mine-ratters' are thieves, right?

Were you acquainted with the two who were arrested?"

"Only by name," Neville said with a grimace. "I'd had a letter from them in answer to my ad appealing for workers to help me out in the workshop. They didn't have any opals on them when the law closed in. Neither did the two who drowned. Not then, at least," he added darkly. "Jed Colby, the fifth man who masterminded the heist, has gone into hiding. Newspaper speculation has it that he's biding his time until he can smuggle the stones out of the country."

"What are the missing opals worth?" Matt asked.

"About ten million dollars, American." Neville got up and started to pace again, his face haggard with worry. "I had never heard of Jed Colby until I read about him in the papers, but Voss and Brightey stayed at my place during The Wet. And, like I said, two of their mates had been all set to come to work for me before that, but the police nabbed them before they could arrive. Now, why would those four crooks want to bury themselves in the back of beyond when they'd just got away with a prize like that?"

"I suppose they could have been lying low until the heat was off," Matt suggested dubiously. "No fence in Australia would have touched those stones. The thieves must have known even before they stole the opals that smuggling them into the States was the only way they would be able to profit from their crime.

"There isn't a lot of honor among thieves," he went on. "My guess is that Colby not only masterminded the scheme but set up the plan for two of his cohorts to apply for jobs at your workshop after you advertised for help. Could be they had a falling out, and he tipped off the police himself as to where they could be found. Once they were out of the way, he sent the other pair. It wouldn't have been hard for Voss and Brightey to fake a convenient breakdown practically outside your door."

Neville groaned. "You figure they had the opals with them?"

"Too right I do, mate." Use of the Aussie slang gave Matt's reply emphasis. "What's more, I suspect you're convinced of that yourself. And now I'd be willing to bet that those gems are stashed in the toys you dispatched to me aboard the *Coral Sea Clipper.* Have you notified the police yet?"

Neville looked like he would rather swim after the ship himself than do anything of the sort.

"Matt, there's something about me you don't know," he blurted, after an awkward pause. "When I was a lad, I all but killed a bloke for raping my sister. The jury figured I shouldn't have been quite so handy with my fists, and gave me five years' hard time. When I got out, I found myself a place to live where there weren't any high walls or guard towers, or crowds of people jammed into tiny cubicles. There's no way I'd ever go back to jail."

"But you didn't—"

Neville cut him off with a gesture. "In this country, ex-convicts are considered scum," he said bitterly. "If the police were to find stolen opals concealed in toys that came from my workshop, they wouldn't look any further for the culprit."

From his own boyhood scrape with the law, Matt knew that Neville had good reason to doubt the justice system. "Got any suggestions?" he asked dubiously.

"That shipment is halfway across the ocean by now. Nuthin' anyone can do until the crates reach San Francisco." The Australian shot Matt a look that was both desperate and imploring. "I was hoping you'd be able to search the toys as soon as they arrive. If the opals really are stashed in the Billabong Babies, you could just—well, pick them out and send them back to their rightful owners, couldn't you?"

"That's the best way I can think of to get us both arrested," Matt replied grimly. "Besides, you're forgetting about Jed Colby. With a false passport, he could have slipped out of Australia and be anywhere. My guess is California. If your suspicions are right, he must expect to collect ten million dollars worth of opals when the *Coral Sea Clipper* makes port in San Francisco late this month."

"Not if he doesn't know which ship they're on," the toy maker argued. "The workshop crew had no information about which shipping line I intended to use, or exactly when those crates would be loaded onto a freighter. I handle all the paperwork myself, and keep it locked up in a safe."

Shock hit Matt like a trembler jiggling a seismograph. That was it! The answer to a question that had plagued him for months. The Australian had just solved the riddle of why anyone would want to break into an empty warehouse.

He'd been way off base in suspecting Russell Kehoe of being the intruder, Matt realized now. The Sutter Street merchant was annoyingly ambitious, but the interloper who had twice stealthily rifled through his papers was involved in a scheme far more nefarious than trying to cut him out as middleman with overseas toy suppliers. Plotting to use Neville's shipments of the Billabong Babies to smuggle the stolen opals into the States, either Colby or one of his accomplices had broken into the warehouse seeking advance information about shipping lines and freighter schedules.

He still didn't know how the illicit entries were managed. But there was no longer the slightest doubt in Matt's mind as to why they had occurred. In order to claim their ten million dollar prize, the mine-ratters needed to know precise details about how shipments from the Outback to San Francisco were handled, and the specific route taken by the cargo.

Matt's mind seethed with possibilities. Did Colby plan to hijack the crates of toys straight off the ship? Or would he wait until they had been transferred to the warehouse, and move in then?

"Except for a couple of crucial points, Neville had the thieves' scheme all figured out," Matt said, when he had finished bringing Penny up to date. "Along with being in the dark as to how the break-ins were managed, neither he nor I have a clue as to who was the culprit responsible. Months ago, when both the intrusions I know about took place, Colby would have had to be on the spot in Australia, masterminding the gang's operations. So how did he manage to break into a San Francisco warehouse twelve thousand miles away at the same time?"

"Does anyone know for sure there were only five members of the gang?" Penny asked in concern. "If those crooks were sharp enough to lay their plans months in advance, they might also have sent one of their mob to California to keep tabs on what was happening at your end."

"Sounds possible," Matt agreed. "But that still doesn't explain how he could have managed to enter my warehouse without jimmying the locks or leaving any trace of his presence except a few disarranged papers."

Their flight from Los Angeles International to SFO was announced before Penny could come up with any helpful ideas on the subject. Mulling over the problem while winging swiftly north high above the rocky Pacific coastline, she knew that their top priority had to focus on safeguarding the warehouse from further intrusions.

"Even with the new security patrols on the lookout, that hoodlum Houdini might manage another break-in," she voiced the concern that haunted them both. "Have you any ideas as to how we can go about outsmarting him?"

"There hasn't been time to think it out. I've had a few distractions lately, remember?" Ignoring her use of the word "we," he slipped his hand into hers and squeezed. "But the *Coral Sea Clipper* isn't due to make port for another week. Hopefully by then I'll have figured out a way to thwart those crooks' plans without risking jail for Neville or myself. It's pretty scary to consider that I'm as likely to come under suspicion for theft and smuggling as he is. After all, those crates of toys are consigned to me."

Remembering the debacle that had occurred another time Matt attempted to help a friend out of a sticky situation, Penny could understand his reluctance to seek official assistance. Even so, the notion that Colby might have a henchman on the scene in California made her decidedly uneasy.

"The authorities can hardly arrest either of you if you report your suspicions and cooperate in retrieving the opals," she tried a bit of gentle urging.

"I wish I could share your confidence in law and order," Matt muttered.

Penny refused to be put off. "Well, then, what if we rig up an around-the-clock stakeout ourselves? Working together, we could catch your intruder red-handed and turn both him and the evidence over to the police. Do you keep a gun in the warehouse?"

Matt hadn't handled a weapon since boot camp. As far as he was concerned, stakeouts and shoot-outs were the kind of things that happened in the movies, not in real life.

Not in his life, anyway, let alone that of the woman he loved.

"No, Penny, I don't," he answered patiently. "I told you before, I run a small, law-abiding operation. But even if I had a couple of Uzis in my file cabinet, I wouldn't want you within a mile of the warehouse so long as there's a threat of danger."

"Matt, I wish you'd come to terms with the fact that I'm not still a seven-year-old weakling who can't fight her own battles," she said, gritting her teeth. "Ethan made sure I had lessons in self-defense. These days, Damsels in Distress give their Knights in Shining Armor some solid backup when it comes to defending the castle from dragons. Really, I can be of enormous help to you."

"You're a wonderful partner," he agreed. "This past week I've learned that I couldn't do without you. But Penny, you're a girl. A sweet, soft, adorable—"

"I'm a woman!" she all but howled in exasperation. "A twenty-four-year-old woman with a black belt in karate!"

The protest seemed to go right over his head. Oh, if only she could tell him the truth about what had happened that day in the ladies' room at the airport when she had foiled a kidnapper! But she had promised Francie never to tell anyone what had really happened that day. Besides, at this point she wasn't sure Matt would even take the revelation seriously.

"Have you forgotten that we're going to be married?" Penny cried pleadingly. "We're supposed to be a team!"

"And we are," Matt agreed. "A great team. But that doesn't mean I'll allow you to risk going anywhere near those crooks."

He yanked his seatbelt more tightly around his middle as the jet swooped in across the water to touch down at SFO.

"Remember, I collected a lot of shiners to keep you safe when I was ten years old."

"So you don't believe turnabout is fair play? Maybe you'd rather I started talking with my old Texas drawl, so you could call me 'Honey-Chile'!"

In outrage, Penny jumped up before the plane had finished taxiing to a halt in front of the hangar. "We promised in writing to take care of each other forever!" Fuming, she snatched her bulging carry-on bag from underneath her seat just as the plane nosed in at the gate. "Let me know when I have your permission to hold up my end of the bargain!"

So angry she could hardly see straight, she blitzed up the aisle. Other passengers followed eagerly, crowding past Matt and leaving him blocked in by the crush of humanity.

Sure that Penny would be long gone before he could make his way out into the terminal, he jerked his own suitcase out from the overhead bin.

Why couldn't he convince her that the situation was dangerous? Twice, at least, the mine-ratter or one of his confederates had managed to sneak into the warehouse. Trying to figure out how the trick had been managed was driving him crazy. Now Penny wanted to stake out the place. Walk guard duty. In fact, she was furious because he refused to allow her to jeopardize her life by getting in the thieves' way.

Her rashness scared him stiff. So did the possibility that he or Neville might wind up in jail. Yet he couldn't just let Colby walk off with ten million dollars' worth of opals.

What the hell was he going to do?

CHAPTER EIGHTEEN

"The plants look beautiful, Inez. Naomi will be thrilled to see how they've thrived when she gets home in a few days."

A little hysterically, Penny wondered what in the world she would do then. She and Matt had planned on living aboard *Gypsy* until they could find a suitable apartment, but at the moment they were barely on speaking terms.

With an effort she dragged her thoughts away from Matt. Inez, she noticed in relief, seemed to be gradually regaining her strength. She expressed her thankfulness at her assistant's improved health, murmured a few trite phrases about Bora Bora, and sent the older woman back to her own little house in the deep Mission District as quickly as courtesy would allow.

Though her brain felt addled from the wearying journey, she was still too distraught to be able to nap. She paced around the spotless apartment, worrying about Matt one minute, fuming at him the next.

A letter from Leeann Jarvis lay atop the small stack of mail on the hall table Inez had collected during her absence. Tearing open the envelope, Penny read that the Air Force had promoted her college roommate from captain to major and assigned her to a base in Spain for the next year. Disappointment flooded over her as she realized that being stationed in Europe might prevent Lee from attending the wedding she and Matt had begun planning.

If there was a wedding!

Growing increasingly depressed, Penny decided that a shower might help bolster her sagging morale. She was letting the needling spray beat on her head when she remembered the water shortage in Bora Bora and guiltily turned off the tap. Then she had to turn it on again to get the soap out of her eyes.

Inez had thoughtfully stocked the refrigerator with a few basic provisions so Penny wouldn't have to shop as soon as she returned from her trip. Knowing she should try to eat, she measured a half-cup of cottage cheese into a bowl, then opened a can of peaches in sugarless syrup to spoon over it.

By the second mouthful she found herself sobbing, remembering the glorious fresh fruit they had enjoyed in the island paradise. What a comedown after that to be eating bland canned peaches—diet-lite, at that!

In her heart, Penny knew the tasteless lunch had nothing to do with her tears. She didn't care what she ate, but she missed Matt. Terribly. Worse, she was worried about him.

What if he decided to try defending his property against a ruthless felon with only his fists as weapons? People had been killed for far less than ten million dollars' worth of stolen gems!

As Penny's sobs diminished, embarrassment took over. Ethan had spent years teaching her to be a courteous, considerate human being. He would be thoroughly ashamed of her for stalking off that plane like a bad-tempered shrew. But not as ashamed as she was of herself.

Her resolve to track Matt down and apologize, restore peace between them even if she had to grovel, hit a snag when telephone calls to both the warehouse and the boat went unanswered. She comforted herself with the recollection that a week still remained before the *Coral Sea Clipper* was due to make port. Plenty of time to try and persuade the man she loved to ask the authorities for help, even if he refused to accept it from her.

Keyed up from jet lag and emotional overload, she headed for the *dojo* where a brisk practice session under the eye of the *sensei* provided a much-needed stress reliever. But afterwards, still unable to reach Matt by phone, anxiety gripped her once more. Hadn't he returned from the airport yet?

Restless and uneasy, Penny decided that going down to her office and checking the tape of her answering machine would be a way of occupying an hour or so. Her pulse raced at the hope that Matt might have left a message for her there, the way he'd written the proposal in her journal at the beach on Bora Bora. Still wearing the casual outfit she had changed into following her workout at the *dojo,* she hurried down the street to the bus stop.

Darkness had taken hold by the time she reached the business park. As she strode around to the rear of the complex, headlights washed searchingly across the petite, auburn-haired woman clad in moccasins, khakis and a long-sleeved cotton T-shirt emblazoned with the legend "Remember the Alamo."

Penny turned and waved at the patrolman making his rounds in the jeep, then continued up the steps to her office. The place was stifling from having been closed up for a week in the September heat. About to prop her door open, she recalled the disapproving lecture a similar action had previously drawn from the grey-haired security officer, the same man she had seen on duty tonight.

In resignation, she pushed the door shut and crossed to the window, planning to open it a few inches for ventilation.

But before she could carry through on this plan, she caught sight of a splinter-thin crack of light twinkling through the split piece of siding in Matt's warehouse.

Relief flooded over her. After all, she wouldn't have to wait much longer to talk to the man she loved. She could be in his arms within minutes!

Pausing only long enough to lock up, she raced down the steps and across the drive. Breathlessly, she pulled up outside the warehouse door and proceeded to beat a joyful tattoo on it, calling out at the same time.

"Matt! It's me, Penny! I've come to apologize. Please, let me in!"

When this plea failed to elicit a response, she kept her patience in check for a minute or two, then started the whole routine again. "Matt, don't be angry," she called, in a tone calculated to carry to the warehouse's interior. "I was just trying to help because I love you. But it's not worth fight—"

She broke off in mid-word, staring down in shock at the padlocks jumping around on their hasps as her fists thumped the door. Both were tightly snapped.

But that couldn't be right, she thought in confusion. Matt would have had to unlock them to get inside.

Unless it wasn't Matt who—

Unluckily for Penny, the realization that something might be seriously wrong came a second too late. Before she could spin around and dash for help, a smooth, heavy object connected with the back of her head. Flashing lights exploded in her brain. She had the sensation of falling. Just as she sank into oblivion, a voice rasped, "Dammit! You promised nobody would get hurt!"

And then . . . nothing.

CHAPTER NINETEEN

Penny came to with a start. One minute she'd been unconscious, floating in a dreamless black void. The next she was awake, lying on a hard, dirty floor with a throbbing pain in her skull. She had no idea where she was, but she had the strong conviction that she hadn't been there very long. It was as if echoes of whispers and footsteps had only just faded, leaving her here alone.

"Here" was evidently a building, small and dark, with rough walls and a splintery wood floor that smelled of mildew. Something moved, swaying against her hand when she reached out. Just in time, Penny choked back a scream of terror. Instinct told her it wouldn't be safe to make any noise.

She forced herself to reach again. Again, the swaying object dangled against her fingers. Steeling her courage, she investigated further, relying solely on her sense of touch to identify the object. It proved to be a pair of baggy denim coveralls, hooked over a nail high up on the wall.

The sight of a streak of starry sky through a gap in the overhead boards brought memory jolting back. She'd looked down from the window in her office, Penny recalled, and seen a ribbon of light through that odd crack in Matt's warehouse wall. It was the only way anyone would have known there was a light on in the place. From any other angle, the warehouse appeared dark and untenanted.

But it wasn't, she told herself, trying not to shake with fright. Someone had been in there. Someone who didn't belong.

As her eyes grew accustomed to the dimness, Penny concluded that she had been locked in a small wooden shack. There was such a building at the rear of the business park, she recalled, located between the warehouses and the docks. The nondescript structure had caught her eye a number of times over the past few months, but she had always just assumed it was a tool shed or a handy spot to store landscaping equipment.

She learned now that it contained no tools, no hoses, no lawnmowers, no brooms. There was nothing inside at all except for herself and that dangling pair of coveralls.

A cautious perusal of the walls soon helped her locate the shed's door. As she had feared, it wouldn't budge. It would have come as no surprise at all to find that it had been locked and bolted from the outside. But this wasn't the case. Instead, a padlock was firmly affixed to the hasp.

On the inside! Penny found that incomprehensible fact almost more frightening than anything else.

With an effort, she got her panic under control. Ghosts, if there were such beings, would have no need of locks. There must be another explanation, Penny assured herself, a logical one, to account for these strange circumstances.

She had the queasy conviction that for her sake and Matt's, she had better find it in a hurry.

Penny had always hated dark, closed-in places. A strong impulse urged her to back into a corner and hide her head. It took grit and determination to haul down those coveralls instead, then fumble through their pockets in search of a key. There was none. But along with a greasy rag and what felt like a small oilcan, she found a book of paper matches.

With unsteady hands she tore one off, missing the sandpapery striking strip twice before managing to get the match lit. The malodorous smell of sulphur filled the shed. The sudden flare dazzled her eyes. It also sparked an answering glint from a metal ring in the floor.

Bending over for a closer look, Penny dropped the sputtering match with a little cry of pain as it singed her fingers.

But it had stayed lit long enough to show her the trapdoor. She tugged on the ring, and lifted the square section of flooring that served as its opening. When the next match illuminated the worn wooden steps leading down into a tunnel beneath the shed, answers started adding up fast.

Shortly after her arrival from San Antonio, Matt had taken her to dinner at a restaurant called Shanghai Sal's. There, he had described one of the wicked practices that gave the old Barbary Coast district along San Francisco's waterfront such a notorious reputation. Vessels hauling supplies to California during Gold Rush days were often marooned in the harbor after sailors jumped ship and ran off to try their hand at prospecting. Many a shady saloon and bawdy house ran a lucrative business on the side supplying replacement crews for these beleaguered ships.

Customers seeking a good time were often slipped a Mickey Finn—knockout drops in their drink—or bashed over the head, as she had been tonight. Quickly, then, they were bundled into an underground passage leading straight to the docks. By the time they regained consciousness, they were miles out to sea.

One of the women in Penny's office building had told her that an infamous gambling palace had once occupied this very property on the fringes of the historic district.

Peering down at the tunnel now, she had no doubt that the high-rolling club had also contributed its share of shanghaied sailors back in the late 1840's and the 1850's, when gold fever was at its peak. Later, the passage must have been closed up and forgotten . . . until Griff Hazelton decided to develop the acreage into a business park.

Why the former fullback had decided to keep the tunnel intact instead of filling it in, she had no idea. Maybe at first the idea appealed to his sense of whimsy. But after Hazelton ran into financial woes and decided to moonlight as an opal smuggler, he had evidently found a new, practical use for the old underground route.

Penny knew it was their landlord who had been getting into Matt's warehouse, snooping through his papers, then passing the information on to his cohort Down Under. Just as she was losing consciousness she had heard Hazelton squawk that he hadn't wanted anyone to get hurt. A savage answer in an Aussie twang demonstrated that the man who'd hit her had no such qualms.

Remembering the story Matt had told her while sitting in the terminal at LAX—was it only a few hours ago?—she decided that she was very lucky to still be alive. It stood to reason that Hazelton's partner-in-crime was Jed Colby, leader of the mine-ratting gang. Anyone capable of masterminding a ten-million-dollar heist was sure to be ruthless.

And she had managed to get in his way!

But it didn't make sense! Penny thought in frustration. The freighter carrying the shipment of toys from Australia wasn't due to arrive for several days yet.

At least that was the information Neville Baker had given Matt. But ocean-going cargo ships didn't sail to an exact schedule the way cruise liners did. It was possible that the *Coral Sea Clipper* had made better time than anticipated.

Had the thieves somehow discovered that fact, and decided to stake out the warehouse earlier than originally planned? Preparing to heist those opals again—this time from where they had been hidden inside the furry little pouches of toy kangaroos and koala bears?

In a rush of horror, she realized that the only way she would get out of this trap was to go find out.

Clutching the book of matches that was her only weapon against the dark, Penny forced herself to descend into the tunnel. The passage was narrow and dank, the footing treacherous. Earth sifted down into her hair with every step she took. A dozen times she was tempted to bolt back to the shed. A dozen times she clenched her teeth and went on.

The outline of the second set of steps leading upward was the most welcome sight she had ever laid eyes on. Regardless of what awaited her at the top of them, it could never match the horror she felt while wandering through this subterranean passageway.

Silently, her moccasins moved up the dusty steps. Just as silently, the trapdoor eased open when she gave it a cautious push. At that moment Penny understood the presence of the oilcan in the coveralls' pocket. The conspirators had been taking no risks of a telltale squeak giving their game away.

Uncertain as to what to expect, she widened the opening an inch at a time. But no one was waiting. Nobody pounced. She levered herself out and tried to quiet her breathing while she got her bearings.

The distinct scent of wool made her think of the engaging toy sheep from New Zealand. The familiar odor removed Penny's last doubt about her present location. She was in Matt's warehouse, very close to the side wall. Mercifully, the only light she could see glowing at the moment

245

came from a powerful flashlight carried by either Hazelton or his fellow criminal. The beam swung back and forth as they walked, clearing the shadows out of the middle and pushing them back against the edges of the building.

Concerned that if the rays swung in her direction the yawning gulf in the floor would be spotted, Penny eased the trapdoor shut. Its outlines vanished, absorbed by the random pattern of plank flooring.

There was no sign of a metal ring at this end of the tunnel. Nevertheless, Penny felt certain there must be some inconspicuous way to gain access to the passageway from inside the warehouse. Perhaps, she surmised, it was operated by some gadget such as the remote control for a TV set. No wonder Matt had never suspected what was going on!

She shrank back as the sound of voices grew closer.

"What's taking him so long?" Griff Hazelton complained.

His companion swung the flashlight in short vicious jabs, as though the shadows held wild beasts that needed fending off. "You'd better hope there's no more complications," he snarled. "That sheila snooping around could have blown the whole show."

"Hell, Colby, she just came over to visit her boyfriend. She didn't see anything."

"Maybe. Maybe not. Either way, there'll be no chance of her identifying us when she tumbles head-first into that tunnel and breaks her neck."

A blackness that had nothing to do with the shadows moved over Penny, chilling her right down to the bone. "Sheila" was Aussie slang for a female. Any female. In this case, her. He had never intended for her to leave that shed alive.

"Your rent-a-cop nearly caught us hauling her off," the man called Colby groused. "Where did you get the crazy notion of hiring a security patrol?"

"Devlin had a hunch something was up," Griff Hazelton defended his actions. "Think I wanted him installing a burglar alarm? Being the thoughtful landlord who hired guards for the protection of his tenants' property will divert suspicion from me. So will the fact that I warned everyone to have his or her locks changed. It's like the old hidden ball trick in football. Keeps the opposition looking in the wrong direction while you tote the ball across the goal line for the score."

"Forget football," his cohort spat. "You might have been king of the hill when we met in that Sydney pub after the Kangaroo Bowl. But this is my show, matey. Once we get those opals, it won't matter who or what Devlin suspects because he won't be able to tell anyone about it. Good joke on the cops if we buried him in the tunnel next to the sheila. Drive them crazy trying to figure out what happened to the two of them."

The mine-ratter's callous plans for her own demise had chilled Penny's blood. Hearing him talk about murdering the man she loved heated it with sudden fury.

No way was he going to get away with it!

When the conspiring pair rambled on toward the rear of the building, she straightened up and eased in the opposite direction. Her objective was the phone on Matt's desk. All she had to do was lift the receiver and tap in "911." There'd be no need to say a word. Just keep the line open until the police homed in on the call's location, and sent a patrol car to investigate.

The rumble of an engine interrupted this plan before she could follow through on it. Sounding obscenely loud against the breathless silence, the motor pulsed and throbbed for a moment outside the warehouse's rear entrance. Then locks clattered. An unseen mechanism set the ponderous door in motion. As it rose noisily upward, Penny saw taillights flare. Before she could blink, an oversized panel truck had backed into the opening between two rows of shelving.

Her heart hit bedrock. Matt wouldn't have rented that truck unless he'd needed it to transport the toy shipment from dock to warehouse. That meant the *Coral Sea Clipper* definitely had arrived ahead of schedule. By monitoring the freighter's progress across the Pacific, the thieves were poised to hijack the shipment containing the smuggled opals the moment it reached its destination.

Thanks to Neville's warning, Matt had been expecting trouble. But not so soon. Exhausted by the long flight from French Polynesia and the emotional tumult of their argument, he'd be unprepared to confront these ruthless adversaries tonight.

Penny yearned to shout a warning that would alert Matt to danger and send him fleeing from the warehouse before the trap could be sprung. The scream was still gathering in her throat when the massive rear door, controlled by a gismo attached to Matt's key ring, began clattering down to close noisily behind the truck.

She swallowed the cry. Too late!

Common sense told her the desperate maneuver would have proved futile even if rumbling machinery hadn't drowned out her words. Matt would have been flabbergasted to find her in the warehouse. He'd have wasted precious seconds asking questions.

Then, being Matt, his immediate impulse would have been to come to her rescue, rather than trying to save himself.

Matt doused the vehicle's headlights, swung open the driver's side door, and stepped out onto the concrete floor. Terrified, Penny watched as two hulking shapes moved out of the concealing shadows to intercept him. Colby's flashlight beam hit him square in the face.

"Evening, Mr. Devlin," the Australian said, with false cordiality. "Aren't you the busy bloke, bringing home the cargo that arrived this afternoon on the *Coral Sea Clipper*!"

"Who the devil are you?" Matt countered abrasively. "And how did you get into my warehouse?"

"Full of questions, aren't you, mate? But mine are the ones that count. Better answer them without any backchat unless you want a bullet in your knee for encouragement."

The menace in Colby's voice was enough to freeze a geyser in mid-spout. Staring at the locked-horned pair from a long angle through half-empty shelves, Penny swallowed hard. A gun had suddenly appeared in the mine-ratter's right hand. With his left, he kept the blinding beam square in Matt's eyes.

"That's better," he gloated, as the young importer saw what he was up against and raised his hands. "If you're really *dying* to know how we got in, maybe you can persuade your landlord here to explain. But first he needs to turn on some lights so we can all see what we're doing."

"How am I supposed to find my way around without the flashlight?" Hazelton grumbled in a sullen tone.

He had been laggardly in stepping forward to confront Matt. Now he sounded as if he regretted ever having become involved in this situation that had unexpectedly turned lethal. Watching the byplay between him and Colby, Penny heard the Australian let loose a string of curses.

"You afraid of the dark, a great big football player like you?" Colby asked with a sneer. "I have to keep the flashlight. How can I hold a gun on our prisoner unless I can see him?"

Penny felt the stirrings of a bold idea as Hazelton turned away from the pair and took a few stumbling steps toward the front of the warehouse. It occurred to her that looking directly at the harsh yellow beam of the flashlight must have destroyed his night vision. He was likely to be disoriented until his eyes adjusted to the dimness. She watched him weave clumsily back and forth, his whole concentration apparently focused on reaching the light switches located beside the door without barging into obstacles along the way.

He wouldn't be expecting anyone to barge into him.

Creeping down a side aisle on a collision course with the lumbering fullback, Penny sharpened her own night vision against the shadows. She moved with determination, breathing deeply, clearing her thoughts, preparing herself mentally and physically the way she had been taught over years of martial arts training. Hazelton outweighed her twice over and was more than a head taller. But she had faced plenty of outsized opponents in the past.

Never with two lives riding on the outcome, though.

Penny timed the approaching footsteps, concentrating hard. Broken-field running must not have been Hazelton's forte during his career with the NFL, because he was still weaving. She let him pass the head of her aisle, then swooped in behind him, hands flashing.

When he went down, the building shook.

Matt Devlin had returned to his warehouse to set a trap. He hadn't counted on falling prey to a deadly ambush himself. Crossing his fingers that the early arrival of the freighter would take his adversaries off-guard, he had hoped to get all the pieces in place before confronting them. It looked now as if he'd made a serious miscalculation. Judging by the stress the Aussie had placed on the word "dying", he didn't intend for Matt to come out of this encounter alive.

Playing for time, he baited Colby. "Did you hear about two of your mates drowning, and the other two winding up in jail?"

The mine-ratter's eyes narrowed. He didn't know how his victim-to-be had learned his identity. But since Devlin was slated for a permanent stay in that crumbling passageway beneath the warehouse, it made no real difference.

"Rotten shame." A grin carved a path across his watchful face. "Fewer people to split with means all the more profit for me."

Taking a casual step back toward the panel truck he'd just driven in to the warehouse, Matt slewed his head toward Griff Hazelton's retreating form. "Is my landlord the only confederate you have left? Or was Neville Baker in on the conspiracy, too? Did he know about the robbery in advance? Plan to help you and your henchmen smuggle those opals into the States?"

"That hermit? A toy maker?" The Australian chortled in disdain. "Hell, no. He didn't know a thing about our plans. I had been planning the robbery since the first of the year. There was no sense grabbing the stones, though, until I'd hit on a way to get them out of Australia. Then I spotted Baker's Help Wanted advertisement."

"Handy. Like the answer to a prayer."

Matt hadn't been able to keep the scorn out of his voice, but Colby took him literally.

"Where I really got lucky was finding out the American destination for Baker's toy exports, and linking up with an old crony at the other end of the line," he bragged. "After

Hazelton agreed to snoop through your papers for a look at the bills of lading, the setup was foolproof."

"You're the fool if you believe that," Matt scoffed. "Hazelton is desperate for money. He got in too deep financially developing this property, and hasn't been able to get more than half the units rented because of the recession. I'll bet he's got plans to keep all the loot for himself."

"I got plans, too." Colby's growl was so menacing it was clear he had never had any intention of splitting the profits with his henchman.

Before Matt could open his mouth to comment on honor among thieves, a resounding crash shook the floorboards.

Colby spun around. "What was that?"

Matt had been expecting some action, but not from down at the other end of the warehouse. He strung Colby along while trying to figure out what was going on.

"Earthquake, maybe?" No fault line had caused that jolt, as Matt well knew. He'd grown up in this city with its frequent tremors, and felt certain a seismograph wouldn't have picked up the thud he'd just heard. It had sounded more like an elephant stubbing its toe and smacking into the floorboards.

Unfortunately, Colby wasn't buying the earthquake theory. "Shut up! Make a move and it'll be your last." Keeping one eye on Matt and his finger on the trigger of his pistol, he swung the beam of the flashlight in the direction Hazelton had taken. Its rays revealed a motionless bulge of humanity sprawled face down in the aisle.

Displaying the lightning-quick reflexes that had helped him elude the police more than once, the mine-ratter began stabbing the strobe-like beam viciously around the warehouse. Watching with bated breath, Matt thought the blinding rays resembled tracer bullets seeking a target. One hit its mark, ricocheting off a shirt decorated with a picture of an old Texas fortress.

"Get over here!" Colby bellowed, before its wearer could whirl away. "Right now, or at the count of three I start pumping lead into your boyfriend. One, two—"

Penny stepped out of a side aisle and raised her hands in surrender.

Colby might have been bluffing, but Penny wasn't about to risk Matt's life by testing that possibility. She knew that even if the mine-ratter hadn't trapped her in the flashlight beam, it wouldn't have taken him long to figure out what had happened. After all, both warehouse doors were secured and the shed that gave access to the tunnel was padlocked from the inside. No one but the woman he had knocked out and left there could have popped up like the embodied ghost of some shanghaied sailor to wreak vengeance on his cohort.

It gave her a great deal of satisfaction to glimpse his stunned expression as she walked toward him. Despite the fact that there could simply be no other explanation, he was having trouble reconciling the notion of such a petite sheila bushwhacking someone the size of Griff Hazelton.

"You do that to him?" he demanded in an incredulous tone.

Penny eyed the burly male on the floor, then disdainfully stepped over him. "Little ole' me?" she feigned astonishment in her best Texas drawl.

Colby didn't appreciate having his chain jerked. Forgetting about Matt for a split second, he swung the gun savagely at Penny.

That miniscule lapse proved his undoing. Half a heartbeat later he was crumpling to the floor, decked by the hardest left Matt Devlin had thrown since he'd finished boot camp.

Penny snatched up the pistol as it clattered to the floor, and flipped on the safety. Then she threw herself into her fiancé's arms.

"What an awful chance to take! Matt, he might have killed you!"

"Me? Honey, you're the one he was getting ready to shoot."

She hugged him even tighter. "You saved my life!"

Over her shoulder, Matt caught a glimpse of Griff Hazelton, who had yet to budge. The former fullback looked as if he had run head-on into the entire 49er defense.

"Yeah, I had to keep up my end of the partnership," he murmured, sounding rather dazed. "After all, I promised to take care of you forever."

"Ummm, yes. As we agreed in Bora Bora, we most definitely need each other."

"That's for sure," Matt agreed. "Reinforcements or not, things were getting pretty sticky. If you hadn't. . . ." His voice trailed off as he remembered Francie Blackburn's father stretched out cold on the floor of the women's restroom at the airport. Both witnesses had insisted the man had slipped on a puddle. Maybe. But there were no puddles here in the warehouse.

"Uh, Penny? . . ."

"Reinforcements?" Penny asked in a puzzled tone. Somewhere in the background, a persistent thumping sound had begun to force itself on her attention. "Did you say 'reinforcements,' Matt?"

"That's right," he answered with a nod. "Today, riding in from the airport, I caught sight of the *Coral Sea Clipper*'s superstructure down at the docks, and realized the time had come to make a decision. The Customs officer I talked to was mighty interested in Neville's story. He tested the theory of the opals being tucked into the pouches of the Billabong Babies on the spot."

"And were they?" Penny asked breathlessly.

"You bet. The toys have been impounded until it's certain that all the gems have been recovered. But I'll have them back in plenty of time to distribute to the retailers before the holidays. Say, Penny, were you serious about . . . ?"

Those thumping noises were becoming positively intrusive. Penny squinted around in the gloom, finally focusing on the vehicle Matt had driven into the warehouse.

"Matt," she asked, "if you didn't haul the cargo from Australia over here with you, why did you need a truck?"

"For the reinforcements," he explained patiently. "Four guys from the Customs Department came along to help me set up a stakeout." A frown flickered across Matt's brow. "I was kind of surprised when they didn't pile out and lend a hand as soon as Colby pulled a gun on me. But since they seemed to be biding their time, I decided to use the chance to get it on record that Neville Baker had nothing to do with the robbery and smuggling plot."

"Neville was an innocent victim, just like you and I would have been if Hazelton and the mine-ratter had had their way." Penny gave the man she loved a hug of thanksgiving. They were both alive!

Then she drew back to gaze earnestly into his eyes. "Honey, I understand rental vehicles aren't always well maintained. Dinah, my former housemate, used to tell some hilarious stories about things that went wrong with cars from her agency. Do you suppose it's possible the inside handle to the truck's rear door might be stuck?"

With his entire thoughts centered on Penny, the frenzied thumping hadn't penetrated Matt's consciousness until that moment. "It worked fine when we started out," he protested. "I watched them test it. But maybe jolting over those speed bumps after leaving the dock—"

He called out loudly, assuring the government agents trapped in the panel truck that he'd be there in a minute to release them. Swiveling around again, his eye fell on the still recumbent figure of Griff Hazelton.

Then he looked back at the woman he adored, determined to get a few straight answers.

"Penny, in about ten minutes I'll be interested in hearing how you and those two clowns got into my warehouse. But first, am I wrong, or did you once say something about having a black belt in karate? Was that what you meant all those times you kept insisting you were able to stand on your own two feet?"

"That's right, Matt." With a radiant smile, Penny twined her arms around her Knight in Shining Armor. "But I wouldn't mind being swept off them long enough to be carried across a threshold. What's more, I happen to know an absolutely perfect room where we can spend our honeymoon!"